Bitters

Bitters

MARY WALTERS

Canadian Cataloguing in Publication Data

Walters, Mary W.
 Bitters

ISBN 1-896300-01-4

 I. Title.

PS8595.A599B58 1999   C813'.54   C99-900971-0
PR9199.3.W3528B58 1999

Editor for the Press: Thomas Wharton
Cover design: Brenda Burgess
Interior design: NeWest Press
Author photograph: Tobin Rooney

NeWest Press acknowledges the support of the Canada Council for the Arts for our publishing program. We also acknowledge the financial support of the Government of Canada through the Book Publishing Industry Development Program (BPIDP) for our publishing activities.

  Canadian Heritage   Patrimoine canadien   Canadä

The author gratefully acknowledges support for her writing from the Alberta Foundation for the Arts. She extends her appreciation to editors Thomas Wharton and Carolyn Ives and the staff at NeWest Press, and thanks the many friends and relatives who provided her with technical advice, moral support, or both while this novel was being written and revised.

This is a work of fiction. Any resemblance in it to actual events or to people living or dead is purely coincidental.

Printed and bound in Canada
NeWest Publishers Limited
Suite 201, 8540-109 Street
Edmonton, Alberta T6G 1E6

for
Daniel and Matthew

1

I first saw Zeke Avery again the night of Archie's nomination. It was a chilly night in the middle of March, but almost fifty people had come out for the meeting: I'd counted them while Archie was delivering his speech. It was a heavy turnout considering that Archie was being returned by acclamation, but a political campaign is like a golf season. There are people so eager to get out, they'll stand around the course and watch the snow melt.

When Archie finished speaking, the applause began. It was loud and enthusiastic, and it went on for a long time. Archie bowed several times in the direction of the audience and then, smiling broadly at the tribute, came across the stage toward us. Cameras flashed and I nudged Ben, and both of us stood up. Archie came to stand between us, putting one arm around my waist and the other around Ben's shoulder. Another camera flashed. I hoped I looked as confident and relaxed as Archie did.

Victor Maxwell, who on the weekend had agreed to be Archie's campaign manager, moved in front of the microphone and without looking at it, lowered it so that it was level with his mouth. He cleared his throat, a small sound, but the applause gradually quieted and then stopped.

I'd heard a lot about Victor Maxwell from Archie, but I hadn't met him until that night. He was a good-looking man, with dark hair and a dark complexion. He was only about five six, not much taller than I am, but even before he started speaking his energy made him seem bigger than he was.

"Ladies and gentlemen," he said, "Archie Townsend's nomination was uncontested." He was pulling down his shirt cuffs, straightening his tie, as if in preparation to speak—as if he hadn't already started. "It was uncontested because we know Archie's work. Because we know Archie's record. Because we know Archie is the best man for the job."

He let the applause interrupt him. He closed his eyes, and when he spoke again his voice had grown more sombre. "Unfortunately," he said, "the election will not be so simple." He opened his eyes and looked around him. "We cannot depend, my friends, on the popularity of the Party for a win. We cannot depend on the popularity of Archie Townsend for a win."

He moved his head slowly, side to side, took a deep breath in, then let it out. "I've worked on a lot of political campaigns," he said. "So have many of you." People began to nod. "Federal campaigns. Provincial campaigns. And we've learned a few things out there." His voice was hypnotic and it was growing stronger, gathering momentum; almost everyone was nodding now. "We've learned we can't let down our guard. Am I not right?" People began to clap. "We can't let it down for an instant." They clapped harder. "Ladies and gentlemen," Maxwell said, and he began to clap as well, evenly, setting up a rhythm, "if I work until I drop, and then *keep* working.... If Archie works until *he* drops..." He looked over at Archie, smiling—Archie was clapping, too, and so was I, "and then *keeps* working.... If you work until you drop—and then you *keep on working*—only then can we be sure." He'd stepped away from the microphone, was shouting to be heard over the pounding, steady applause that he himself was leading. "If every one of us works until we drop—and then *keeps* working—then we will *win*." The audience exploded. "We can *only* depend on *us*."

Raising his hand in Archie's direction, he waited for the applause and cheering to subside. When it had, he said, "Ladies and gentlemen, our work has just begun."

I was impressed. Victor Maxwell was not only energetic, he

was completely self-assured. Members of the audience were already making their way toward the stage, eager to talk to him. Victor would get things done. He would take control. That he'd agreed to come all the way out here to work on Archie's campaign made me more confident that defeat might not be inevitable after all—a man like Victor would never back a certain loser, no matter how much he was paid.

I was more pleased for Archie than for myself—the last thing I wanted was to be married to a public figure for another three or four years—but maybe Victor's presence would help to alleviate the terrible uncertainty, the fear, I always felt when Archie was campaigning.

John Majewski, the constituency president, stood up—still clapping himself—and indicated the tables of refreshments at the back, and the sign-up sheets for campaign volunteers.

"I want to go home," Ben said into my ear.

Archie had moved off, and he and Victor were surrounded by a group of people who were clapping Victor on the back, clapping Archie on the back, shaking one another's hands. They were pumped, excited.

"I have a math exam tomorrow."

"It won't be long now," I said. "There's juice back there. Why don't you go and get some?"

"I don't want juice," Ben said. "I want to go home."

"Ten minutes," I promised him.

Miffed, he went to sit backwards on a chair near the back of the stage, facing the curtain. I sympathized. He'd done well to be here this long, and he'd borne it graciously enough for him. It was even harder to be the fifteen-year-old son of a politician than it was to be the wife of one.

I headed down the steps from the stage, intending to get him the juice he didn't think he wanted. In the aisle a short, well dressed woman with crimped bright reddish hair who looked to be in her early sixties stepped in front of me. I recognized her from previous campaigns.

"Bill can't be here tonight," she said, "but Archie can count on his support. Mine, too, of course." She was holding a cup of coffee and she raised it as if to make a toast, then lowered it again.

I thanked her, wishing I could remember her name. "We're very grateful. Please thank Bill as well."

She walked with me toward the back. "Your son doesn't look too happy."

I paused and turned to look at Ben, whose back was still defiantly turned toward the hall. "You know what kids are like," I said. "They hate the limelight—at least when their parents put them in it."

"You must get tired of the limelight, too."

"It's okay," I said, smiling down at her. "You get used to it." There was a fat brown mole in the part-line of her hair, and the hair itself was an intense and unnatural shade of orange-red.

"It's not just the public eye, is it?" she said. "It's the insecurity, too. I couldn't stand not knowing whether Bill might have a job next month or not. Sure Archie's popular, but you never know for sure, do you? Even people who say they're supporting him could vote against him. You can't ever know for sure."

Her name came back to me: Edna Lazenby. Edna and Bill Lazenby. He was a self-made millionaire—real estate or something—and this was what Edna did: offered support one moment and took it away the next.

I turned back to her, smiling. "Oh, he'll be fine, Edna," I said, using her name now that I'd remembered it. "With such a wonderful team—people like you and Bill…. How could he possibly lose?"

"Well, good for you," she said comfortably. She glanced toward the stage again and nodded. When she finally wandered off, I felt the kind of disproportionate relief I often feel when I'm being Wife of Archie the Politician—as though I'd been released from a trap just before it became necessary to chew some part of my body off.

On the tables at the back, Dagmar had arranged several plates of cheese and fruit and crackers, a tray of vegetables, a coffee urn. There was a press of people against the tables but they let me in, and I got a box of juice for Ben and a cup of coffee for myself.

"Hello, Maggie," a voice behind me said as I turned back toward the stage.

I'd noticed him earlier—a man in blue jeans and a long black overcoat. He'd been sitting with his arms crossed at the back of the room, but not exactly in the back row—he'd pulled his chair a little away from the others. The brim of a dark felt hat had obscured his face. He'd seemed uninvolved in the proceedings, and as he'd rocked slowly, leisurely back and forth on his chair during Archie's speech, I'd wondered what he was doing there.

I still wondered what he was doing there, but now I knew who he was, and I was too surprised to speak.

"Maggie Hunter," he said.

It had been years since anyone had called me by my maiden name; it was even more astounding to hear it uttered by that particular voice.

"Zeke?" I asked at last, my face hot with surprise and awkwardness.

He gave me a slow smile. "You remember."

"Of course I remember."

Since I'd seen him last, the sharp features of his face, all angles and planes, had become etched with lines, especially near the eyes. Perhaps to help my memory, he'd taken off his hat, revealing closely shorn grey hair, an earring. He was watching me, still smiling.

"How you doing, Maggie?"

"I'm fine," I said, still awkward. My elbow was pressed against my side to keep the coffee steady in the cup. He seemed aware of my nervousness, amused by it.

"What are you doing here?" I glanced at the stage, and saw that Edna Lazenby was watching us. I turned away again, putting my back toward her.

He shrugged. "I was in the neighbourhood."

"I thought you lived down east."

"Moved back last winter. I've got a place outside of town." He was looking at me appraisingly. "You haven't changed much, Maggie."

I looked down at my dark red suit, my black leather heels, thought of my short, dark hair. What was he talking about? Last time he'd seen me, my hair had gone half way down my back. I'd lived in tattered old blue jeans and various oversized shirts. He, on the other hand—well, aside from the lines on his face, aside from the greying hair—he could have walked straight out of then.

His face was strong, the nose and cheekbones hard and strong, and there was a small scar over his left eyebrow. He had an almost disproportionately large, expressive mouth, and even teeth. How well I remembered those grey watching eyes, the look of guardedness and distance. He'd always seemed older than he was.

I still didn't understand why he was here—only Party members could nominate a candidate, only members in the riding. "Have you become a Conservative?" I asked him.

"Hardly," he said, smiling a little.

"Mom?"

My heart leaping in surprise, I turned and found my son standing at my elbow. Awkward again, I introduced them.

Zeke put out his hand, perfunctorily, not interested in Ben.

Ben shook it with equal indifference. "I have to study," he said to me.

"Big test tomorrow," I told Zeke.

Zeke nodded, as uninterested in tests as he was in sons. He was looking beyond Ben, at the stage where Archie and Victor were still talking with a group of other people.

"Not a test," Ben said, a note of exasperation in his voice. "It's a mid-term. An *exam*. And I'm going to flunk it if I don't...."

"Okay, okay. I'll take you home," I said, embarrassed. "Mr. Maxwell can bring Dad. Here." I handed him the juice box. "You go and get your things."

I turned back to Zeke. "I have to go."

He was looking thoughtfully in the direction Ben had gone, but now he looked back at me. "Why don't I give you a call?" he said. "We could get caught up."

"Sure," I said, surprised. "Why not?"

"What's your number?"

I waited for him to pull out a pen, but he kept his eyes on me. I could have told him that the number was in the book, under "Townsend, A.R." Instead, letting my eyes meet his, and feeling the flush in my face intensify, I said the number aloud.

He repeated it, and nodded.

I left him there and went back to the stage to tell Archie that Ben and I were leaving. He paid me no attention, but Victor assured me he'd bring my husband home.

When I turned again, Zeke was already gone.

2

At home, Ben checked for messages, handed me the phone, aimed the remote at the television set, and dropped onto the couch.

The message was from Archie's mother, Millicent, saying they'd be back from Phoenix Friday. She gave the arrival time and flight number. No need to pick them up, she said—just thought we'd like to know. She and Edward hoped the meeting had gone well.

I went up to the bedroom to get changed.

Zeke Avery. It had been a long time since I'd even thought of him, but during the drive home—Ben silent, sulking in the passenger seat—more than two decades had dropped away, and for several moments the sense of loss I'd felt when he had disappeared had grown as keen and new as if it had just happened.

Now I looked into the closet mirror to try to see what Zeke had seen tonight, to try to see how different I looked from the way I had back then. I could remember less about how I'd looked than how I used to feel when I was with him and the others in his group, which was awkward and inadequate. My awe of them had almost always reduced me to confusion, silence.

I gazed into the mirror, but found it was impossible to conjure enough of my younger self to compare it to my current one. I knew I was only a few pounds heavier than I'd been at university, and there was still very little grey in the dark brown of my hair. It was blunt now, smooth and neatly trimmed above my shoulders, where once it had been so long. I had wrinkles at the corners of my eyes—but then, so did Zeke. Otherwise, the slackening elasticity of my skin was more something I was aware of than something anyone else could see.

I changed into a sweatshirt and sweatpants, washed my face, then went back downstairs, where I nagged Ben about his exam until he finally got mad and went up to his room. A moment later, I saw the telephone-extension light come on: some big exam.

At the back of the liquor cabinet I found a nearly full bottle of Grand Marnier, and poured myself an inch of the liqueur. I wandered with it through the empty, dim-lit main floor of the house, remembering how I'd met them.

Zeke and the others had occupied—possessed—two tables in the coffee room in the basement of the old Students Union Building. I remembered them in that half-lit basement room, six or seven regulars and always a few hangers on. Smoke rising from their cigarettes and pipes, intent on their conversation, they leaned into cup after cup of vending-machine coffee—coffee that tasted of cardboard no matter how much white or sugar you got the machines to put in. Stalwartly black-clad in the era of the hippies, they were the intellectuals.

I discovered them during my second year, late one Friday afternoon as September was drawing to a close. On my way to the bus, I'd run into a girl I'd met in a first-year course—anthropology, I think it was—and she'd suggested a cup of coffee. She led me out of strong sun and a biting wind into the darkness and warmth of SUB, down the stone stairs with its wide oak banisters, and into the smoke of the coffee room.

There were four or five of them there that afternoon, standing about as though they were on the verge of leaving but not making the actual break for the whole time we were there. The sun did not penetrate that room, which was hazy with their smoke, and a dim fluorescent overhead light gave inadequate lighting. Save for them, the room was deserted, and we chose a table in a darkened corner, twenty feet from them. It was as though I saw and heard them through a gauze, and I couldn't take my eyes off them. In my efforts to hear what they were saying, I almost ignored the woman I'd come in with.

Intense. They were always so intense—all of them, although Zeke, a little taller than the others, his voice more certain of itself, distinguished himself immediately from the others. They were arguing that afternoon, as they were to do again in the weeks to come, about a production of *Happy Days* they'd seen the night before, over whether it had succeeded in creating an illusion of boredom, as the author had intended, or whether they had actually been bored. Zeke supported the latter view, yawning once or twice to prove it, before coming to life to point out that the "tragic pruning" of creative genius that occurred between the mental image and the page was bad enough: the play as a creative form put integrity at risk a second time through translation from page to stage. Someone else didn't think creative artists had the choice: "Inspiration's inspiration. A play's a play. It's not a novel."

This was the way I'd imagined university would be before I got there. Instead, during my first year I'd found my classmates no more interesting than the people I'd known in high school. And, after all, I'd realized with disappointment, that was what they were, most of them—high-school seniors, one year older. Now two years older. Just like me.

Zeke and his group were of a different order, an order that seemed to have evolved where we had not. They looked smart, talked smart, but there was something more: determination, even ferocity. Surely these were the thinkers of the future, the poets and the critics, the kind of people who were supposed to be at universities. And Zeke was always at the centre. Almost as though they were unaware that they were doing it, the others would go quiet when he said something, turn in his direction, give him the final word.

During the weeks that followed, as winter began to close in, the mere thought of them—of the way they looked, the way they talked—drew me down to the basement of SUB again and again to see if they were there. I was never disappointed: I always found at least a few of them smoking, arguing, complaining. It didn't occur to me then to wonder why some of them never seemed to go to classes, but afterward I saw that they'd been more concerned about themselves as intellectuals than as scholars. Maybe I learned this truth through contrast: Archie was the other way around.

At first I pretended my arrival in the coffee room was accident, coincidence. I'd bring a book and open it and stare at it as I ate my bag lunch or slowly sipped a coffee. Increasingly unable to resist the draw of them—even missing a class or two myself to be there—I began to worry that they'd mind, that one of them would come over and tell me to eavesdrop somewhere else. I identified the few I thought were capable of that—Zeke was one—and prepared myself for flight.

But instead of sending me away, a couple of women in the group began to raise their hands or smile a greeting whenever I came in. One afternoon Nola, a small, bright chattery woman with wiry red hair who seemed to take pride in being able to swear as well as the men—she's now a lawyer well known for her work with the less than privileged—came over and asked why I didn't come and sit with them. Katherine, taller, quieter, but no less forceful or intelligent when she did decide to speak—patted the wooden chair beside her that Nola had just vacated. I went over and took the seat, feeling terribly awkward—not least because I was attempting to balance a coffee on an open textbook and a stack of binders. But I made it, put my things down on the table, sat. Nola pulled up another chair. The others—Zeke among them—waited, uninterested, until I was settled and then resumed whatever discussion my arrival had interrupted.

I began soon after that to go with them sometimes, with groups of three or four of them at least, to lectures on economics, paleontology, psychology, given by visiting scholars, grad students, scheduled at odd hours when I should have been studying or in class. It didn't seem to matter what the subject was or who delivered it: their greed for knowledge, for opinion, was scattershot. I went with them to films and to the folk concerts that were held in the lounge two floors up from the coffee room. Often feeling like a third-grader—and I was younger than most of them—I tagged along when they went for coffee afterwards, or to someone's room for wine and beer, and listened to them take apart and examine what we'd just seen or heard. I attended a couple of real parties with them, too, in dark sweet-smelling places. Heard their music, watched them finally unwind.

I felt privileged to be so close to them, to learn from them— even, let's face it, to appear to outsiders as though I were a part of them, although I never really felt I was. They had read so much, seen so much, done so much that I had not. Still haven't.

By the time Archie came in, I'd poured myself a little more liqueur.

"I thought it went well," I said, following him into the family room. The extension light on the phone was off at last.

"It did go well," he said, slipping off his suit jacket and picking up the newspaper from the ottoman. "We were preaching to the converted, of course, but Maxwell's going to make a difference. He's full of good ideas."

"You were right about his energy," I said.

"Loads of energy," he agreed, nodding. He shook out the paper, reorganizing it so that the front page was back on top, and sat down in his armchair. "Did I tell you he's never lost one?"

The word "yet" hung in the air between us, but neither of us said it. Archie was telling me to relax, which I was unlikely to do, Maxwell or no Maxwell. The term that was just ending had been marked by cutback after cutback, and even though the most recent budget had balanced and the polls were showing a definite change in public sentiment, I still had my doubts. A lot of people had been laid off as a result of government decisions in the past four years: how could they so easily forgive, forget?

I'd spent weeks imploring whatever gods might be listening to convince Archie not to run again, but either there were no gods, as I suspected, or their attentions had been focused somewhere else.

Archie was reading the paper and watching Letterman at the same time, his reading glasses perched at the end of his nose. He was—is—a large man, big-boned, just over six feet tall. If he'd continued teaching, he'd probably have been overweight and soft. He'd been tending in that direction six years before when he got it in his head—or his father put it there—to run in the by-election.

He took good care of himself now, partly because he wanted an image that reflected self-control and restraint, partly because he needed to stay one step ahead with the Party and physical condition mattered there, and partly because he didn't want to die of a heart attack the way his predecessor had. He'd taken up jogging, and lifted weights a couple of times a week. With his still-thick sandy hair and blue eyes, he looked good. He looked powerful. He was a presence.

The presence was looking at me over his reading glasses.

"What are you doing?" he asked.

"Doing?"

He nodded at the glass.

"Having a nightcap," I said.

"On a Wednesday night?"

I shrugged. "I was cold when I came in."

He folded the paper back down on the ottoman, stood up and said, "I have a seven o'clock breakfast meeting with Maxwell. I'm going to bed."

And so it starts, I thought. Even before the writ has dropped. Not that it made much difference any more. He was absent often enough during term as well, especially now that he had a portfolio, that Ben and I had grown used to operating as a twosome.

I told him I'd be right up, and went to turn out the lights in the living room, my attention caught briefly by the family portrait over the fireplace. I wondered how long I'd have to leave it there, and decided that the answer was probably until something fatal happened to Millicent and Edward. They'd gone to a lot of trouble to have it done, and quite likely a lot of expense, as a gift for our anniversary.

The artist had worked from a photo portrait that Archie had insisted we have taken the previous summer for our Christmas cards. The photo itself had been unremarkable and, I'd thought, inoffensive. But in translating it to canvas, the artist had managed to render all three of us less attractive and certainly more flat-headed than we were in reality. Archie and I looked middle-aged, settled and predictable, while Ben's "likeness" was that of a somewhat mischievous but basically angelic young teenager— the kind who was likely to be carrying a slingshot in the back pocket of his trousers and harbouring a frog inside his half-buttoned jacket.

As if, I thought, turning out the light.

I'd have worn something entirely different if I'd had any idea what Millicent and Edward would eventually do with the photograph. Something black, perhaps, or red. Certainly not the rose-pink suit that suited my colour in reality, but made the skin of the reproduction look sallow and unhealthy. Made me look fifty-five instead of forty-one. Made me look like a 1950s housewife. Made me look boring and somewhat stupid. I hoped that was not what Zeke had seen when he'd looked at me tonight.

I drained the glass and put it in the dishwasher, then turned out the rest of the downstairs lights. As I went upstairs, I saw that Ben's light was still on.

I knocked lightly on his door. "It's after midnight," I said.

"I'm *studying*," he said, his voice hard.

Archie was in bed, his light out, but he'd left mine on. I felt warmed and a little tipsy. As I was taking off my clothes he asked me mildly, half asleep, "Who was that guy you were talking to tonight?"

"When?"

"At the hall. Just before you left. He looked familiar somehow."

"Just someone I knew at university."

"Did I know him?"

"I don't think so. Zeke Avery. He was part of that group I hung around with for a while in second year." I'd met Archie a year and a half after Zeke had disappeared.

He nodded, his eyes still closed. "The hippies."

I turned out my light and lay down on my back, my hands behind my head. "Not hippies," I said. "They were more like throwbacks to the Fifties. Beatniks or something." I shook my head. "Haven't seen any of them in years."

A few years earlier, Archie and I had attended the re-dedication of Rowland House, as the old Students Union Building is now called. It has been carpeted, panelled, furnished with teak and indoor trees, and today it houses the university's senate chamber and the administration offices of the president. The reception was on the second floor, but I'd gone down to the basement just to have a look. I'd found more offices, more waiting areas, more partitions, and more potted trees. Nothing looked or smelled familiar: there was no sign that there'd ever been a coffee room down there.

"Avery. He the one got arrested for possession?"

"No."

That was Andrew Parker—right group, wrong person—but I found myself feeling protective and didn't say the name. Archie's as opposed to drug use as it's possible to get, and you never know. In politics, you run into a lot of people.

Archie sighed. "I've got to get some sleep."

A few minutes later, his voice already slowed, he said, "Boyfriend?"

"Who?"

"Avery."

"Oh, no. He was just part of the group."

I didn't remember if I'd ever talked to him specifically about Zeke, but if I had he seemed to have forgotten so it didn't matter anyway. I'm sure at the stage when I might have, I would never have let him know how much I'd once longed for someone else. Once we'd run into Nola on the campus, and I'd steered Archie away as quickly as I could—before she could ask, "Have you heard anything?" Before I could say, "Have you?"

Apparently not finding it unusual that someone I hadn't seen in more than twenty years had showed up for his nomination meeting, Archie was soon asleep, his breathing regular and even. I lay awake for a long time. Not tossing and turning. Just thinking and remembering.

3

Zeke called on Friday morning—
the first day of spring—as I was heading out the door.

"Bad time to call?" he asked. He didn't identify himself. He didn't need to. His voice was at once familiar and unfamiliar, a little rougher and deeper than it had been twenty years before.

Flustered, I said, "Oh, no. It's fine." Then I looked at the clock on the stove. "Except that it's not," I said. "I'm going to be late for work."

"Where do you work?"

"The Purple Parrot."

"The 'Purple Parrot'?" he repeated, amusement in his voice.

"It's an arts shop," I said. "Arts and crafts. It's pretty well known." I sounded defensive, felt embarrassed.

"I haven't been back that long," he said. "Lot of new places around. Where is it?"

I'd been listening again to the timbre of his voice and I had to think for a moment before I answered.

"Old Watchford." I looked at the clock again and thought, A

neighbourhood at least fifteen minutes away from here. "I've really got to go," I said. "Can I call you back?"

"Let's meet," he said. "For coffee."

I hesitated, asked, "Today?"

"Today," he said. "Why not?"

Today.

Millicent and Edward were arriving at the airport at five. They'd said not to bother to pick them up, but they'd be astounded if I didn't. I was meeting Alana for lunch, which meant an extra hour at the shop; I'd never get away before four.

"I can't today," I said.

I worked again the next day, Saturday, and Ben had hockey. Sunday there was the requisite church appearance, no doubt dinner with Millicent and Edward. Shit.

"Then when?" he said.

"I'm sorry," I said.

For some reason it didn't seem right to meet him on the weekend anyway.

I was growing panicky—all this thinking was making me later and later.

"How's Monday?" I asked. "Or Tuesday?"

"Monday's good," he said, as though it didn't really matter one way or the other after all. "What time?"

"I'm off at three."

"All right. That's fine." Then, "Where?"

I named a coffee shop near the Purple Parrot, and told him where it was.

As I put the receiver into the cradle—my hand, I noticed, trembling—I remembered Ben's dental appointment: Monday at four-thirty. I pulled the phone book out of the drawer and flipped through it to the Averys. Nothing that could be a Zeke. I looked at the phone. There was a number I could call to find out what number had just called me, but I had no idea what it was. Ben knew, but Ben wasn't home.

We'd only have half an hour. Forty-five minutes if I pushed it. That wouldn't be long enough. Nowhere near long enough to catch up on twenty years.

I took a deep breath, took my keys from the counter, and started again for the door. It would be enough, I told myself. It was only coffee. It was no big deal.

I was only ten minutes late for work, but Fiona was in a temper. My mind still on Zeke and the others, it took me a while to realize that her anger had nothing to do with my lateness. After three years, I knew something about Fiona's moods, and when I paused to consider it I realized that this one was well entrenched, likely hours old. It could be a rejected story, a plumbing problem, anything.

Fiona Delaray is not a beautiful woman. Her nose is a little long, her lips a little thin and wide. But her hazel eyes are beautiful, and she knows how to use make-up and clothes to her advantage. She's tall and slender and that day, with her long dark curly hair pinned up on her head, and a dark brown A-line dress that came nearly to her ankles, she looked even taller and slimmer than usual.

That morning everything about her, from the long skirt of her dress to her long white fingers with their perfect tips of bronze, contributed to the drama of her gestures—which included stalking in and out of her private office at the back, dashing papers and notebooks onto the sales counter, and scooping up others that seemed, from her expression, to have been deliberately avoiding her.

I knew not to ask if anything was the matter. If I did, she'd snap. I waited, and I was relieved when she got a phone call about eleven and suddenly went out.

Fiona was not that much easier to work with when she was in a good mood, but she had fewer sharp corners then. I had learned to coexist with her, to work around her. I must admit I admired her flair, even envied it. She had an artistic temperament. She *was* an artist, a writer to be exact. In the past year, she'd had four short stories published; at the age of thirty-two she was "on her way," she said, and I believed her.

I watched the way she was not only in an effort to keep the peace, but also out of professional interest. I had started doing a little writing, too. I hoped the impulse that had got me started had more substance to it than the mere flattery of imitation, but I wasn't sure.

I hadn't mentioned my writing to Fiona, or to anyone. I was waiting until I got better at it. What I came up with now seemed dull and amateurish to my eye, and I had no idea why I kept at it.

I'd begun to wonder if you needed a temperament like Fiona's to actually be any good.

I'd started out attempting to write stories. Fiction. Most of them were about middle-aged women who were trapped—by marriages, aging parents, children. I wasn't positive, because I saw so many women now who seemed to have it all together, people like Fiona and other artists at the Purple Parrot, and even Alana, and several who were in the Legislature with Archie, but I was fairly certain that there would be some readers who would be able to identify with women who felt trapped, even in the Nineties. But as I wrote I saw that I had no idea how to release them, or how they could release themselves. After several pages their lives seemed boring anyway, trite, and I lost interest in them. They depressed me. I ripped them into shreds, releasing them that way.

Then several months before, I'd wakened early from a dream, and it was as though Gran had been near enough me to touch. It had been years since I'd dreamed of her, and I couldn't remember much of the dream I'd just wakened from, but in the early darkness I felt utterly secure in her presence, and at the same time fully aware that she was not there. I was no longer small. This house was not her house: our house. She had grown feeble and old, incapable of protecting me, or of teaching me, years and years before. My awareness that it was illusion made the feeling of her closeness painful, but I was reluctant to let it go.

But it did go, within moments, caught and stolen off by thoughts of what lay ahead of me that day. Dusting shelves at the Purple Parrot later in the morning, it had occurred to me that I might conjure her deliberately by writing about her—writing down not only what I remembered of her, but what she'd told me of her life before I came along. My memories of her memories: the thought amused, intrigued me. There was lots to write, when I thought about it, and I became eager to get at it.

The piece grew gradually from its starting point, both back in time and forward. It was made of fragments: memories invention-smoothed, inventions that slipped in so easily I could in places barely remember where the truth began or ended. The whole was truth, but parts of it were not. I had no idea how long this would go on, or how I would describe it when it was finished: it wasn't fiction, it wasn't, strictly speaking, memoir. Nor was it biography or autobiography, poetry or essay. It was all of these.

The content was reflected in the medium, scribbled bits of paper stuck here and there throughout a small bound notebook which I'd wrapped in two elastic bands and carried always in my handbag. I still didn't think my writing was very good, but engaging in it had given me those glimpses I had hoped for, brief contacts with the woman who'd been both parents to me, and that kept pulling me back to it.

I worked at it only when I felt like it, when memory occurred, and never when there was anyone around, which meant I didn't work on it very often. Almost everything I'd written had been done in short bursts at the Purple Parrot, in quiet times when Fiona was away and there were no customers. Things tended to pop to mind while I was dusting, filing, sorting. Once in a while something longer had started, and I'd been tempted—or at least it had crossed my mind—to turn the little sign on the door around so that it read "closed" instead of "open," and write on. But I could never really do that, in case even one customer escaped: the hopes of our artists were attached more securely than the price tags to the objects in the Purple Parrot.

There were a lot of objects. The walls were nearly covered with framed sketches and watercolours, bright quilts, wood carvings, brass rubbings, small hooked rugs and painted masks. Two dozen white shelving units arranged at irregular angles throughout the two-thousand-square-foot shop held pottery bowls and vases, candlesticks, teapots, hand-crafted pencil holders, straw kitchen witches, keepsake holders with hinged and needle-pointed lids, and dozens of other items that had caught Mark's or Fiona's fancy at one time or another. Near the glass-topped counter—on which stood at the moment both the "old" and the "new" computer, as well as the papers and file folders Fiona had tossed there earlier—hung gold-coloured neckbands and necklaces, hammered-silver arm and ankle bracelets, and brooches and earrings set with stones, and beside the jewellery racks stood boxes of hand-made paper and packages of note cards featuring drawings of local historic sites.

My regular hours at the Purple Parrot were ten to three, three days a week, and all day Saturday. I also worked at other times when Mark and Fiona needed me. On days like this, when I went out for lunch—which I didn't do very often because I'd been hired in part to cover Fiona over the noon hour—I worked an additional hour to make it up.

Working with Fiona could be difficult, but in three years I had never regretted the impulse that had made me ask about a rumour I'd heard that they were looking for some help, and I had never stopped being grateful that Mark and Fiona had hired me. I wasn't paid a lot, but it was more than a job. It was another way of looking at the world, a different way from the way people in Archie's world, and mine at home, looked at it. Now that the place was also connected with my writing, I felt some kinship with the artists. It just *felt* right to be there.

I left the paperwork I might have done and put on a new CD. As Rampal's flutework filled the shop, I started dusting shelves and merchandise, and let my mind wander back to Zeke. When I'd been talking to him on the phone, I hadn't been able to see his face, but now I could. I remembered how he'd been at the nomination meeting, the way that time had layered over the younger man, and gravelled his voice as well, without really altering anything about him.

Zeke had disappeared before the end of the Christmas break, part way through his third, or maybe fourth, year of Honours English. I'd been one of the last to see him.

Katherine had insisted I accompany her to a party one night during the holidays: someone she wanted to meet would be there. I had gone, knowing she'd likely asked me only because most of the others were away, knowing I'd likely have to make my own way home alone. That was me, back then, with them.

The party, at the apartment of a couple I didn't know, was crowded and too hot, and everyone there seemed to know someone else but me. Katherine soon found the person she'd been looking for—who, to my surprise, although I did not appreciate the implications until later—was a beautiful but severe-looking woman who appeared to be in her late twenties. The two were deep in conversation, heads close together, in the doorway to the kitchen. Less than hour after we arrived, feeling awkward and alone and as usual too young, I began to think of leaving. And then—about ten o'clock—Zeke Avery walked in.

He was wearing something very much like what he wore to the nomination meeting, a wide-brimmed hat and an overcoat that was dark and long and flowing, far too light for winter. His arrival had an impact—there was a momentary hush, and several people crossed the room to greet him. He surveyed the gathering in his haughty way, his eyes slipping over Katherine and her conversation partner and then stopping briefly when they came to me. He raised a hand in greeting. I nodded back, my heart pounding from surprise and pleasure. At that moment someone handed me a glass of wine, and I leaned back against the window sill and decided to stay put.

Within a few minutes Zeke, who had moved only a few feet from the doorway and still had his coat on, but was now also holding a glass of wine, was delivering an impassioned talk to a group of people I didn't know. It looked as though he'd had a few drinks before he came in, and I watched with a mixture of longing, fascination and concern as he moved deep into his subject—tossing his head back, using his free hand to make a point. I had no trouble hearing most of what he said, despite all the people between us. He was continuing a theme we'd heard quite a bit about in SUB before the Christmas break, and here as there it was raising a few hackles.

For some reason, he'd decided early in December that universities were elitist, and that the intellectual discourse that took place in them was artificial. The others in our group had been hurt when he made it plain that his wide-ranging disenchantment extended to us. They thought—we thought—that what happened down in SUB was about as meaningful as life could get. The unwillingness of the others to accept his point had made him unhappy, alternately distracted and withdrawn, argumentative and fierce.

"The credits should go to those who are working on the docks and in the fields," he said now. "Picking cabbages in the hot sun for minimum wage or less. The hookers and the foot soldiers— they should be the ones who get degrees. What do we know about life—reading poetry, tamping tobacco down into our briar pipes, drinking a glass of wine, pronouncing...? What do we know about anything?"

He took his pipe out of his pocket, as much to underscore his point as to begin the process of lighting it. An older man who looked like he might have been a prof—he might also have been our host—sniffed and said that Zeke was being silly. He said that the very point of universities was to provide a place apart from a raucous world, a place where contemplation and thought were possible.

"But what do we have to think *about*?" Zeke asked. "What do we have to contemplate? Most of us have been in *school* for our entire lives."

Uncomfortable at the potential evolution of this debate, and increasingly worried about how long I'd left Gran alone at home, I finished the wine and put the glass down on the windowsill. In a bedroom I found my coat at the bottom of a great heap and put it on, then made my way through the crowded living room to the door—waving at Katherine and casting my eyes at Zeke as I went by. Neither of them seemed to notice. Zeke was deep in argument, eyes blazing, and his adversary looked almost murderous.

The temperature outside had risen by several degrees in the past few hours and I set off for home, happy to be outside. I had gone less than half a block when there was the pound of feet behind me. I turned. It was Zeke, running to catch up.

"You're a wise woman," he said. "It was very hot in there."

It must have been the wine: I laughed.

He considered me for several moments, and then he laughed as well. A small laugh, but it was something. It didn't happen very often.

I cast about for something else to say but could think of nothing. He walked along beside me, lost in thought, turning a corner when I did. Finally, I asked him where he was going.

He looked at me and said, "I have no idea. How about you?"

"Home," I said.

He nodded. After another little silence he said, "Tell me why you hang around with that bunch."

"What bunch?"

"Nola and Katherine," he said, looking across and down at me. "Andrew and the others. What do you get out of it?"

Unable to think of a more sophisticated answer, I told the truth. I said how impressed I was by them, how much I'd learned. I told him about the books I'd started reading and the music I had turned to, thanks to them. How I felt my education was really taking place in the basement of the Students Union Building, not in class.

He nudged me along with questions—when had I first thought about university? How had I expected it to be? What was the most important thing I'd learned in high school? Things like that. When he stopped asking, and fell silent again, I said, "Tell me about yourself." But he shrugged in a way that said he didn't want to talk about it.

We were off the main streets now and I slowed the pace, brushing away the obligation I always felt to get home as soon as possible to Gran. She would have to survive without me for this once.

It had snowed a lot in the days before, and there was a moon. It was a beautiful evening—the most perfect winter night, I decided, that I'd ever seen.

Suddenly, he began to laugh. It wasn't a mocking laugh, but a happy one. It was infectious, too, and I began to giggle along with him until both of us were laughing, laughing, filling up the moonlit winter night and the deserted streets with laughter. We laughed until my stomach hurt and I was walking bent and crouched.

"This is my street," I gulped at last, as we reached the final turn. And he stopped and caught me, took me in his arms and I can feel even now the way the laughter went away as his big coat came around me, can feel the warmth and taste of him as he bent and kissed me, a long and gentle kiss, his lips against my lips.

"Thank you," he said, then he let me go, raised his hand and waved, and walked back the way we'd come.

I watched him go, that coat out like a cape, his head down, lost again in thought.

By the time classes resumed, he was gone. No one knew where, but the others didn't seem concerned about his health or safety. Perhaps they assumed that his vision and his promise were just too great to snuff.

"He's Kerouacked," someone said with envy. "Hit the road. Gone off to find real life."

I had begun to dream, to hope, to fantasize in those few days since the party, and a great emptiness opened up inside me when I learned that he was gone. Needing to be near the others, I tried to conceal the extent of my devastation, but I probably didn't have to: consumed by their own feelings of bereavement—all of them but Katherine, who'd fallen in love that night too—no one seemed to cared how I felt.

I went over and over what I had said to him that night, wondering what I might have said differently to alter what had happened. He had seemed so happy. I couldn't understand it. Gradually, loss turned to guilt and shame, and then to a depression that took a long time to lift.

The group's enthusiasm and energy faded rapidly—whether because Zeke had vanished or because we thought we should have vanished, too, it wasn't clear. By the end of February, it was over. The size of the group in the coffee room dwindled, became knots, then pairs. At the end I, and no doubt others, would occasionally come down the stairs, take a look around, see no one we knew, and wander off to class or to the library. There were no more parties or plans to go to films. Some of us got down to work, a veil having lifted to reveal or to remind us—and my re-realization was accompanied by a good-sized dose of panic—why we had paid tuition. Others just seemed to drop away.

Fiona came back to the Purple Parrot just after noon, carrying a clear plastic container with a salad in it. She pulled bank books out of her handbag and dropped them on the counter.

"Mark call?" she asked.

"No," I said. "Was he supposed to?"

"He had his meeting with the City this morning," she said, impatient with me for forgetting.

No wonder she was tense.

"Maybe the news is good," I said after a moment, "and they're working out the details."

"Maybe," Fiona said, glancing over at two women who were examining a woven hanging on the back wall. "And maybe a rich relative just died and left me a million dollars. Have those people been helped?"

"They said they didn't want help," I said, putting the feather duster away under the counter. I straightened and turned to her. "While you were out, a woman came in and spent nearly fifty dollars."

This information was intended to cheer her up, but it had no visible effect. "If you're going out to lunch," she said, "you might as well get going."

I went to get my coat and handbag, and Fiona went over to chat up the two women. She was pretty good at doing that, turning on the charm. The conversations she started with customers almost always came around eventually to her writing—she was building a future audience for her books—but she usually managed to make a sale as well.

I left her to it, and went to meet Alana.

4

Alana took a sip of Diet Coke and said, "There's something going on between Ken Swimmer and Marianna Johnson."

"Who?" I asked, thrown off course by this announcement. I'd intended to launch our conversation with my own news—had been, in fact, so eager to tell Alana in person about seeing Zeke at the nomination meeting that I'd resisted the temptation to tell her on the phone two days earlier, when we'd arranged this lunch. I'd thought she'd be interested to hear about the group at university, to learn something new about my past after all the years I'd known her.

"Ken Swimmer—"

"I know who he is," I said. Swimmer was a real-estate lawyer in the firm where Alana did paralegal work. She did quite a lot of work for him, and she mentioned him often. He'd come across to me as a good looking but arrogant man who didn't like to admit he was wrong, and who was more interested in training for triathlons than practicing the law. "Who's Marianna Johnson?"

"She joined the firm about six months ago. I'm sure I've mentioned her. She's beautiful, she's smart. Actually, I really like her." Alana shrugged, leaning forward to peel batter off a piece of cod before she ate it. Her multi-coloured earring dangled close to her plate. "I'd have thought she was too intelligent for this."

In the course of twenty years, Alana had raised herself above the level of the rest of the support staff at Sanderson and Lebel, but she was not a lawyer. In a niche of her own, she had no social peers at work and I'd become a repository for so much of her office gossip that I felt like I knew half of the lawyers and staff myself.

Alana's long black hair was rapidly turning white-grey, but it was no less unruly than it had been when she was younger. She'd caught some of it back today in a bright red ribbon. She was given to brightly coloured clothing—big patterned shirts and flowing skirts and flashy pieces of jewellery. I often thought that her appearance must alter the whole tenor of that office full of lawyers, who I tended to visualize as clad entirely and consistently in grey.

She'd been battling a weight problem all her adult life—battling it successfully enough that it never got completely out of hand, but neither did it ever go away. She loved the kinds of foods that tended to put on weight, and she was always trying to figure out ways to eat them without ingesting the calories that came with them. Hence the stack of batter that was accumulating at the edge of her plate today.

"Swimmer's about our age, isn't he?"

She nodded. "Married, with two kids." She put a French fry into her mouth. "Two teenagers."

I finished the bowl of vegetable soup I'd ordered, put down my spoon, and sat back in my chair. As soon as I'd opened the menu, I'd realized that I didn't feel much like eating. Zeke's call had made me nervous and now, with the turn the conversation had taken, I was beginning to wonder if I should mention him after all. Not that the two subjects were related, but I didn't want to put any ideas in her head.

"What gets me is that it's so bloody typical," she said. "Middle-aged man, younger woman. It happens so damned often."

"What makes you think there's something going on?" I asked,

thinking that I could tell her about the nomination meeting, maybe, without mentioning that I was planning to meet him for coffee. She would definitely raise her eyebrows at me if I told her that.

"Give me a break," she said. "You'd have to be blind. They think they're being so careful, but you can practically feel their hands all over one another when you get anywhere near them. I can't get over it. Swimmer's such a self-centred dork. She could have any man she wanted. It makes me feel like shaking her." She looked at her watch and started on her coleslaw. "They're working on a few files together. They've got endless excuses to 'consult,' if you want to call it that."

"There's no accounting for tastes," I said.

"He's *married*, Maggie. Both of them should know better."

Alana could afford to be censorious when it came to infidelity, I thought. After seventeen years of marriage, she and Vern were still madly in love with one another. They did things together, just the two of them, without the kids—went to concerts, went on picnics—because they wanted to, and it even sounded as though they still talked to one another. I envied them their closeness and companionship, which I attributed to good luck. In my experience, couples didn't often have common interests, common tastes, or similar dispositions. I'd concluded long ago that whatever functions of the brain were involved in the selection of a mate, thinking was not one of them.

Alana looked up from her ravaged lunch and said, "Anyway. What's new with you?"

"Not much," I said, and waved to the waiter for a refill on my coffee.

She was looking at me. "You okay?" she asked.

"Sure I am," I said, looking her directly in the eye. "Why?"

She lifted a shoulder, making an earring glint in a beam of sunlight that had reached our table. We moved onto other subjects, starting with the standard comparison of notes on child-rearing. We'd met on a parent committee when Ben and Zachary had been in the same play school a dozen years before, and we'd been friends ever since. From the beginning—at least, until today—I'd always enjoyed Alana's nerve. She knew exactly what she thought, and she said what was on her mind. Even her clothes made a statement, unlike anything I owned.

Archie and Vern had met only once or twice, early on when Archie was still teaching, but they didn't have much in common. We'd given up on them after a couple of excruciating evenings, and a few years later we'd finally stopped trying to get our kids to get along. Now we just met for lunch, the two of us, every few weeks or so.

My decision not to tell Alana about Zeke was disturbing me, but I was trying not to show it so she wouldn't ask me again if something was the matter. I couldn't tell whether I felt guilty because I was going to see Zeke again, or because of how Alana might interpret the fact that I was going to see Zeke again.

I said a silent prayer of thanks to Ken Swimmer and Marianna Johnson when she turned the subject back to them, and then another one to the waiter when he finally brought the bill.

When I got back to the Purple Parrot, Mark was sitting at the sales counter, looking through the contents of a file folder. He rarely showed up during the day, but I was always pleased to see him. He nodded and smiled at me as I put away my coat and handbag and, since there were no customers in the store, I went over to talk to him.

Mark Scales, like Fiona, has a taste for trendy clothes. That day he was wearing dark green trousers of some expensive-looking cloth, soft leather loafers, and a camel jacket. He'd perched his wide-brimmed hat atop the computer monitor, and his thick brown hair, which showed a few more threads of grey than when I'd met him, was shining in the glow of the light above the sales desk. Some men seem to enter their primes, appearance wise, as they approach their forties, and Mark is one of those.

Before I could ask him how the meeting with the City had turned out, Fiona came bursting out of her office with a thick file folder in her hand. She slapped it down on the counter next to the one Mark was reading and said, "They're fucking Philistines."

"It's not the end of the universe, Fiona," Mark said dryly. "They don't have any money; that's all there is to that."

"They have money for trade missions to Japan, don't they?" Fiona said. "They have money for potholes. What do they think we're doing here—selling day-old bread? This is culture. *Local* culture."

"I told them," Mark said. "So did the army of loyal supporters who took time to call or write on our behalf. All five of them." He glanced at me. "We didn't win the appeal."

"I gathered," I said. "I'm sorry."

I really was sorry. It wasn't just the job, although I was worried enough about that: I couldn't imagine my life without its regular shifts at the Purple Parrot. They were like fixes. They kept me sane. But I was almost as worried that the Purple Parrot itself would have to close. It was like an institution in the city.

I'd watched the decline in customers in the past year or so and wondered how long Mark was going to be able to keep it running. He was obviously subsidizing it to some extent already, and he'd had to lay off two part-time staff in the past twelve months or so. Now, aside from Fiona, there was only me and Bill Bold, the university student who helped out evenings and weekends.

Mark seemed to be pretty well off, but that didn't mean he'd want to keep throwing good money after bad—especially in this economy. His grandfather had established one of the city's first printing companies—Scales Printing and Graphics, it was called today—a highly successful and well respected firm. Mark now ran the company, his father having taken early retirement after Mark's mother died. Today, Hugh Scales spent most of his life sailing and scuba-diving from a huge house on Maui, which he had built and now lived in with his new, much younger, wife. Mark and Fiona went there once or twice a year, and brought back pictures.

Before all this had happened, back in the mid 1980s when Mark had more time on his hands, he'd responded to some artistic longing of his own by buying the Purple Parrot. It had been established five years previously by an artists' collective, but the artists had been disorganized, poor business managers, and even in times of plenty had been unable to make a go of it.

Mark had hung a brightly coloured six-foot plastic parrot out over the street, applied a couple of coats of paint inside, and mounted a canny promotional campaign that emphasized the Purple Parrot's funkiness. He'd quickly turned the prospects of the place around, and for several years people had come in droves—from as far away as Paris, France, I'd heard—to have a look and to take away something—almost anything—contained in a piece of Purple Parrot wrapping paper.

In the middle of all this, Mark met and fell in love with Fiona, and he installed her as the Purple Parrot's manager when the time came to turn his full attention to the printing business. Even before her arrival, I'd become a regular customer. Just knowing that the gift I'd bought had come from the Purple Parrot made me more confident about giving it.

Fiona had gone off to answer the private phone which was ringing in her office.

"Are you going to be all right?" I asked him.

"The grant would only have meant a couple of thousand dollars," he said. "Hardly sink-or-swim, despite what I let them think." He leaned back on the stool and stretched. "The city manager's right in one way—keeping the Purple Parrot open isn't like road maintenance. If people want what we've got, they'll buy it. If they don't, maybe we shouldn't be in business." He looked around the shop. "The truth of the matter is it's been pretty slow around here. I've been so busy at work I've been trying to ignore that." A couple of customers wandered in and he raised a hand in greeting. "I got into the Purple Parrot because it was a challenge. I enjoy turning things around." He sighed, then raised his eyebrows and looked at me with a bright smile. "I'll just have to find the time to turn them around again."

"But there's a principle involved, Mark. You've been getting a grant from the City for a lot of years."

He shrugged. "Governments can't afford principles any more." He glanced up at me. "Sorry," he said, and smiled.

I took a breath and said, "Speaking of governments...."

Fiona came back at that moment with the news that Bill had called in sick. "I can't believe this day. Maggie, can you work tonight?"

"Sorry," I said. "I can't. I've got to pick up Archie's parents at the airport and get Ben to a hockey practice."

"It's okay, Fiona," Mark said. "I can come back later." He was looking around the shop.

The door chime went, announcing the arrival of two of our artists. Behind them were two more customers, an older couple.

"Business is picking up," I said quietly to Mark.

Fiona went off to help the customers, giving me a look that

suggested I should do the same.

Before I did, I finished what I had to say to Mark. "Archie won the nomination Wednesday night," I said.

"Is it that time already?" he asked, his eyes now back on the open file folder.

"The election hasn't been called or anything. It's just a matter of being prepared."

"Well, good for Archie," he said, looking up. "Give him our congratulations."

"Who?" said Fiona, coming up beside him, a plate in her hand and customers behind her ready to pay for it.

"Archie," Mark said. "He's been nominated again."

"Don't give him *my* congratulations," Fiona said.

"Come off it, Fiona," Mark said.

"It's all right," I said. "The point is that I don't know how much extra time I'll be able to put in here."

Fiona, ringing in the sale, looked up at me. "'Extra time' or 'time'?"

"Extra," I said. "I want to work my regular hours. It's just that it'll be busier than usual at home. There'll be things I have to do. It's the extra time I'm worried about: I don't want to let you down."

"We'll manage," Mark said firmly, looking at Fiona.

Fiona shrugged her shoulders, switched on her charming face, and turned to the customers. "That'll be fifteen-sixty," she said.

I started off to talk to the artists.

"Don't worry so much," Mark said behind me.

I turned back, but he was looking at his papers. It was impossible to tell whether he'd been speaking to me, Fiona or himself.

5

On Monday at three, I left the Purple Parrot and drove four blocks through slush. It was a dreary kind of day, overcast with a chill breeze. I found a parking spot in the street behind the Java Mia, then picked my way around puddles to the coffee house.

There was no sign of Zeke. I bought a coffee and sat at a table near the back, where I could see the door. I didn't take my coat off, and I kept looking at my watch. I would give him until three twenty, maybe three twenty-five, then I'd leave. I couldn't tell any longer whether I was hoping he'd show up or hoping that he wouldn't. I was nervous about this, had been nervous about this all weekend. More than anything, I wanted the nervousness to stop.

I watched for him through a plate-glass window that was scummed and streaked with dirt and smoke. Beyond, tattered notices and playbills fluttered half-torn from telephone poles and power boxes. Rivulets of water ran across the sidewalks, down into the gutters where bits of garbage had accumulated.

The city—the world—used to be a cleaner place. The world,

or at least the part of it I knew, used to be a lot of things it wasn't any more. Cleaner, simpler. Simpler—oddly enough—when there were more possibilities. As I grew older, the options narrowed, disappeared, and that made everything more complex. It should have been the other way around.

When I thought back to my first few years at university, before I met Zeke and even later, Archie—when I was studying, attending classes, going home to Gran's small house—I remembered the outside world as lighter, brighter.

The bits and pieces I was writing about Gran were that way, too. Gran declaring, bus tickets in one hand, the other firmly gripping a wicker basket packed with hard-boiled eggs, apples, cheese and lettuce sandwiches—determined against my protest that I wanted to stay home—"When I was a girl we went on picnics": taking me in imagination back to that other childhood, hers, which I saw as sunlit and newly swept. The farther back I imagined, the brighter and more pristine Gran's world became—its lightness and simplicity increasing in direct proportion to the distance from the present. The trees took on a fullness as they disappeared in time. The streets grew wide and empty. The blue of the sky washed cleaner with the disappearing years, and even the clouds were lighter, fluffier, whiter than they ever seemed today.

It was no doubt accurate in some ways—there was less pollution then—but it was also nostalgia and imagination letting it be known, if you paid attention, that they could not be wholly trusted.

But it was worse now, definitely worse in the past few years. Everything looked drab and slightly worn. Battered by cutbacks and hard financial times, people cared less about keeping things clean, repaired, attractive.

Three twenty-five. I took a swallow of the coffee and prepared myself to leave.

Zeke came by the long window beside me, his head into the wind, moving quickly, his big coat blown tight against knees. I sat back in my chair.

He was dressed as it seemed he'd always been—black coat, blue jeans. He pulled open the door to the coffee house, came in and looked around, his expression lightening when he caught sight of me. Heart thudding, I watched him come across the room.

"Maggie," he said. "Hi." He pulled a package of Players from his coat pocket and tossed it on the table. "Sorry I'm late."

That gesture with the cigarette pack took me back even more effectively than my earlier attempts to pry loose memories had done—I could suddenly see the lattice of carved letters in the heavy blond oak table where we used to sit, smell the smoke from their cigarettes, taste the watery cardboard-flavoured vending-machine coffee.

"It's great to see you," he said.

"You, too," I said. It was the truth.

He glanced down at my mug. "What are you having?"

I looked again at the pack of cigarettes. "Coffee," I said. "Milk and sugar."

While he went to get the coffee, I looked at my watch and did some fine calculations involving speed limits and traffic flows. When he came back I said, "I have to leave in fifteen minutes."

"Are you kidding me?" he asked, pulling out the chair. "Fifteen minutes? Shit." He sat down. "Sorry. I was working…. I lost track of the time."

"I've got an appointment at four thirty. I forgot it when I talked to you last week."

"Can't you change it?" His eyes met mine, grey eyes. That little scar.

I shook my head. I watched him stir his coffee, asked "What were you working on?"

"A paragraph. A sentence." He shrugged. "Nothing that important."

"You're a writer?"

He looked up at me. "Yeah." He sounded surprised.

"What kind of writing do you do?"

"I'm a novelist. I'm working on a novel." He paused, then said, "My fourth."

"Okay," I said, embarrassed. "I don't keep up too well." That wasn't exactly true—I kept up as well as I could.

He shrugged and fixed his eyes on something in the distance, beyond the dirty window. "It doesn't matter. This is the big one, coming up." He looked back at me. "The others were just practice."

"A writer. I always figured you'd do something like that."

"Why?"

I looked down at my coffee, up again at him. "It was the way you talked about books and films. You always wanted to figure out what the author was trying to do and how he was trying to do it. It seemed like how the idea was coming across was even more important than the idea itself."

"Well, *as* important, anyway," he said, and smiled. "You've got quite a memory." He nodded. "I guess I'm still obsessed with that, with the creative act—how the idea manifests itself creatively. But I've learned a few things in twenty years."

"Like what?"

He shrugged. "Oh, like that criticizing can be easier than doing it yourself." He shifted a little in his seat so he was facing more toward me. "How about you, Maggie? Tell me what you do. What have you become?"

"Not much," I said, feeling my face flush. I found his eyes on me intense and disconcerting. I had a husband, a son, a job: I really couldn't think of anything to tell him that he didn't already know. "I'm still working on that," I said. "I'd rather hear about you. Tell me where you went after you walked out on us. Start there."

"Walked out on you?"

Afraid that I'd said 'me' instead of 'us,' I said again, "On us. On us: The group."

A look—like he was trying to decipher my words, or remember something—moved across his face.

"Come on," I said. "One day you were there, the next you weren't. We did notice you were gone."

Focusing on me again, he nodded. "I was walking along the beach in Vancouver the day you all went back to class. Wondering who was saying what to whom." He looked amused. "How *did* they all react?"

They. I thought for a moment. "Well, they were mystified, to start with."

He shook his head. "They shouldn't have been that. If they'd been listening to me...."

"And hurt, I guess. That you hadn't told anyone. Envious. Some of them, anyway. Andrew knew before the rest of us—he'd tried to call you at home a day or two before classes started. I guess your dad...."

I saw a shift in his expression. "Anyway," I said, "somehow we all survived. And you went to Vancouver. Were you there for long?"

"A year or so. Then east." He sighed and leaned back in his chair, pulled out a cigarette and lit it.

"Without ever coming back?"

"Not for a long time."

"Why?"

"You make a break, you make it. I wanted to be gone. All we were doing here was yattering, all day, every day. I got impatient, itchy to get going. Had to move, do something, see something—" He looked up at me, shrugged. "There were other reasons, too."

Tapping ashes into the glass dish at his elbow, he said, "You look great, you know," he said. "Just looking at you is great."

"Thanks," I said. "You, too."

"Yeah," he said, looking away and shifting in his seat. "This is what I needed." He looked back at me. "I've been thinking quite a bit lately, about that time back then."

"Have you looked up any of the others?"

He shook his head. "I've been working—most of the time, anyway—since I got back. Haven't had much time."

Why me, I wondered, but I didn't ask.

"I work with a writer," I said. "Fiona Delaray. You've probably never heard of her." I wondered if Fiona had heard of Zeke.

With a jolt, I suddenly remembered Ben and looked down at my watch.

"I've got to go," I said.

He looked up at me. "Five minutes, Maggie. Please?"

Ben would be waiting outside the school....

It wasn't that cold....

If I drove quickly....

"Three," I said. "Three minutes."

"We'll plan better next time."

I laughed, nervous again. Next time. Yes.

A young woman appeared at the table. "Excuse me, sir," she said, "but this is a non-smoking restaurant."

He turned and looked up at her. "It is?"

"Yes, sir."

He took a deep breath, leaned forward, and I watched him transform himself into someone I remembered well, someone harder, colder than he'd been a moment before. "A non-smoking restaurant," he said slowly, sardonically.

"Yes, sir." The girl looked evenly at him.

He extended a finger in the direction of the glass dish he'd been using as an ashtray. "Then tell me. What is that?"

"It's a candle holder," the girl said.

"I don't think so," he said lazily. "I think it's an ashtray."

I shook my head, remembering that edge to his voice, remembering how it gathered strength, then zeroed. Fear of his contempt used to keep me quiet but the girl, barely older than Ben, carried innocently on.

"No, sir," she said. "This is a no smoking restaurant. It's a candle holder."

"But there's no candle in it," Zeke said.

"We put candles in at night," the girl said.

"You put candle holders that look like ashtrays out during the day, but you only put candles in them at night?"

I flashed back to the guy who came to talk about racial conflict in the southern States at the McAllister Lecture Hall. Zeke and Kevin Pine and a couple of the others were in a twist ahead of time because the guy was white, and they leapt up on some predetermined cue and started in on him—throwing out quotes from Eldridge Cleaver and Malcolm X and generally insisting that a white guy had no right to try to represent the Black perspective—which he was yelling back that he wasn't trying to do. I'd been mortified, scared—figured they'd start a riot and that we'd all get killed.

"People steal them when they're not lit," the girl was saying. "They're those fat kinds?" She raised her thumb and index finger in the shape of a C, to indicate the size. She giggled. "You know. They cost money."

I looked at my watch. It was ten to four. I had to leave.

I stood.

To my surprise—and the girl's, too, it seemed—he stubbed out his cigarette immediately. "I'll walk you to your car," he said, standing, lifting on his coat. "What kind of appointment is it?"

"Dentist," I said, heading for the door.

"You?"

"My son. Check-up. It's been booked for months."

I felt angry. At fate. At the waitress. At Dr. Leggatt. At Ben.

"Why did you do that?" I asked him in the street.

"What?"

"With the girl. Tease her like that." Waste our time, I thought.

He shrugged. "Incorrigible," he said. "I love to make a scene."

"I hate scenes," I said.

He nodded. "You used to blush."

We were walking with our heads down into the wind, our hands in the pockets of our coats. Every few steps his elbow would touch mine and a little shock would start through me.

Zeke Avery. Here. I still had trouble believing it.

I led him in a jay-walk across the street, reaching into my handbag for my keys. I reminded him of the incident at McAllister Hall. "You backed off that time, too."

"I didn't 'back off' this time," he said. "I wanted to walk with you." He shoved his hands deeper into his pocket. "McAllister." He shrugged. "After we got started, Kevin and I, it hit me that we had no more right to be yapping than the guy did at the front. That's what got me going on that whole train of thought about how all we did was think and talk. We had no idea what we were talking about. We had no idea of what was real."

"So you went to find out?"

He shrugged. "That was the idea."

"Did you?"

"Find out?"

"Yeah." I presumed if anyone had, it would have been Zeke. But he only laughed.

When we came up beside my red Tempo, he said, "Is this your car?"

I told him it was, pulling back my coat sleeve to look at my watch. Four o'clock: I should have been at the school.

"It's a sign," he said.

"What do you mean?" I asked.

He pointed at the vehicle ahead of mine, an aging and battered pickup truck, once brown and white, now rusted half way up the doors. "That's mine," he said. He looked back at me. "When will I see you again?"

His eyes on me, his voice, made me catch my breath. Tonight, I thought. Tomorrow morning.

I shook my head. "I'd better check my calendar this time," I said. "Can I call you?"

"Sure."

"I couldn't find your number in the book."

"It isn't there," he said.

I found a pen in my handbag, he a surprisingly dry scrap of paper in the gutter, and he wrote down the number. He handed me the ragged slip and said, "Call soon."

He held the handle of the car as I climbed inside. When I looked up at him, rolling my window down a little, he said, "Did we walk down this street that night?"

"You remember that night?"

"Of course I do," he said. "Of course."

I looked out the window on the far side, through the windshield at the front. "Not this one, I don't think. But not so far from here."

He nodded, pushed my door shut.

"I'll see you soon," he said.

6

I drove fast and distracted to the school, my mind now on Ben and Dr. Leggatt, both of them waiting for me—why couldn't dentists ever be behind schedule?—and now on Zeke, who I'd left standing in the street as I pulled away.

He'd told me to call him soon, and I wanted to. There was more to it than wanting to catch up on old times, and I was alarmed by whatever it was that was turning around inside me. I'd been attracted to other men since Archie and I got married—not that the attraction had ever led to anything—but this was different. Powerful. It made me want to act.

Ben was waiting on the sidewalk in front of the school, rocking on his heels, alone, hatless, his jacket up against the wind. I pulled up to the curb in front of him, and his hand was on the door handle before I'd completely stopped.

"Where the hell have you been?" he asked, throwing his book bag onto the floor of the front seat and climbing in after it. "Do you know how cold it is?"

"I got held up," I said. "Sorry." I looked over at him. His ears were red with cold. "Why didn't you wait inside?"

He sighed with dramatic depth. "You told me never—"

I cut him off. "All right, all right." I remembered the last time I'd picked him up—waiting, waiting, finally putting the car in park and running inside to find him.

"There's a balance, you know," I said, "between being half a mile inside the school and standing outside in the wind."

"Where were you anyway?"

"Work," I said. "There's some stuff I need to put on the new computer, addresses and so on. It's a big job." That part was true enough.

Ben pressed himself into the seat beside me as I made my way through almost-rush-hour traffic.

"Why don't we just skip it?" he asked in a voice he'd made to sound rational, adult. "We're going to be late anyway."

I didn't answer.

"There's a phone booth," he said, pointing. "We could call and cancel."

"Of course we could," I said.

"Why don't we have a car phone? Everybody has a car phone."

I clenched my jaw and pulled out from behind a bus, into the next lane.

He started in about the game of street hockey he was missing and it wasn't until I was pulling up in front of the medical-dental building that I realized he'd stopped talking and was looking at me.

"What's up with you?" he asked.

"Nothing. Get out. I'll park."

I felt a moment of relief when he was gone and then, immediately, contrition, and then again the fear. I was his mother. I was Ben's mother, and I was Archie's wife. This was what I did.

When I got upstairs I apologized to the receptionist for being late, then went into the bathroom down the hall. I looked into the mirror as I washed my hands.

I felt elated, lifted from my life…. All these years, he'd remembered that night as well as I had. He'd been thinking about that time, and here he was again. He'd called me. Not the others. He'd needed—wanted—to see me.

I grinned at my reflection.

I remembered how unreachable, untouchable, he'd seemed when we were younger. Not letting anyone near him, not that I'd ever noticed. He'd been a solitaire. Dark and distant, utterly and assuredly alone. Until he'd leaned down and kissed me that night—the memory made me close my eyes against my reflection the mirror, draw in breath....

I wanted to be kissed by him again.

I went back to apologize to Dr. Leggatt for having made Ben late. He, however, had checked Ben's teeth, handed him over to the hygienist and left while I was in the bathroom.

"He had an appointment he had to get to," the receptionist told me. "He said Ben's teeth look fine. He'll call you with the X-ray results tomorrow."

While I waited for Ben, I found myself wondering where Leggatt had gone in such a hurry. I found myself thinking about Ken Swimmer and Marianna Johnson. Maybe it happened all the time, to everybody.

"Ben. Salad."

"I don't want any."

"It's good for you."

"My teeth hurt."

"They'll hurt you more if you don't eat salad," Archie said. "Do as your mother says."

I don't need your help, I thought.

"Later."

The phone rang. Ben leapt up to get it, but it was for Archie. Jack Armstrong from the Legislature office. Archie listened, then thanked Jack and told him to go home to dinner. He came back to the table.

"Problems?" I asked him.

"Nothing serious."

"You were on the news again tonight," Ben said, disapproving.

"You were watching the news?" Archie asked with mock incredulity.

"Flipping channels. Saw you with a microphone in your face."

Archie shrugged at him. "Sometimes you have to step on a few toes in order to get things done." He reached for the crab-apple jelly and the spoon. "Nobody likes it, but that's the way it is."

"What were you on the news for?" I asked.

"Oh, it's just a little communications contract," Archie said. "We're privatizing, and a few people are upset. It's no big deal."

I got up to carry my plate to the kitchen. "This isn't a great time to be privatizing, is it? With an election coming up? I thought all that was over."

"It's a small thing, Maggie. Housekeeping. The voters support privatization anyway." He opened the *Maclean's* at his elbow and started flipping through it.

I studied him, wondering at his motivation. There'd been rumours that a few other MLAs had been critical of his low profile when the major cuts were going on. That some of them felt he was protecting turf when he should have joined shoulders with the Party.

"May I be excused?" Ben asked.

"Not till you eat some salad," Archie said, not looking up.

"I did," Ben said.

Archie, lost in an article, didn't respond. I put a cup of coffee down in front of him.

"Mom?" Ben pleaded. "I've got homework."

"Go ahead," I said. He still hadn't eaten any salad, but I let it go. When he was still quite small, I'd started insisting on such things as bed-making, salad-eating, toy-straightening, face-washing—nagging away at him until at last he would give in a little: straighten one sheet, eat one piece of lettuce, put one truck in the toy box, wipe clean one half of his chocolate-smeared chin. That had been all I'd wanted at the beginning, only some gesture of cooperation. I'd reassured myself that as he grew older I would insist on more and more. For a number of years, I had, but now that he was fifteen and beginning to move away from me, the process seemed to have reversed itself. Or worse: I often found myself backing off completely. It was as though I feared that some minor domestic dispute might suddenly push him out of reach completely, drive him into adulthood and out the door before I was ready for it.

"Oh, by the way," Archie said suddenly, "Maxwell says to be there by seven on Saturday."

"For what?" Then I remembered. The fund-raising dinner. I

couldn't get out of that one.

"I've got a game Saturday night," Ben said, coming back from the kitchen with a glass of juice.

"One of us should be at the game," I said quickly. "We're getting close to playoffs."

"Not this time," Archie said. "I want you at the Park Regency with me. Ben, arrange a ride."

"Child abuse," Ben said. "Neglect."

Archie looked up from the magazine. "We've got an election coming."

Ben shrugged. "I hate elections."

So do I, I thought.

My notebook was in my handbag. I decided that after the dishes, after Archie had gone out and Ben had gone upstairs, I'd open it at the kitchen table and at least look over what I'd written.

Zeke would be doing that kind of thing tonight. Writing. We would both be....

"You look a million miles away," Archie said. I turned, startled. He was looking at me mildly.

"Just thinking about work," I said.

7

When I got into the Purple Parrot on Wednesday, Fiona was standing at the sales counter with Sylvie Monod and Anna Perry, two local artists who had been displaying their artwork at the shop for several years. Fiona was dressed in one of her most flattering outfits, an olive-green suit with a skirt that fell neatly to her ankles and a jacket that gathered at the waist. The older women looked slightly dowdy, even dumpy, beside her.

Fiona was slowly turning pages of the customer-information printout, but she didn't appear to be reading it. Anna and Sylvie greeted me awkwardly and then stood silent, looking at one another, as I went to hang my coat in the back. My arrival had obviously interrupted a conversation; when I came back, the three of them were heading for Fiona's office.

Fiona asked if I could manage the front.

"Of course," I told her.

They closed the door behind them.

I was mystified. Sylvie Monod and Anna Perry were two of

Fiona's least favourite people, and when they appeared at the shop—which was fairly regularly; they liked to drop in for a chat—she normally disappeared.

Fiona considered them to be without talent. It had been Mark who'd approved their work for the Purple Parrot, which probably added to Fiona's negative feelings about them. It irritated her no end when Mark authorized new artists without her approval, which he did from time to time without malevolence, but also without any apparent idea that he might be offending her. I could see what made him do it—he did, after all, own the place. On the other hand, he could have been more subtle.

I didn't mind chatting with Sylvie and Anna, although I shared Fiona's assessment of their artistic talents. They were both widows in their late sixties, healthy and well heeled. They'd met in a watercolour class half a dozen years before, and had been fast friends ever since. Together they seemed to be urging everything they could from life. They were always taking some course or another—I'd heard all about their experiences with Introductory French, Asian Cooking, Archaeology and Gymnastics—or heading off on a bus tour or a cruise.

While they were delighted to have their work on display at the Purple Parrot, their regular visits to the shop were more social calls than business ones, which is why Fiona preferred to disappear. Their attitude had its advantages as far as I was concerned—unlike many other artists we worked with, they never seemed too concerned when they learned that nothing of theirs had sold. I sensed that they didn't worry much about anything at all. The two energetic women made me smile. Anna, in particular, reminded me a bit of Gran.

Fiona's office door was closed for more than half an hour, during which time I helped a few customers and continued the long process of inputting names, addresses and phone numbers onto the new computer. Both the customer and the artist databases needed to be transferred by hand because no one could figure out how to get the information from the old computer onto the new one any other way. The two computers had sat next to one another on the counter for several weeks as one technical wizard after another—located through Mark's network of connections—stopped by and attempted to achieve a union. On the weekend, Mark had given up and had instructed Fiona to proceed with the "long-hand" method. Fiona had passed the instruction on to me.

It was work you could do with your brain half-dead, which mine was. The day before, my day off, had passed in a similar fog, and I'd accomplished quite a lot. I'd put through several loads of wash, dusted, cleaned the floors, ironed, defrosted the freezer, and knocked off a range of other household chores which, like the task before me now, required a modicum of concentration and no actual brain-power.

My thoughts were consumed by Zeke and now, most precisely, on how long I should wait before I called him. Dear Miss Manners: what is the appropriate length of time a woman should wait before she calls a male acquaintance she recently met for coffee and desperately wants to see again? Dear Wife and Mother: I think you know the answer to that question.

I did, but that didn't stop the question from going round and round.

I looked up when Anna and Sylvie, looking purposeful and determined, came out of the back office. Again they seemed awkward with me, giving me only the briefest of greetings before they left.

Fiona had followed them part way through the shop, and she watched them go and then stood with her arms crossed, distracted.

"Everything okay?" I asked.

She turned, looking somewhat startled. "Sure," she said.

She cleared her throat and came over to the counter. Indicating the computer, she said, "We're going to need this system up and running. How long do you think it'll take to finish what you're doing?"

"I'm only at 'D' on the customer list. There's still all the artists to do."

"How long, though? Hours? Weeks? Days?"

"Days."

"Well, then," she said. And then said, "Days?"

I nodded.

"Well." She sighed. "You'll just have to keep going, I suppose. Do it as fast as you can."

She watched over my shoulder as I input names, addresses and phone numbers. Her close attention made me uncomfortable, but I said nothing. When I'd done three complete entries she said, "It does take time, doesn't it?"

"To do it accurately? Yes."

"Can you work on it tomorrow?"

I fought down disappointment—realizing only at that moment that a plan had been forming that involved Zeke and my next day off. "I don't see why not," I said. "For a few hours? Sure."

"Good," Fiona said. "That's great."

The warmth in her voice encouraged me to ask if she'd heard of him—of a writer named Zeke Avery.

"Ezekiel Avery? The novelist?"

"I guess so," I said, surprised at how quickly she'd answered. And by the name. Ezekiel Avery. "Yes."

"I've read a book or two of his."

"I went to school with him. I just found out he was a writer."

"He's not too bad," Fiona said. "He hasn't published anything in years though, has he?"

That was what they'd said at the bookstores when I'd called around. They'd said they didn't have anything of his in stock, that his books appeared to be out of print.

"I guess not. The thing is, I've never read his stuff, and I wondered if you might –" I shrugged. "If you might have any of his books. Just out of curiosity, you know?"

I turned around and looked at her.

"I don't think I ever bought anything of his. Tried the library?"

The library. Of course.

"Good idea," I said, turning back to the computer. "I'll have to stop in there sometime."

I'd reached the 'F's when Mark called. He was returning a call from Fiona. She hadn't answered the private line, and he wondered how soon she'd be back.

"She went out to buy some envelopes an hour ago, said she'd be back in fifteen minutes." I wanted her to show up myself so I could go home.

"Get her to give me a call."

I told him I would, and was about to hang up when I heard him say my name. I raised the receiver back to my ear.

"Did you say something?"

He paused. "I was just going to say that this situation is probably going to be a little tricky for you."

"What situation?" For one heart-stopping moment I thought he was talking about Zeke.

"This Bellamy and Cato thing."

"Bellamy and who?" I asked, my heart starting up again.

There was a long pause at the other end. "Bellamy and Cato." Another pause. "I guess you didn't see the news last night."

"No," I said.

"Or the paper."

"What are you talking about?"

"I guess you should talk to Archie about this," he said, sounding embarrassed. "I figured you had by now."

"Mark," I said. "What is going on?"

I could almost hear him considering at the other end. "No," he said at last. "Just go find a newspaper."

I tried to call Archie to ask him what had happened, but Mrs. Embury, his secretary, told me he was out. A high-strung woman who was highly effective in her work because she spent so much time making sure that nothing she was doing could possibly come back later to alarm her, Mrs. Embury tended to panic when I called and Archie wasn't there. This was partly because I called so rarely: when she heard my voice, she was always sure it must be an emergency. I called even more rarely than I felt like calling because of the reaction I knew I'd get from her. And so it went.

She said she'd get him to call me back the instant he came in. I told her not to bother. She said of course she'd bother. I told her I would be very grateful if she did not. "I won't be here," I said. "I won't be anywhere. That's reachable by phone, I mean."

She told me I should get a car phone. I said I would consider it.

It was after three o'clock and I shut down the computer and waited for Fiona to get back. There was no doubt in my mind that Fiona knew what Mark had been talking about—not that I was going to ask her—and that Sylvie and Anna knew as well.

8

I sat in the car on a side street and skimmed the paper I'd bought from a corner box. The item was on the second page of the second section.

Privatization Process Angers Printer

At least one local company is reacting with anger to the government's decision announced earlier in the week to turn over management of print-material production to the private sector.

Mark Scales, president of Scales Printing and Graphics, says the move will effectively shut down several small businesses in the city.

"It's going to hurt us, no doubt," Scales said. "But it's going to be worse for a lot of smaller companies out there. Not to mention writers and editors and so on who depend on government contracts for at least some of their income."

Public Works representative Jack Armstrong defended the move, which will see Bellamy & Cato Communications assume responsibility for the production of all government print materials. "Everything was done according to Hoyle," Armstrong said. "We tendered the contract, and Bellamy and Cato offered us the best package. It's going to be a more efficient system, and it's going to save us money."

"I'd like to know who was invited to tender," Scales said. "We weren't."

Armstrong said the tendering process was a confidential matter. Public Works Minister Archibald Townsend was unavailable for comment.

I drove home slowly. Mark was right—"tricky" was a good way to describe the situation. But why had Fiona been tiptoeing around it? No mock sympathy, no barbed comments—nothing but concern about my progress at the computer.

Fiona normally acted as though I were at least partly responsible for every government decision she didn't like, and there had been a lot of them. Like most of the artists who hung around the Purple Parrot, she opposed on principle the massive cuts and wholesale privatization that had marked government policy in the past few years. She normally went stony silent with me following announcements she didn't like, while at the same time denouncing the government to other people in my presence. In the past year or two, she'd spoken out quite eloquently within earshot of me on behalf of seniors, liquor-board employees, laundry workers, environmentalists, nurses—whatever group had been affected. Now, when my husband had, at least indirectly, caused a reduction in the income of the man she lived with, she'd been almost friendly. Why?

And what had she been talking about with Sylvie and Anna for so long? The older women would be concerned for Mark—they were very fond of him—and it was logical that they would offer him their emotional support. It was even logical that they wouldn't want to talk about it in front of me. But the way Fiona had gathered them into her office, and stayed with them for so long—that wasn't logical. It was ominous.

Mark was no big-C conservative himself, but his political attitudes were slightly to the right of Fiona's, probably because he owned a business. Like Fiona, however, he seemed to assume that Archie's politics and mine were identical. This irritated me, but to set them straight would have sounded disloyal to Archie so I never did it.

In truth, I'd stopped discussing my political opinions with anyone, including Archie, years before—basically because I had none. Or if I did, they didn't seem to fit any model I'd ever heard about. Sometimes I could see both sides of a question, sometimes neither. Often as not when I did know where I stood, I'd find my position completely inconsistent with how I felt on other issues.

When it came to party politics, I was mostly cynical. Exactly the same party that had handed out millions of dollars ten years before for hospitals and highways in order to buy votes was now taking the dollars away in order to buy votes. Corporate leaders talked about reducing government intervention, but that was because they wanted lower taxes. Artists supported social programs, but that was because most of them were poor. Nobody I'd ever talked to ever seemed to have a political philosophy that was at odds with their own self-interest. Not, at least, since the days in the basement coffee room at SUB.

With this communications thing, it seemed to me that the government—or Archie, to be precise—had hit a sector for which there was not likely to be much public sympathy, in order to be able to boast just prior to the election that it had saved another few thousand dollars. I disliked those kinds of tactics but if I said so to Archie, he'd say something to the effect that savings were savings, and that cow-towing to the victim mentality was what had got us into trouble in the first place.

There was no one at home, but the phone rang as soon as I got in the door. It was Archie.

"I got a message that you called."

He was the last person I wanted to talk to.

"It was stupid," I said. "Really. I was trying to call Alana. Dialled the wrong number. Can you believe it?"

"Everything's all right then?"

"Everything is fine."

"Ben?" he asked.

"Not home yet."

"But there's nothing wrong with him? Mrs. Embury sounded worried."

"Mrs. Embury always sounds worried."

Finally—with no mention, to my relief, of Mark Scales or Bellamy & Cato—he let me go.

There were still at least ten minutes before Ben would get back from school. I pulled my wallet out of my handbag and removed the slip of paper from the pocket where I'd hidden it on Monday. I closed my eyes, took a deep breath, opened my eyes again, looked at the number, and dialled.

"You have dialled a long-distance number," said a cheerful voice, recorded. "To reach this number, first dial one or zero, plus the area code. Thank you."

I almost did, realizing just in time that a long-distance call would show up on the month-end statement.

Damn.

Long distance. He'd told me at the meeting he lived outside of town—I'd thought he'd meant the suburbs.

I plugged in the kettle.

I wondered if you could still use coins to make long-distance calls from a phone booth. There was one near the convenience store a couple of blocks away.

And then the phone rang and it was him.

9

"You must be psychic," I said.

"Why?"

"I was just about to call you."

"I'm glad to hear it," he said. "It's taken you long enough."

"It's only been two days."

"Long enough."

I leaned back against the counter, smiling. "What have you been up to?"

There was a small pause. "Not much. Working."

"On the book."

"Yeah."

"It's going well?"

"Well enough. I don't like to talk about it."

"Sorry," I said.

"It's only superstition."

"Nothing wrong with superstition," I said. Then, "You don't live near the city."

"I've got a cabin about fifty K west. Near Waldham. Ever been to Waldham?"

"No."

"You haven't missed much. It's south of Osier."

"It must be pretty out there in the country. At this time of year."

"You could come out and have a look."

The back door opened and Ben came in. I turned away from the door, disappointed at his timing.

"I could do that, I guess. Sometime."

"It sounds more romantic than it is," he said. "It's a rented cabin, and it's a good deal the worse for wear. But the price is right, and it's far enough away from the rest of the world that I can get some work done."

Ben dropped his book bag and his jacket in the back hall and came up into the kitchen. I raised a hand in greeting as he headed for the fridge.

"Sounds great," I said.

"I liked talking to you the other day."

"So did I," I said evenly. "It was good."

"When can we do it again?"

"Why don't I call you back on that?"

He should have guessed from my words and tone that I had an audience, but he didn't seem to notice.

"How about tomorrow?" he said. "I'm coming into the city."

"I'm working tomorrow." Damned computer. I should have trusted my instincts.

Ben had pulled bread and margarine from the fridge, peanut butter from the cupboard. I could tell from the angle of his head, the way he was moving, that he was listening.

"Maybe I could get away at noon. For a little while."

"Good." He sounded pleased. "Where?"

"We could meet at the coffee shop."

Ben was slathering peanut butter on slice after slice of bread. He laughed. "We can meet there, but I'm not going in."

I smiled. "Okay. Outside then."

"I'll be there at twelve."

"Who was that?" Ben asked when I'd hung up the phone.

"Alana," I said. "Mrs. Drummond."

I watched him stack sandwiches onto a plate and drop the knife into the sink. He'd have no room for dinner. I felt light and happy, disengaged from such concerns.

As he headed for the family room, told him I was going to the library, and asked if he wanted to come along. He looked at me as though I had a screw loose, which was what I'd hoped he'd do.

As soon as I got to the Purple Parrot the next morning, I told Fiona I'd be gone for an hour at lunch. In order to say this calmly—like I was going out to buy shoes or something—I'd deliberately put Zeke out of my head and reminded myself that it was in fact my day off. But Fiona seemed distracted; it didn't seem to matter to her.

I settled in at the computer. I'd slept badly, and been too rattled to eat anything for breakfast. The fact that I was rattled made me even more rattled, and by the time Ben and Archie had left, I'd been feeling almost nauseous. I'd taken a teaspoon of Angostura Bitters to settle my stomach and then stood in front of my closet for ten minutes, trying to decide what to wear. Nothing I owned seemed right for meeting Zeke. Ezekiel Avery, the author.

I'd found one of his books at the library, and had sat with it in my lap in the library parking lot for a few minutes before I'd headed home. *Bergmehl*, it was called, the word written above his name. And on the back cover, a photo of him against a wall of rock, looking a little younger than he did now. Beneath the photo there was praise for his first novel: "Cutting edge." "Uncompromising." "Avery breaks the boundaries of language."

On the back flap there was a disappointingly brief author note: "Ezekiel Avery lives in Toronto. This is his third novel. His first, *Kapstone*, won the Vista Fiction Award for 1984."

At home, after Ben and I had eaten dinner—both of us picking at our food, but for different reasons—I'd taken my handbag to the living room and pulled out *Bergmehl*. An hour later I was no more than a dozen pages into it, and I had no idea what it was about. His vocabulary was prodigious, but even when I looked up the words I didn't know, I had no greater understanding of the whole. Half pages of solid text turned out to be single sentences that meandered here and there and turned back on themselves and twisted out again in new directions. I found them impossible to follow. By page fifteen, where I'd given up, defeated—my eyes travelling the same line over and over again, my mind drifting away to Bellamy & Cato, to Ben, to what I'd make for dinner the next night—no characters had yet been introduced. Parts of *Bergmehl* had to do with mountains and history and geology and wind, but what Ezekiel Avery had said about those subjects, or anything else, I had no clear understanding.

I remembered Fiona's comment about his work—"Not too bad"—and envied her whatever background or intelligence had allowed her access to his writing. My own work, the piece about Gran, seemed hideously obvious in comparison—as it did to Fiona's writing, too. At least with Fiona, who wrote about mutated microbes and cyberspace rendezvous, I could understand what she was talking about.

Fiona came out of her office to ask if we could just print out the customer list from the old computer.

"Do you want this copy?" I asked her, indicating the printout I was working from.

"No," Fiona said. "You need that one."

"We'd have to reconnect it all," I said doubtfully, looking at the pieces of the old computer which had been moved to the floor behind the counter. "Even then I'm not sure: They've been mucking around with it so much." I looked at the stack of papers at my elbow. "You could make a photocopy of this one."

Fiona shook her head. "The pages are a mess: it would never feed through a copier. The print's too faint anyway." She sighed. "Never mind. Just carry on."

The morning passed too slowly and too quietly. There were no customers, and Fiona spent most of the time in the back office. The only sound I was aware of was the click-click of the computer keys at my fingertips, and the churning sound the computer made when I told it to save an entry. I longed for some distraction that would give time a bump and make it move more quickly.

When the minute hand at last released me, I hurried the few blocks to the coffee shop. The clothes I'd finally decided on—ankle-high black boots, jeans, a black sweater and, over that, my heavy grey hooded jacket—were at least warm. An overnight change in the weather had been dramatic, the temperature having fallen at least fifteen degrees, and the sky was cloudy, promising snow.

He was waiting outside the Java Mia, hatless this time, his hands deep in the pockets of his long, thin overcoat. I wanted to put my gloves up to his ears, to warm him.

"Where to?" he asked.

"Doesn't matter to me," I said.

"How long have you got?"

"Till one or so."

"Let's go for a drive," he said.

We hurried along the sidewalk, avoiding frozen pools and rivulets of ice, until we came to his truck. He got into the driver's seat and leaned across to unlock and then open the passenger door for me.

I climbed up and in, and pulled the heavy door shut. Immediately we were closed in there together, I felt the air change: as though the space inside the truck was both too great and too small for the two of us to be contained within it.

I looked around the wide bench for a seat belt. There wasn't one.

He turned on the ignition and the heater, then shoved his bare hands back into the pockets of his coat and shivered. "What happened to spring?" he asked. But the truck was already warm, and it wasn't long before he was ready to drive out.

I cannot remember a time with Zeke when I was surprised to find him watching me. Always, it seemed, I felt his look the moment he turned his eyes toward me. Now he glanced over at me as he pulled out into traffic and said, "It's good to see you."

"You, too," I said, meeting his look.

He turned his attention back to the road and asked me how things were going at work.

I was looking at his profile, at the wide cheekbones, the angle of his brow—remembering them, and at the same time seeing them for the first time. I looked away, out at the road and said, "I'm doing data entry. It's taking me forever."

I felt unsecured without a seat belt. It had been a long time since I'd been in a vehicle without one.

"Is that what you do there? Clerical stuff?"

"Not normally." I told him a bit about the Purple Parrot, its history, about Mark and Fiona.

"It's a good place for you to work," he said.

"What makes you say that?"

"The way your voice sounds when you talk about it. It's a good place for you to be."

"You're right."

When I talked about the Purple Parrot to Archie, he either looked at me condescendingly or tuned out. At least that's the way he used to react—as though he thought my job was "cute"— until I got tired of it and stopped talking about the shop.

Zeke shoulder-checked, changed lanes. "How long have you been working there?"

"About three years."

He drove smoothly, well, and I felt myself beginning to relax. "It was a gift I gave to myself, that job," I said. "I'm not that keen about putting mailing lists onto the computer, but you're right. Most of the time it's great."

We were driving through the river valley, and small flakes of snow had begun to blow around the truck.

"Look at this," I said. "It's probably spring down east by now. What brought you back to this?"

"I needed a change," he said. "Toronto was getting claustrophobic."

I smiled. "I can see getting claustrophobia here," I said. "Toronto's a big city."

"Not when you've lived there for a while. Toronto's like anywhere—it's a bunch of communities. Not only geographic ones, but other ones—ethnic communities, economic communities, political communities, artistic communities, whatever. Unless you keep moving, you're bound to get caught in one or two of them, and eventually they're not big enough. Plus the weather comes down on you like a vise. I started to miss the open spaces." He shrugged.

"How long were you there?"

"In Toronto? Fifteen, sixteen years I guess."

"A long time," I said, and then, "I found one of your books at the library."

He nodded.

"*Bergmehl*," I said.

He looked at me amused, corrected my pronunciation. "It means 'mountain flour'."

"That's pretty."

"Not 'flower.' 'Flour.' F-l-o-u-r."

"Oh."

"Bergmehl's a geological term."

I sighed, feeling awkward again, and stupid. "I haven't read it yet."

"I'll give you a copy. Autograph it for you. I've still got one or two."

He'd pulled off the road and into the parking lot that served the River Valley Golf Club in the summer and cross-country ski buffs and hikers in winter. In this in-between season, the lot was nearly empty. He pulled the nose of the pick-up against a snow bank and put the truck in neutral, leaving the engine running.

He took my gloved hands in his and said, "Maggie, I can't stop thinking about you. I feel you with me when I'm writing, and when I look up from it, all I want to do is be with you."

His grey eyes were on mine. I knew that I might discourage him with as little as a look, or the withdrawal of my hands from his, and also that I would not. He must have known it, too.

"The way you were the other day," he said, "and the way you were that night we walked together all those years ago—they've become layered over one another in my mind. It's very power-ful." He looked out through the front windshield. "Women can... distract me from my work," he said. "This is almost the reverse." He looked back at me. "It's because I knew you when all of it was starting. It's put me back in touch with where I was. How I felt. Some of the dreams I had."

I looked away. I said, "I was—disappointed—when you left."

"Were you?" He sounded surprised, pleased. After a moment, he put one of his hands up, under my chin, and I felt its coolness like a shock. He turned my face toward his. "It isn't too late," he said.

I wanted to lean right into him, sink into him, but I drew away and shook my head. "It is too late. I'm married, Zeke. You know that." My eyes moved down the horizon to where the bank of the river rose into the dome of the Legislature Building.

He pulled a pack of cigarettes and a lighter from his inside pockets, took a cigarette from the package, lit it. He leaned back into the seat and blew out smoke, his eyes going in the same direction mine had.

"How'd you end up with a politician?" he asked, exhaling smoke. "A Conservative politician, of all people."

"I didn't start out with one," I said. "He was... quite different then." How could I phrase it without sounding disloyal? Even what I'd said already wasn't exactly true. Archie had always been this way—it was just that I was only figuring that out in retrospect.

Zeke's eyes were moving across my face as though memorizing it, but he was also listening, waiting.

"He *looked* different anyway," I said, smiling at the memory. "He had this big blond-red beard, hair in a ponytail. You might have noticed him around campus. He was everywhere, involved in everything."

He shook his head. "Doesn't ring a bell."

"He was in Education, studying to be a teacher. He wanted to go to Africa or South America or somewhere to teach kids. I was going to go with him."

Zeke had wrapped his fingers around one of my hands, and I looked down at his wide nails.

"But you didn't."

I shook my head.

"Are you disappointed about that?"

"Not really. I think I liked the idea more than I would have liked the reality. I don't think I'm much of an altruist."

He smiled. "Me either."

"I know." I smiled too, then looked away, down the river-bank corridor. "Anyway, Archie's not that different in some ways than he used to be—obviously he's still getting involved in things—but his politics have changed a lot. That's not so unusual. It's happened to a lot of people our age. You must have noticed that."

He shrugged, so maybe not.

"It happened pretty gradually. He had to pay off some student loans before we went travelling, so he decided to teach here for a year or two. He had a hard time getting a position when he graduated, but finally he did and one thing just led to another the way it does—house, mortgage, baby. More debts. I guess money was always the bottom line."

He was watching me talk, which made me shy. I looked away from him.

"For a long time I felt like it was my fault—Ben's and mine, at least—that he didn't ever get around to fulfilling that vision of his. But I don't know about that any more. He'd never admit it, but I don't think he ever really liked teaching, so when the idea came up that he should run for office, the prospect of doing something else wasn't exactly loathsome to him." I looked up again in the direction of the Legislature Building.

"How'd you feel about it?"

"Me?" I gave a small shrug. "At the beginning, I was scared to death."

"How about now?"

"I'm still scared to death." I smiled. "No. That's not true. It's faded back to a nice, consistent state of alarm: most of the time, anyway. I hate the public eye. It wasn't my idea. But Archie's good at what he does, I have to give him that, and it seems exactly the right thing for him. He's always liked politics, and he's sincere about what he's doing now. Probably a lot of the left-wing stuff he was doing in university was just a reaction against his parents. They're both dyed-in-the-wool Conservatives. I watch Ben now and I see what happens...."

There was a silence. Finally, I said, "I guess I don't know the answer. I met him. We fell in love. We got married. And here we are."

"You don't sound exactly passionate about him."

"I'm not." I looked away. "That's normal, Zeke. It doesn't mean anything. We've been married a long time." I looked back at him, and his eyes met mine.

Passionate. Funny word. A funny feeling.

"What about you?" he said. "What about what you want?"

I couldn't answer without saying more than I wanted to, without making a decision. Archie and I had very little in common: we never did have. But that wasn't his fault, and we were married. And right now I was on treacherous ground, and knew it.

I looked at my watch. "I've got to get back."

Zeke looked away. "I want more time with you."

I looked out the window, too, at the grey expanse of snow and sky. "It doesn't seem possible."

"No one needs to know."

I shook my head and looked up again at the Legislature Building. "That's not the point."

He squeezed my hand, then let it go. "Okay," he said. "I'm sorry."

"Don't be," I said. "It's just the way it is."

He straightened and put the pickup in reverse. He leaned his arm across the seat—not touching me—and turned to back out of the parking spot.

As he crossed the bridge, taking us back to the south side, I said, "Did you ever get married?"

"No," he said. "Not married. I knew myself too well, I guess. At least when it came to commitment." He smiled. "They never passed the writing test."

"The what?"

"When the attraction breaks the writing down, it's doomed. It's not doing that with you."

I watched the side of his face. His eyes were on the road ahead. He wasn't that good looking, really. But attractive: yes. The angular cheekbones, the short grey hair, that tiny scar. More attractive than when he'd been younger.

I longed to touch him. I looked away.

"How about kids?" I asked when we were driving past the university.

"One. A son."

"How old?"

"Eight. He lives in Toronto with his mother."

"Do you see very much of him?"

He shook his head.

"That would be hard."

He pulled out another cigarette from the pack that was now on the seat between us.

I sighed. "I really think we'd better let this go."

"Don't decide that now."

Following my directions, he pulled his truck into the alley behind the Purple Parrot and stopped. He turned to me. "I want...." He shook his head. "I want to see you again."

"I know," I said.

I opened the door and slid out, shut the door and waited, watching, while he drove away. Then I stood in the alleyway, snow blowing cold onto my face, and closed my eyes to imagine—to allow myself for a minute to imagine—before I went inside.

10

"You do know that Mark Scales owns the Purple Parrot," I said on the way to the fundraiser.

Archie paused for a moment, digesting this, then said flatly, "Great. Why didn't you tell me?"

He'd dressed carefully for the evening. Over his charcoal suit and the deep red tie, the egg-shell shirt, he was wearing a black wool overcoat with a soft, creamy scarf folded across his neck. He'd gone for a haircut late in the afternoon, then for a jog and a steam at the club. He looked neatly trimmed and healthy.

"What difference would it have made?"

"I like to know what's going on in my own house."

"It's not like I've been keeping it a secret," I said. "I've mentioned his name a hundred times."

"Not in the past few days, you haven't."

"I didn't think I needed to," I said. "I've been working at the Purple Parrot for three years."

I'd been waiting since I'd seen the article on Wednesday for him to raise the subject. After a day or two, I'd stopped feeling wary and started feeling angry: I'd be damned if I was going to make the connection for him. His silence on the subject, clearly innocent, showed how little attention he paid when I talked about my job.

"I don't know why you want to work there anyway," he said. "Serving people. It's not like we need the money."

"You *serve* people, too."

"I don't wait on them."

I wouldn't have raised it at all, except that morning there'd been another item in the paper about Bellamy & Cato—the media weren't leaving it alone. They'd managed to find several independents in the communications field who were as upset as Mark was, and they'd tracked down Donald Bellamy, president of Bellamy & Cato. He'd said the smaller independents' fears were groundless. There would still be contracts, he insisted— Bellamy & Cato couldn't possibly manage all of the work themselves. Archie had been quoted, too. He'd said that the government was committed to saving taxpayers' dollars, and that one of the foundations of the open-market system was the opportunity to get the best value at the lowest possible price.

"Well you're working for a fool," he said.

"He doesn't seem like a fool to me. He's a successful businessman, among other things."

"I know how successful he is, but I don't now how he got that way if this is the way he thinks. Privatization is the way things work these days. The way things have to work. Any entrepreneur worth his salt supports that approach."

"I think he's pissed off because he wasn't asked to bid."

Archie looked over at me. "He said that to you?"

"I read it in the paper." I picked a bit of lint from the skirt of my dark blue dress coat. "I haven't seen Mark once this week, and we never discuss politics anyway."

He had pulled the Blazer into the underground parking lot at the Park Regency, and found a spot close to the elevators. He turned the engine off and turned to look at me.

"Well, for the record, the bidding process was carried out exactly the way it's supposed to be." He pressed the button to release his seat belt. "Just in case he asks."

"He won't ask," I said.

He nodded. "Well, if he does ask. Just so you know." He

glanced in the rear-view mirror, smoothed his hair. "In the meantime, we'd better go up." He got out of the car, came around to my side and took my elbow.

"Ready for the big entrance?" he asked, eagerness to get to the dinner already lightening his voice.

"Ready as I'll ever be," I said, sounding more grim than I'd intended. "Sorry," I said more brightly. "Of course I am."

Victor Maxwell and a few others met us in the lobby, along with a piper in a green and purple tartan skirt whose skirls we followed up the escalator, down the mezzanine hall and into the private dining room. I kept my eyes on the backs of the bare knees above the piper's sand-coloured socks, embarrassed at our intrusion into the quiet of the hotel.

When we entered the dining room, a cheer went up as though the campaign were over and Archie had already won. The place was packed with people, and the atmosphere was festive. Round tables had been arranged throughout the room, draped in pink and set with glass and silverware. Maroon napkins rose in fans from water glasses, and in the centre of each table a glass-and-silver bowl was filled with yellow daisies and carnations. In the air above us and against the walls moved bouquets of ribbons and balloons, pink and maroon and yellow.

Someone took my coat and someone else my elbow, and for the next half hour I greeted people, many of whom I hadn't seen since the last election. I asked them how their children were, how they thought the hockey season would turn out, how the accounting course had gone, if they'd been anywhere since their trip to Osaka. My ability to listen and remember meant that I could nudge conversations back to life even after intervals of several months or years. It was a talent Archie did appreciate: it had been useful to his career as a teacher, and was even more so now that he was a politician.

I didn't pay attention for his sake, particularly, or for the sake of the people I listened to. When I was younger, my disinclination to speak had been born of shyness—or, as it had been in the coffee room of SUB, fear that I might say something stupid if I said anything at all. Now it was more often self-protective. At events like this one, if I kept other people talking, I wouldn't need to talk about myself.

Dagmar, who ran Archie's constituency office and would also run his campaign office, came over with a glass of wine and handed it to me. She asked the couple I was talking to to excuse us for a moment; instead they wandered off.

"We want you and Archie to lead off the buffet in about ten minutes," she said. "Is that okay with you?"

I told her it sounded fine.

"Shall I tell Archie?"

"I can," I said.

I watched her go over to talk to one of several people from the hotel staff who were wheeling out trays and chafing dishes. An attractive, solidly built woman in her late twenties, Dagmar had two degrees—one in French history, the other in biology. And yet I'd watched her supervise a coffee table capably and charmingly, as though ensuring that everyone had adequate supplies of cream and sugar were her primary concern in life. That's the kind of woman a politician should marry, I thought.

An arm came around my waist, tightened and released me. "Looking good," Victor Maxwell said. "Looking good."

"Thanks," I said, but from the way he was looking around the room I decided maybe he'd been referring to the gathering as a whole.

You could feel Victor's energy when he stood near you. It gave him a presence that was unexpected, given his relatively small size. Tonight he was dressed in an expensive-looking black suit with a soft sheen to it, a very white shirt, and a gold-coloured tie with a small black-diamond print. He wore a gold wristwatch and a gold and black signet ring on his right hand. His eyes moved constantly, seemed to take in everything.

"Great turnout," I said beside him, also surveying the room.

"It's the follow-up that counts," he said in a voice low enough that he wouldn't be overheard. "The three-punch."

"Three punch?"

"We're here to turn dimes to dollars," he said. "We want these babies to stick with us. We want 'em to carry the word out there, and we want 'em to come back. Gotta wow them. What's more, we're gonna do it." He made a fist against his side and twisted it. "Got a killer for them tonight."

"What kind of killer?"

"The speech," he said, looking directly at me for the first time.

"Really?" I asked. "That's great." Archie hadn't even mentioned the speech: I wondered if he thought it was as important as Victor obviously did. "Who wrote it?"

His eyes flicked away from me, out at the room again. "Archie," he said. "Who else?"

Right, I thought, an instant before he added, "With a little help, of course."

"Of course."

Victor's hand in the speech was obvious mere moments after Archie took the mike. It was as much in his delivery as in the words themselves. He stood straighter than usual, used more gestures—forceful gestures: a stabbing finger, a fisted hand against a palm. During the twenty minutes of the talk, he never once looked down, never broke eye-contact with the audience.

He was talking about the Party's goals, and his goals for the future. He sounded utterly confident that the Conservatives would form the government, and utterly confident in himself. His new manner was assertive. Not aggressive or offensive, but stronger than what I was used to hearing from him.

"Support for small business is primary," he said at one point, which made me think of Mark and the other printers, and to hope that no one else was thinking about them. "We will examine and moderate the laws that now stand in the way of small-business owners. We will provide entrepreneurs with greater access to the services they need, and create tax incentives that give them greater financial flexibility. We will be paying particularly close attention to those who have chosen to establish small businesses in their homes."

Which they wouldn't need to do—said Fiona's voice in my head—if the goddamn government hadn't unemployed them. But no one in the audience looked in the least perturbed, and I realized that worrying here was silly: these were not the unemployed, nor were they people who were concerned about losing their jobs. Their incomes were secure enough that they could donate money to a campaign. Furthermore, having already bought seats in order to hear him speak, they were unlikely to be overly critical of the candidate.

Finally, I began to relax, leaning back slowly in my chair at the head table so that no one would notice the change. The speech wasn't what I'd call a "killer," but it was getting a good response.

I thought about Zeke's surprise at my being married to a politician. If someone had told me twenty years ago what the future held, I wouldn't have believed it either. It just sort of snuck up on me.

I met Archie just after Gran died, the summer before I started my final year at university. With the help of an elderly lawyer who'd been working for the family for years, I'd sold the house and then found myself a small apartment. Without Gran to think about, I should have felt free, released. Maybe I would have if I'd let it go a little longer. Instead, her death began to hit me after school began again, and mostly I was feeling lonely, scared and insecure. I felt protected by Archie's big, kind, bearded self, and I would have followed him anywhere in the world.

We made elaborate plans for teaching overseas, but before we could go away there were the loans, his loans, to deal with. Unlike just about any other student I ever met, he was determined to pay them off as soon as possible—and he felt an obligation to make major inroads on them before he left the country. That should have warned me what kind of man he was going to turn into, but I doubt it would have made a difference at that point.

After a year of blue-collar jobs—which he'd hated—not to mention a haircut and a shave, the school board finally hired him. He asked to be assigned to an inner-city school, but he was sent instead to an alternative-type school in a fairly affluent neighbourhood, a neighbourhood very much like the one where he'd grown up.

I was surprised after everything he'd talked about at university to discover that he had no real empathy for his students. He didn't even seem to like them very much. He did like committees, however, and in no time he was on the executives of in-school committees, district committees, conference committees, curriculum-development committees and a lot of other committees. He was rarely home.

I was working as the coordinator of leisure activities in a seniors' residence. I had a miscarriage, and my doctor told me to quit my job the next time I became pregnant. It took two years, and when it finally happened, I quit immediately. I didn't work for pay again until I started at the Purple Parrot, when Ben was twelve years old.

It wasn't that we ever made a decision not to go to South America to teach; we just finally stopped talking about it. I can no longer remember when that happened, any more than I can remember when Archie's attitudes started changing. Maybe "solidifying" was a better word.

The teaching did some of it. The students were hard to control, and vandalism was an increasing problem at the school. "No respect," he said. He thought they had it too easy. More discipline was needed, he said, more rigour. He was critical of a system which passed kids even when they didn't get the grades, of a system where students were constantly being excused from classes so they could go to track meets, piano recitals, on field trips to radio stations.

As he became, to my mind, increasingly self-righteous and his views increasingly entrenched, I learned to avoid raising subjects that would lead to fruitless arguments. He had more stamina for argument than I did, and easily dismissed my opinions on subjects that ranged from affirmative action to abortion to whether boys should take dancing lessons. I wished I were better equipped to hold my own—wished that I'd learned more about the finer points of debate in the coffee room in SUB. Not that it would have helped much: It's hard to win an argument with someone who is absolutely certain he is right.

It seemed that we had stopped talking about anything important even before Ben was born. Now the countries we spoke of visiting were not nations in development, and Archie's list of terms for the group he once referred to as "the disadvantaged" had grown at about the same pace as his sympathy for most of its members had diminished. By the time he'd decided to run for office, he was the consummate conservative.

But like I'd said to Zeke, it wasn't as though I'd fallen in love with Archie because I thought he was a liberal, and had felt betrayed when he turned out not to be. It was nothing as morally justified as that; it had had nothing to do with politics or philosophy. I'd needed him when he came along, we'd fallen in love, and we'd been married. I'd always figured that what had happened after that was just the way life went.

When Archie was finished speaking—he got a standing ova-tion, which made Victor, who was sitting beside me, look more smug than pleased—Werner Hoeppner got up and reminded everyone of the costs involved in running a campaign. The dinner was a "wonderful, remarkable start," he said, "but...." He made it sound as though an additional contribution would be like buying a ticket in the lottery: the grand prize would, presumably, be Archie.

Werner was Minister of Advanced Education, a man in his sixties, well respected. As he spoke, Victor sat back in his chair, his eyes closed. I had the sense that he knew every word that Werner was going to say before he said it, too.

After the speeches, I escaped to a bank of phones that over-looked the hotel lobby. I wanted to find out how Ben's hockey game had gone, but there was no answer at home. Back in the Tulip Room, there was entertainment yet to come, smiling and nodding yet to do, but I found myself standing at the railing, looking down at a young couple who were seated in two big armchairs at a low round table in the piano bar. They were partly concealed from my view by the fronds of one of the trees that grew in pots around the bar, but I saw them lean toward one another. The man put his hand up and cupped her chin, as Zeke had cupped mine in the truck.

I imagined his cabin, small and warm, snug inside a stand of trees—lights from the windows through the darkness. I imagined him inside it, writing at a roll-top desk, looking up from time to time—to thoughts of me, he'd said. That seemed incredible, a miracle. Zeke Avery—the thinker, the writer. He'd won awards, met people, moved in circles.... The life he'd lived in Toronto had the Purple Parrot's ambience beaten ten times over, I was sure of it. I imagined him at gatherings in lofts with deeply angled ceilings, saw him in small, dark restaurants where he'd gone to meet fellow writers in the middle of the night—when their work for the day was done. Imagined the people he'd associated with down there, the filmmakers and poets, the playwrights and the sculptors—people who, I was sure, had started out in basement coffee rooms like him.

The couple in the bar moved apart and looked over as two kids appeared, boys about ten, running along the low stone wall that enclosed the bar. Loosely wrapped in towels and dripping water from the pool, they leapt down from the partition, ran across the lobby and punched the elevator buttons. The doorman was on them, shaking his finger at them, pronouncing phrases I couldn't hear. They nodded at him big-eyed and solemn, but laughed the instant he turned away.

I took a deep breath, felt time lifting off my shoulders. Even thinking about Zeke made me feel younger and more hopeful— as though a great deal of my life were still ahead, and I had the power to control where it would go.

The elevator had whisked the kids upstairs. The young couple were putting on their coats. The doorman was now speaking to a woman in a long dark dress with a black scarf tied around her head, who was standing near the registration desk. She was holding a baby in one arm, and trying with the other to hang onto the hand of a wriggling toddler. Looking shy and tired, she shook her head at the doorman and indicated a man wearing a yarmulke who was arguing with the clerk.

So many lives. All accidents of fate: accidents like the one that had landed me here tonight against the mezzanine railing at the Park Regency Hotel.

Every impulse told me to step onto that escalator, descend into the lobby, slip out into the night. To find him. I resisted, and went back to the Tulip Room instead.

11

I sat in the living room of my in-laws' home, trying to resist the urge to raise my sherry glass to my lips and up-end it to get the final drops. If I did that, Edward would certainly leap to action and refill my glass, but the breach of manners would be noticed—and interpreted.

My daily life seemed increasingly tedious. Sharing Sunday dinners with Millicent and Edward was an excellent example of the kind of thing that I didn't necessarily want to do, but did, over and over again. I wondered if they felt the same way.

I was fortunate in the in-laws I'd been dealt, and knew it. But it wasn't as though we contributed anything of substance to one another's lives in these almost-weekly sessions. Most of our conversations had been repeated so often I could recite them, and the menus had reached the point of predictability where if Millicent or I—depending on whose turn it was—had served rice rather than potatoes with the roast, everyone would have noticed and made a comment. Which is maybe why we didn't.

I often had the urge to have an extra drink at these family

dinners, and the urge was particularly acute tonight. I sat bored as Archie and Edward argued about Victor Maxwell, my hand around my small and very empty glass. Edward's drink was at his elbow, almost untouched. I could hardly get up and help myself.

Edward Townsend was a tall, good-looking man in his early seventies—lean by nature, unlike his son who had to work at it. His skin was tanned from the time they'd just spent in Phoenix, and his grey hair was thick and healthy looking. Edward had taken to retirement with alacrity and ease, having owned and operated the same successful drugstore in the west end of the city for forty years, and having sold it for a substantial sum. He'd enjoyed his career as a pharmacist, and now he was enjoying a well earned, permanent holiday.

The life Edward had chosen to lead had worked out well for him, and had made him a confident man with considered but strong opinions on just about every subject. An active supporter of the Conservatives long before they came to power, he knew exactly what they should do as a government—which meant that he also knew how his son should run his campaign. For the most part, I felt he'd earned his convictions. For the most part, I respected them.

He was very unhappy about Victor Maxwell. Bob Sanders, a friend and contemporary of his, had run Archie's two previous campaigns. Despite his successes, Archie had decided to approach Victor instead of Bob to manage the campaign this time. He'd done this while Edward and Millicent were down in Phoenix—not by coincidence, I thought—and now he was facing the music. This argument was hardly unexpected.

Archie was trying to convince his father that the new economic climate required a harder, leaner approach to political campaigns, one that Sanders wouldn't understand.

Edward shook his head. "Wrong," he said. "We've had enough of hard and lean in the past three years. Not that it wasn't necessary. All those cuts. Had to be done. Most of them anyway. But voters are voters when it comes election time, and Sanders knows what he's doing. He's a team leader. He's astute. He doesn't scare people off."

"Victor doesn't scare people off."

"He scares me," Edward said. "Makes me afraid for the campaign. You can't talk to Maxwell—he doesn't listen. He's high strung, like a bomb about to go off. You want a man like that running your campaign?"

Archie, looking at his glass—his, rum and coke, was still half full, too—didn't answer, but I knew he was thinking, 'yes.'

"Bob Sanders...." Edward leaned back in his armchair and sighed. "Well, I don't have to remind you who won the last two elections for you."

"I thought maybe I'd had something to do with it," Archie said dryly.

His father grumbled and took another damnably small sip of scotch.

"Victor's never lost a campaign, by the way," Archie said.

"That means nothing," Edward said. "Without a context, that means nothing."

Archie gave him context, listing and describing other campaigns that Victor had worked on. Most of them had taken place in other provinces, so this evidence held no sway with Edward. He believed the province he'd lived in all his life to be unique—especially when it came to politics. Others shared his opinion. There were whole books on the subject.

"The only campaigns Bob Sanders ever ran were mine," Archie said.

"He knows the constituency," Edward said. "He knows you."

"It's not like I don't want his input, Dad."

"You're not likely to get even that. Especially not if he hears about this from someone else before he hears from you."

There was a moment of silence and then Archie looked over at me and said, "Shouldn't one of us be helping Mother?"

Archie would rather be harangued to death by his father than help in the kitchen: I knew who he meant.

"Ben's out there with her," I said evenly. "I'm sure he's giving her a hand."

At that moment, I didn't feel like being anywhere near Ben. For reasons I couldn't fathom, he seemed to hold me personally responsible for the fact that his hockey team had lost the night before, and I was tired of listening to him. Or of not listening to him, to be precise—he was making a big point of not talking to me. The whole thing—for no good reason—made me feel guilty. Ben can make me feel guilty in a way that no one else can.

Alana says that parenting guilt is based on the assumption that the miseries and defects of our offspring are totally our fault. She says if we want to be effective as parents, we have to resist that line of thinking. The difference between us is that Alana thinks the assumption is erroneous, while I think it's probably correct.

"Maggie!" Edward said. "Your drink is empty." He stood up, smiling at me. "You're too polite. You should have said something."

"That's all right," I said, sitting forward, picking up my glass to hand it to him. But he'd turned toward the dining room and I turned too and saw Millicent coming from the kitchen, carrying a fork in one hand, a pot holder in the other, looking warm and happy. She'd worn her hair exactly as it was now for as long as I had known her—pinned up softly at the back—but it had gone completely grey only in the past few years. Nearly a head shorter than her husband, her lifelong habit of daily walks kept her healthy and reasonably fit, and in both appearance and energy, she was younger than her age... something she was proud of.

"We're almost ready," she said. "I've had a lovely chat with Ben, and he's offered to set the table."

Wonders never cease, I thought.

"Aside from that," she said, "and putting things in serving dishes, there's really just the gravy."

"We don't need gravy," Edward said. "The cholesterol is bad for all of us."

"We do need gravy," Millicent said to me. Meaning: we always have gravy, don't we?

"Why don't I make it?" I said, avoiding Archie's eyes. I stood up and went to help in the kitchen.

So much for the drink.

Edward considered it his privilege, as no doubt it was, to hold forth on subjects of interest to him when he presided at his dinner table. He wielded his words with as much care and attention as he did the carving knife and fork, but that didn't stop Archie from interrupting him whenever he paused for longer than a single breath. Millicent, Ben and I occasionally tried to say something, but we never got very far, and Ben and Millicent usually ended up having conversations of their own. That night, my mind wandered back to Anna Perry, as it had been doing off and on all day.

The previous morning, Anna had dashed into the Purple Parrot, picked up a thick envelope Fiona had left for her—I knew it was a printout of the new customer list, although I hadn't actually had anything to do with putting the package together—and dashed away again, with barely a word to me.

Anna had never been lacking in enthusiasm, but there was a new focus to it. You could see it in her eyes, and in the way she moved. Almost overly sociable on most occasions, yesterday she'd been self-absorbed, looking neither left nor right but only at the package she had come to get.

By now I was sure whatever she was up to had something to do with Bellamy & Cato, and I wondered if I should have mentioned that to Archie, too, the night before. It wasn't until after we'd come home from the fundraiser and I was lying awake in bed that I'd begun to think seriously about what Anna might be up to—Anna and Sylvie and Fiona. But I had no real evidence that there was any connection to Bellamy & Cato, and even the thought of mentioning it to Archie was offensive. Anna and Sylvie were my friends, not his: it would have been like telling tales.

Millicent looked up from her chat with Ben, smiling broadly, and interrupted Edward to announce that Ben had gotten eighty on a math test. Amid the congratulations, I shot Ben a look of annoyance, or maybe jealousy, because he hadn't mentioned the test result to me. Ben pretended not to see it.

Archie did, though, and he looked from Ben to me and back again, mystified. Finally he said, "Your mother seems to feel you could have done better."

"I didn't say that," I said. "Eighty is fine with me. Eighty's just great, in fact."

"Well, then," Archie said. "That's fine then, isn't it?"

I nodded at him.

Archie said more confidently, "Very good work, Ben. Now eat your vegetables."

Ben rolled his eyes.

Millicent said, "It's all right, Archie. They're a little overdone."

"Why should I anyway?" Ben asked Archie. "Mom's not eating anything."

Millicent looked at my plate, then looked up at me. "He's right," she said. "You've hardly touched your dinner, dear. Aren't you feeling well?"

"Pre-campaign jitters," I said lightly, glancing down at my plate. "You know how I feel about campaigns." Roast beef, gravy, mashed potatoes, and waxed beans—only the latter overcooked, but none of it appealed to me. I wasn't about to mention that this was nothing new: my appetite had been practically non-existent for several days.

"You mustn't worry about the campaign," Millicent said. "Archie will do just fine." She looked over at her husband. "Look what you've done with all your fretting."

"It isn't him," I said. "It's nothing."

"It's always tough ahead of time," Edward said, "but Archie's very popular. You know he'll do fine." He glanced at Archie. "Although of course we'd all feel better if Bob Sanders were involved."

"Stop it," Archie said.

Edward looked back at me. "You'll feel better once the campaign starts, when you have more to do."

"She doesn't need more to do," Millicent said. "She's already working and running a household." She looked at me. "Maybe you're working too hard."

"I'm not working too hard," I said, picking up my knife and fork and starting in. "Really, nothing is the matter. I just wasn't hungry." I put beef and now-cold potatoes in my mouth and indicated pleasure.

"You'd have to work pretty hard just to keep that place together," Archie said dryly. "With that guy for a boss."

I glared at him.

"Who's your boss?" Millicent said, interested.

"Fiona Delaray," I said firmly. "Archie must be confused."

To my relief, Archie shrugged and let it go.

"I thought you liked your boss," Ben said accusingly to me.

"I do," I said. I looked around the table. I looked back at Ben and said, "Weren't we talking about *your* beans? Why don't we get back to that?"

Millicent said, "The beans are cold now. He won't want to eat them."

"Right," I said. "Okay." Avoiding Ben's eyes, Archie's eyes, everyone's eyes, I put down my fork, and got up to clear the table.

As we went out to the Blazer to go home, I told Archie how little I liked being embarrassed in front of his parents. He said he hadn't been trying to embarrass me: he'd been trying to pay me a compliment.

"Sure you were," I said.

Ben came out and got into the driver's seat, Archie got in beside him to give him his driving lesson, and I climbed into the back, which meant that we didn't have to say anything else to one other on the way home.

When we got there, Archie went into his den and Ben turned on the television set. I poured myself a drink—the refill I hadn't got from Edward, I told myself—and went up to the bedroom and closed the door. I'd hidden *Bergmehl* in my lingerie drawer, and inside that the scrap of paper with his phone number on it. Now I took out the little piece of paper and sat and looked at it while I sipped my drink.

It seemed ironic that I should feel closer to a man I'd been with for no more than three hours in the past twenty years than to the one I lived with every day, but I did, and I needed to talk to him. Not about anything in particular—not about what had happened over there at Millicent and Edward's, not about Bellamy & Cato—just to talk. Just to hear his voice.

When the glass was empty, I slipped the paper back into the book, and the book into my handbag. I checked my purse for change but found only some pennies and a two-dollar coin. I chose a few dimes and quarters from the bowl where Archie emptied his pockets every night.

I left the two-dollar coin to cover the change I'd taken. Then I went downstairs and told Archie we were out of milk, which wasn't true at all.

12

Soon after I got in to the Purple Parrot Monday, I looked up and saw Sylvie manoeuvring her car into a parking space out front. Anna was beside her in the passenger seat. A sense of foreboding overtook me at the sight of them, as though they'd been involved in some unremembered dream.

Their appearance was not, in itself, unusual. They often came by on Mondays, knowing there would be few customers about, to see if any of their work had sold. It was just Sylvie, and just Anna, I told myself: two watercolourists—one of them with no sense of perspective, the other nearly oblivious to proportion.

Sylvie came through the door carrying several envelope-sized boxes; Anna, behind her, had an armful of cardboard tubes. They'd left the trunk of the car open: there was more to come. Their arrival set off the tinkle of brass chimes.

I moved forward to help, but Sylvie raised an index finger in warning. "We can manage," she said.

She was wearing a thick brown down-filled jacket, the fake-fur trim of its hood standing up around her neck. Anna's jacket was turquoise, hip-length, meant for spring. They were both wearing blue jeans which looked brand new, and clean white running shoes. I couldn't remember having seen either of them in jeans before.

They headed resolutely off in the direction of Fiona's office.

"Fiona's not here," I said, intending only a warning but sounding sharp. I followed them around the shelves and tables. No one except Mark ever went into Fiona's office uninvited.

But Sylvie called back, "Don't worry, dear. It's fine."

Anna opened the office door and found the light switch. Sylvie turned briefly back to me.

"She knows we're here," she said.

Anna was putting her boxes down on Fiona's floor. Reluctantly, I left them to it.

When they came past on their way outside again, Sylvie smiled at me. The smile looked artificial. They gathered up more tubes and boxes and came back in, this time closing the trunk of the car behind them.

I could hear them talking in Fiona's office, but I couldn't hear the words. I was inputting the names, addresses and phone numbers of the artists and craftspeople the Purple Parrot dealt with. I hoped that by the end of the day, the new system would be finally up to date.

At some point I realized that Anna and Sylvie had stopped talking, and I turned to find them standing silently outside Fiona's office, looking at me. Sylvie had taken off her winter coat and was carrying it over one arm. She was wearing a short-sleeved maroon T-shirt, untucked, under a dark blue cardigan. Under her jacket, Anna was wearing what appeared to be an identical T-shirt.

Both women were relatively short—perhaps five-four—but aside from their heights they didn't normally look alike. Today, however, with their white hair—Sylvie's straight and thick, Anna's short and curly—and their pale, wrinkled faces, their dark purple T-shirts, their new jeans and running shoes, they looked bizarrely twinned.

The phone rang at my elbow, making me jump. I answered it, and an unfamiliar voice asked if he could speak to Sylvie Monod. He said her name hesitantly, as though reading it. I put the call on hold and said, "Sylvie, it's for you."

I'd expected that she'd be surprised to get a phone call here, but she didn't appear to be. Nor did Anna exhibit any surprise as she watched Sylvie walk up to the counter and lift the receiver.

I pressed the button.

"Sylvie Monod," Sylvie said in her dry voice. Then, "Yes, Jacob." She glanced up at Anna and said, "It's Jacob Peterson." Anna, her eyes on me, did not respond, and the name meant nothing to me.

After a pause Sylvie said, "I need to talk to someone before I place the order. Can I call you back?"

She turned the message pad around and I handed her a pen. She wrote down a name and number. When she hung up, she turned and looked again at Anna. Anna's eyes were narrowed on Sylvie now, beaming some message at her. Determined.

Sylvie sighed and turned to me. "Anna feels we must explain to you."

"Explain what?" I asked.

Anna came closer.

"We heard Mark on the radio last week," Sylvie said. "Or I did, rather, first."

Anna nodded, her eyes moving back and forth between Sylvie and me, and said, "It's really the last straw. You understand."

"When you think what Mark's done for this community...." Sylvie turned to Anna, apparently at a loss for words. Anna had moved up beside Sylvie now. They were on one side of the counter, and I was on the other. I could smell their dusky breaths.

Anna swallowed, nodded. "The Purple Parrot is a good example of the economy—how it works—or how it should, at least."

Sylvie nodded. "The trickle-down effect."

"We had no idea then...." Anna glanced at Sylvie. Sylvie looked away. "We didn't know that this man Townsend...."

I nodded.

"That you...."

I nodded again.

"Until after we'd made the appointment."

"Appointment?"

"To see him," Anna said.

Sylvie looked away.

"You're going to see Archie?"

"Wednesday afternoon," Anna said.

"Anna," Sylvie said, turning back. "I think we've said enough."

"We didn't want you to think it was deliberate."

I shook my head. "I wouldn't think that."

"You've been very good to us." I noticed Anna's use of the past tense. "It's just something.... Well, it has to be done, you see."

"Anna," Sylvie said. "We have to leave."

"But it's not personal or anything."

"I understand," I said. I watched them go, wondering what I did understand.

I forced myself back onto the computer, but customers began to wander in, distracting me. The weather was bringing people out. It had improved again—become unseasonably warm—and each time the door opened, I felt the draw of spring and wished I were with Zeke.

"If you won't come out tonight," he'd said on the phone the night before, in a slow deepened voice that made my knees buckle and inclined me to agree with everything he said, "at least come out tomorrow.... To hell with work, Maggie. You can ditch it, can't you? You need a holiday. I need a holiday. A mini holiday...." And then, "Maggie, I want to see you."

I was meeting him Tuesday morning at a coffee shop in Osier.

Fiona returned just after one thirty. She was dressed today in white and lemon yellow: even her full-length coat was yellow. She spent a huge amount on clothes, I realized, and wondered how she managed it. Mark couldn't pay her that much to run the Purple Parrot, and she was always complaining about how little she got from her writing. Maybe Mark was subsidizing her as well as the Purple Parrot.

She stood at the counter glancing through her messages, looking elegantly tense, while I told her about the morning's business. I thought she'd be as pleased as I was about the sale of a Paul Yee jewellery box. Paul was a favourite of us both, a highly talented young man who did not yet see how good he was. It had given me great pleasure to phone and let him know that we'd got the price we'd been asking, which he'd insisted was far too high. That kind of moment made me love this job.

But Fiona merely looked up and said, "Mark's coming by at two. He wants to talk to you."

"To talk to me," I said.

"He'll explain," Fiona said. "Is two okay with you?"

I looked at the wooden wall clock and nodded. Fiona started for the back.

"Sylvie and Anna were here," I said. "They left some things for you."

Fiona nodded and kept going.

"They left them in your office," I said, keeping my voice even. "They said you were expecting them."

She turned. "I was expecting them, for God's sake. Not in my office."

I said nothing.

"Nobody goes into my office," Fiona said. "You know that. Nothing goes...."

"They insisted."

"Those old bags are going to drive me nuts." She shook her head and strode away. "Shit. I don't believe this."

Mark appeared at exactly two o'clock. There was no one else in the shop, and by then Fiona had cleared her office of boxes and tubes and shut herself inside.

"Got a minute for a chat?" he asked, slipping off his dark brown outer coat. He was wearing soft brown trousers and a pale blue shirt the colour of his eyes, open at the collar. "We can talk in Fiona's office."

"I'm not so sure that's a good idea," I said, keeping my voice light. I told him about her reaction to Sylvie and Anna's intrusion on her space.

Instead of looking amused, he said, "It'll be all right."

He led the way. He gave Fiona's office door a light rap with his knuckle, and opened it. I stood back, but Fiona seemed quite calm when she came out.

"I'll take the front," she said, meeting Mark's eyes, not mine.

The office was spotless, the desk clear of clutter. Mark closed the door behind me, then hung his coat on the rack beside Fiona's yellow one. He sat in the swivel chair behind the desk and indicated the chair across from him. I sat down, too.

Mark was obviously tense. He picked up Fiona's computer mouse and turned it over. He rolled the ball with his fingertip, then put the mouse down and began to move it back and forth across the mouse pad.

When I couldn't stand it any more, I said, "Shoot me. Get it over with."

He looked alarmed. "I don't want to shoot you."

"Then what is it, Mark? What are we doing here?"

He sighed. "It's this Bellamy and Cato thing," he said quietly, looking even more uncomfortable.

"That's got nothing to do with me."

"I know it doesn't." He looked up. "Not directly, anyway."

I looked away. "It's Archie's problem. And yours."

"Other people are involved as well."

"You mean Sylvie and Anna." I looked back at him. "They told me about the meeting."

"Okay. Good. Well, I've got it covered. My sister's coming in Friday, so you don't have to."

"Friday?"

"For the meeting."

"Mark, what are you talking about?"

"What did Sylvie and Anna tell you?"

"That they had an appointment to see Archie. On Wednesday."

"They do?" He laughed, caught himself, said, "Sorry. But they're quite the pair."

"What's happening on Friday?"

He took his hand off the mouse and crossed his arms, leaned back in the chair and looked at me. "Sylvie and Anna are organizing a small letter-writing campaign. They're upset about this Bellamy and Cato business. Not for the same reasons I am, but that's beside the point."

"Why, exactly, *are* you so upset about Bellamy and Cato?" I asked him. "It doesn't sound like the contract's going to do any real damage to your business."

"No." He shrugged. "Scales Printing and Graphics will survive. We've had long-standing contracts with the government, and we're going to miss them, but it's the smaller companies that are going to feel the pinch."

"So you're just being altruistic? Speaking out for those smaller companies?"

"That's part of it."

"But it said in the paper that Bellamy and Cato would be sending contracts out to them, the same way the government did. What difference does it make…?"

Mark had closed his eyes, and I stopped speaking.

He opened them again and leaned forward. "It's not as simple as that, Maggie."

I waited.

"Let me tell you about Bellamy and Cato." He leaned forward, resting his arms on the desk. "Bellamy and Cato Communications has five offices in the prairie provinces, and more than a hundred employees. Graphic artists, typesetters, writers, editors, you name it. They also have a huge sales department." He looked down at his fingertips. My eyes followed. I noticed how clean his nails were. "The company was established four or five years ago. Five years ago, I think." He looked up at me. "Already it's sucked up several small independents and put a few others out of business. Some have survived only because of their government contracts. And now, poof." He closed one hand into a fist, opened it again. "All the government work is gone. To them."

"But if they contract out.…"

He shook his head. "They won't. At least not to the extent your husband—the government—imagines. If Don Bellamy and Maria Cato have any ethics, I've never seen them. I'm suspicious about how they got this government thing in the first place, and I have no confidence they'll contract anything out at all. They're known throughout the industry for their questionable tactics, Maggie. They start rumours about other companies to get contracts for themselves. They steal employees. They rip off ideas. They've managed to turn themselves into a megalith, but they've done it by being underhanded and unprofessional. In my admittedly unobjective opinion, they're a pair of scum bags." He'd managed to keep his voice fairly even and controlled until this last part, but now the anger gathered. "Some people might call what they do 'business.' Or 'competitive behaviour.' I don't." He stopped. After a moment added, "Sorry. But that's the way it is."

"Why don't you tell that to the Department of Public Works?" He looked at me, and I realized how naïve I sounded.

I took a very deep breath and let it out. "Okay," I said. "I see." I asked him how Sylvie and Anna fit into all of that.

"Through the back door." He shook his head, and his face relaxed again into amusement. "They have their own tactics. They've gone to bat for the Purple Parrot. The way they see it, the Bellamy and Cato contract is taking business away from me, and that's bad for the Purple Parrot."

"Which isn't true."

"Not directly. But it could be: they've got the right idea. None of what they're doing was my idea, but I'd be an idiot to put a stop to it." He looked up at me.

That's why they needed the customer list, I thought. For phone numbers.

I took a breath and said, "Do you want me to quit working here?"

"Are you kidding?" He looked genuinely surprised. "God, Maggie. No. Not at all. Fiona would go nuts without you here— I don't need that, for several reasons." He looked at me. "Do you want to quit?"

I shook my head. "I like it here. You know that."

He nodded. "I was just trying to protect you. Regarding Friday, I mean. And let you know what was happening."

"I appreciate it."

"Just keep in mind that this whole thing's Sylvie and Anna's idea, this letter-writing thing. I'm providing the space for the meeting, but that's it."

"It is tricky," I said, and sighed. "I can see both views: yours and Archie's." I shrugged, looked at my watch. "I should get back to work."

He nodded.

I stood up, then turned and said, "I can't really keep this 'letter-writing thing' to myself, you know. It would be sort of like I was supporting it."

"I understand that perfectly," he said, nodding. "I don't imagine they're depending on the element of surprise."

"It's not like I'll be here for the meeting or anything."

"No. That's the whole idea."

"It's not the Purple Parrot that's initiated it."

He shook his head. "Not at all. Anna and Sylvie."

"And it's a small campaign."

He nodded.

I took a large breath and said, "Okay."

As I went back into the front, I found I was angry with Archie. He couldn't have done a better job if he'd intentionally set this whole thing up to invade the one space that was mine. Knowing that such thinking bordered on the irrational didn't help at all. I looked around the Purple Parrot, the warm, bright cluttered place, and swallowed back the tears.

That evening, when I had finished telling Archie about Anna and Sylvie and about their impending visit to his office, and hesitantly started to add a few words about the small letter-writing program they were planning, he whipped the ball he'd just made out of his dirty socks across the bedroom.

"I am sick to death of hearing about this stupid contract," he said. "It's a nothing, Maggie. Nothing."

It didn't seem like an appropriate time to explain to him how Mark felt about Bellamy & Cato.

13

We were to meet for coffee at the shopping plaza in Osier, a large town about thirty kilometres west of the city. It began to drizzle when I reached the highway and I was early anyway, so I drove slowly. I calmed myself by concentrating on what I was going to say to him about his book.

By then, I'd picked up *Bergmehl* again and flipped ahead a little way, and I'd found the names of people and some bits of dialogue here and there. It seemed that eventually something was going to happen to someone. Reassured, I'd started again at the beginning, and this time I found the going somewhat smoother. Now that I knew that the long beginning part was preparation, setting, a second reading had left me with awareness of the place—of open land and rocky outcrops, of wind. It had left me with the sense of being in it, untenured and exposed. I hadn't understood it all, but it was as though I'd been there. Somewhere. Now I'd be able to tell him that I liked the way he'd done it: that much I could say.

I wanted to tell him about my work, too, but it seemed

pointless. I hadn't even looked at it since I'd run into him again. What kind of writer never did any writing? I'd thought about it, even felt drawn to it sometimes, but I couldn't so much as open the notebook, much less take up the pen. The new confusion in my life devoured my attention and my energy. Compared to what Zeke did, my work seemed too simple anyway, too ordinary. Too bogged down in reality. The same way I was.

Before I'd started writing, the memories of Gran's final years had overwhelmed what came before, so that I was unable to remember the better times. When I'd think of Gran, I'd think of helping her to dress for my high-school graduation, of helping her step by step from the taxi to the school auditorium, of worrying from the stage about her safety in the press of younger people. Of hating the need to worry.

I'd remember the overwhelming apprehension when I went out at night to university dances, parties, movies—that Gran might fall, or leave the kettle on, or go to bed with the door unlocked. I'd remember the excuses I'd needed to invent so I could go home early, and returning to find the house and Gran secure, and indulging my self-pity by clamping my teeth on pillow cases, releasing groans as quietly as possible into feather battings.

I'd remember, too, the sense I'd had at the beginning that this fragility was temporary, that Gran would recover and go back to the way she'd been before, that order would return and I'd be able to get on with my life. And how, as awareness grew that it would not—that she would not—I'd begun to see how utterly alone that made me. How much I feared aloneness.

Those memories could easily swallow what had come before, and I had no urge to put them down on paper. Instead, when I was writing I'd move back to times when I was younger, when she was as well, and even back again—through my memories of her memories—to the sixty-one years of her life before she found me thrust upon her.

The writing had given me comfort. But now it seemed too personal. Zeke and Fiona didn't mix such intimacies into what they did. And they were real writers, published writers: they knew what they were doing.

Gran would never have approved of this, this—way I felt for Zeke—but she would have prescribed bitters for the way I felt.

It was her standard prescription for disorders of the stomach. "Your father had a nervous stomach," she would say with a hint of disapproval. Until those last few years, Gran herself was rarely bothered by disorders of any kind.

The drizzle had become rain, and I spotted his pickup in the plaza parking lot through the wet windshield. I was drawing my car in beside the truck before I realized he was sitting at the wheel. He opened the passenger door and I was out and ducking through a yard or so of downpour, climbing up into the truck and pulling the door shut behind me. His arms were around me, mine around him, his lips on mine, the engine running, the windshield wipers slapping, slapping. I could barely breathe from longing and surprise.

"Not here. Not here," I said, starting to pull away from him. "Zeke, no. I can't touch you here."

"Come to the cabin," he said into my hair. I nodded.

He drove fast, past fields still patched with snow—me barely knowing where we were—one of his hands holding mine tightly, as though to give me courage. The windshield was wet with rain and skimmed with fog, and he looked from the road across to me, then back to the road again. He was wearing jeans, as I was, but he wore cowboy boots, a heavy grey-wool sweater and a toque. The toque made him look younger than he had in the city, more vulnerable. Softer.

"Jesus," I said finally. "How far is it?"

"Too far," he said, his voice tight. "Too far." He glanced over at me. "I want you, Maggie."

His words sent a tremor through me. I nodded.

But still we kept driving, and at last I began to smile. Then laugh.

He glanced over at me again and said, "How can this be funny?"

"You'd think a building was on fire."

"Not a building," he said, but he smiled too.

We were a little easier after that. He pointed out Waldham, a summer village on the edge of a lake still white with ice and snow. The cabins and cottages looked deserted; so did a small, two-story hotel—"Waldham Inn," said a sign in need of paint.

He'd needed to release my hand to shift gears through the village, and when he took it back I turned and put my other hand on his thigh. He sucked in breath, looked over at me and said, "I haven't felt like this in a long time."

"This good?" I said, teasing.

He moved his head to confirm that that wasn't what he'd meant.

"You're not looking at the road," I said. "You want me to move away?"

"I want to pull over and have you right here in the back. Right now."

The idea appealed to me. In theory, anyway.

It was at least ten minutes more before he turned off the secondary highway and onto a poorly maintained side road. About a kilometre later he turned again, onto a drive that seemed to be little more than rutted mud. We bumped and skidded along through a copse of bare birch and alder until we rounded a corner and a small cabin appeared in the rain.

It was set in a stump-pocked clearing littered here and there with junk—rusted and weed-ridden bits of farm equipment, a pile of tires, a water trough shot through with holes. The cabin itself was a red-brown colour, its windows small and green-shuttered, its roof dark grey, uneven, gleaming wet. The tilt of the building was at variance with a big front porch which looked relatively new, a light cedar with newer and more even shingles, but it was impossible to tell whether the cabin or the porch was out of plumb. Steam rose from a chimney the colour of gun metal, and water from the roof splashed into large wooden rain barrels, one at each corner of the little building.

"It's not what I imagined," I said.

"It's pretty bad," he agreed. "But it costs the way it looks, which was a selling point for me."

He stopped the truck, turned it off, and put his arms around me. With a small groan, he opened his door and got out of the truck, and came around and pulled me out from my side by the hand, and we were running through the rain and pushing our way into the cabin—it smelled of furniture polish and fresh coffee—and we were pulling at one another's clothes as he edged me, edged with me, into the bedroom, into his bed.

It was over so quickly the first time that he apologized, his face against my shoulder. I didn't mind, I told him, running my hand over the stubble of his hair, down the smooth of his back, and after a while he went to get us coffee and came back, handing me a mug to put on the upended orange crate beside the bed. He sat on the edge of the bed and lit a cigarette. I ran my hand over his bare shoulder, down his naked back. He was so different from Archie. His body was long and lean, and the hair on his chest and legs—it was greying a little on his chest—was the same dark colour as the short-cropped hair on his head. He moved in a loose and careless way that put me in mind of something leonine. Archie always seemed pale and deliberate, tight somehow, even inside his skin.

Zeke turned and smiled down at me.

"We'll get better," he said.

I nodded, smiling too. "It really doesn't matter," I said. "Just being here –"

"It does matter," he said, and after another few drags he put out the cigarette and turned back to me. He was sure and patient, and my nervousness went under as he seemed to fold me inside out. I surfaced once, at the sound of my own cry, to hope there was no one else around, and then sank back, deepened and gave in—and then for a moment felt utterly at peace, alone, and then complete, with him.

Afterward, he slept against my shoulder and I watched him, watched his chest rise and fall against my paler skin.

When I knew I had to go, I moved.

"Don't go," he said, his eyes closed. "Please."

"I have to," I said. "It's getting late."

In his bathroom, I found lukewarm water, cool air and rough towelling. I dressed, brushed my hair, touched makeup to my still-pink face. Then I went out to see where he lived.

The bedroom and the bathroom ran along the east side of the cabin; aside from them, there was only one room. The kitchen was at the back of it, at the north end, and the living area was at the front. On a long table, clear of clutter, in front of a small west-facing window—through which I could see the trunks of trees and underbrush, stretches of pale brown stubble, dark earth and strips of dirty snow—there was a computer and a printer, a brass table lamp, ceramic mugs holding pens and pencils, a few closed notebooks. No roll-top desk. I'd been silly to imagine one. Only amateurs wrote by hand.

The bookshelf beside his work area held a small stationery store—packages of paper, boxes containing pens and pencils, paper clips and staples. The rest of the small room was designed for function, too. It was threadbare, but clean enough, and contained a worn maroon couch, a low, cheap-looking coffee table, an armchair that matched the couch, but was covered in a throw printed with gold and purple flowers. There were a few braided rugs, a floor lamp with a paper shade, a small chrome-legged table with four cream-and-gold vinyl-seated chairs. Behind the couch was a low bookcase, full. More books were stacked neatly on the floor beside the armchair. Beyond that was the kitchen area. It looked spotless. The cabin smelled as though it had been newly cleaned.

There were three windows, one over the sink, one looking out onto the front verandah, and the one he looked out of when he wrote, but the day had made the cabin dark. I wanted to turn on the desk lamp to see how it softened the room, but I didn't dare approach his work area.

He came out of the bedroom and put his arms around me, his lips against my neck, nuzzling, tingling my skin.

"I like it," I said, leaning into him. "It must be a good place to write."

"It's cold and dark," he said, moving away from me. "Do you want another coffee before you go?"

I said I couldn't. A feeling had started in my stomach and my throat that I'd known was bound to come—although it felt more like fear of discovery than guilt. I had to get home before anyone noticed I was gone.

He filled a travel mug with coffee.

The rain was no more than a light mist now, but the day seemed darker than it had before. It was after one o'clock. He put the plastic coffee mug on the seat of the truck between us, and the sound of the engine starting brought me some relief. I held the mug steady, and when we reached the secondary road I lifted it off the seat and moved closer to him.

Slowing into Waldham, he said, "When can you come back?"

I thought, How can I come back?

"I shouldn't be here now," I said.

"This feels so right. To me," he said after a moment, glancing over at me. "Doesn't it feel right to you?"

"That's not the point," I said. I took a deep breath, holding out my hand flat, seeing my wedding ring, closing my hand again and pressing the ring into my lap. I thought of Ben, of Archie—oddly, of Victor Maxwell. The election. "It's dangerous," I said.

"A little danger never hurts," he said lightly. "It's good for your soul."

I shook my head.

"Okay," he said. "I'm sorry."

When we'd passed the edge of town and he was picking up speed again, I said, "Why is it right for you?"

His eyes on the road, he considered for a long time, then took a breath and said, "Every moment is made up of three times, Maggie: the past, the present and the future. You're here in the present with me, and the future too, I hope—falling in love is always about the future—but you're also part of my past. That's critical. Not only to me as a human being but also to me—particularly to me, right now, as a writer. When I'm with you, that time at university is real. All the time that was gone is still ahead. You've given me back memories I haven't had in years." He glanced at me. "You've given me time, and will."

"Recaptured youth," I said. "That's how I feel, too."

"It's more than that," he said. "When I'm with you, I am then, but I am also now. I can see the track I've been on—where I've stayed with the vision I once had, and where I've veered away. I can see where I was naïve when I started out, but I can also see where I was right, and I can see that I'm getting somewhere—that I've got somewhere." He sighed. "So much of it is perspective. I'd been dwelling too much on what other people had accomplished, feeling like I'd failed in contrast. I don't feel that way now. When you've got all three together—past, present, future—all together and in the right perspective, you've got everything you need."

Feeling swamped in the wake of his thinking—a familiar feeling—I said, "And here I thought it was my smile."

He laughed and looked at me with affection. "It is your smile," he said. "And your voice. And your hands, and the curve of your

neck. I love the look of you—you make me wish I could draw."
I nodded. "I'd draw your eyes," I said. "You have most wonderful eyes." I smiled. "It was such a shock—to look up and find them looking at me that night, at the nomination meeting."
He reached to take my hand.
"What were you doing there?" I asked.
He raised his eyebrows. "Looking for you. What else?"
"But why me? Why then?"
"I had a dream a month or so ago about you. About that night we walked." He looked at me. "It was an important night."
"The night of the dream, or the night of the walk?"
"Both, I guess. The dream now, the walk then. The walk consolidated things for me. All those wild and crazy thoughts I'd been having for years got harnessed—like they'd been galloping all over the place in every direction and suddenly gathered and headed for the chute. I could see where they were going. Where I had to go."
"Which was someplace else."
He nodded. "I had to do, and write. I knew I'd had enough of studying, looking at other people's thoughts, but that night gave me focus. And now seeing you has given me focus again." He lifted a shoulder. "It's important."
I sighed and leaned back into the seat. "When you left—it was almost like the fates had taken you or something. Like it hadn't been your decision. I always assumed you were part of a larger picture—some guiding system. For me, things just happened. One after another. Plan-less." I took a deep breath. "Like this."
"This?"
"Well, I never would have planned this. But you did."
"Not this," he said quietly. "I planned the meeting. I had to see you. But I thought it would be only for coffee or something. I didn't intend that I'd feel the way I do. That you'd have such an effect on me. I didn't plan this part."
After several moments, I said, "I started to read your book last night."
"Damn," he said, hitting the heel of his hand against the steering wheel. "I meant to give you one. I've got a whole box of them back there someplace."
"I like it," I said. "So far. I like the way you've used the words."
He laughed.

"I mean the images you make with them."

"No," he said. "That's a wonderful review. 'I like the way you use the words.' I'm very satisfied with that."

"You must be pleased with it yourself."

He shrugged. "*Bergmehl* is history. It's gone. The new one's all that matters."

I looked over at his profile, put out my hand and touched his cheek, withdrew it. I thought briefly about not seeing him again—about deciding not to see him again—and knew I couldn't do that. I turned away from him, toward the passenger window. For a clear moment, I felt—felt, rather than imagined—what I was about to do: to my life, to my husband, to my son—and shuddered. I had no courage for all that.

I pushed the feeling off, and asked him what it was about, his book.

"You okay?" he asked.

"Yes. Why?"

"Your voice sounded—different—for a second."

I nodded. "I'm all right," I said. I cleared my throat. "What's the book about?"

He shook his head. "Sorry, but I can't. Like I told you. Superstition." He glanced at me. "You ever done any writing?"

"Not really." I felt my face redden. "Not like you do. Or Fiona."

"But something."'

"No," I said. "Not really. Nothing."

He smiled. "Let me have a look at it."

"Absolutely not," I said, aghast.

He laughed. "That's a good sign."

"What is?"

"That you don't want to show it to me."

"Why?"

"It's just a good sign, that's all." He still looked amused.

"That I don't want to show it to you specifically, or that I don't want to show it to anyone?"

"Doesn't much matter. Which is it?"

I thought about that, then said, "Both. Although you'd be worse."

"Thank you."

I could see the buildings of Osier in the distance, and I looked away from them.

"Sounds ridiculous, doesn't it?" I said. "I climb naked into bed with you, but I'm afraid to show you a few sentences I put down on a page."

"That's not ridiculous at all," he said. "That's perfectly natural. There's intimacy and then there's intimacy. Your instincts are sound." He looked over. "Especially about climbing into bed with me."

He pulled in beside my car, pulled on the brake, put the pickup into neutral. He took my hand in his. "I want you back soon," he said.

I looked into his eyes, then looked away. I didn't want to leave.

"I'll phone," I said.

He leaned forward to kiss me, but I shook my head.

I opened the passenger door and stepped out into the parking lot. I closed the door, part way, slowly—and found even that small act of separation more difficult than I could possibly have imagined.

Slowly I opened the door again and said, "I guess I will be back."

He nodded and said, "That's good." Then, "When?"

"I don't know," I said. I felt my stomach sink—I knew I'd crossed a line. "How's Friday?"

"Too far away," he said.

14

A week or so ago I'd been resentful of the amount of time Archie would be gone because of the campaign; now it was like a gift that I'd barely seen him in two days.

"We're going to be late," I said when he finally got into the driver's seat of the Blazer on Wednesday evening.

"I'm here," he said evenly, slamming the driver's door closed. "That'll have to do."

I didn't want to be late. We were on our way to a school play in which Ben was a stage hand. Edward and Millicent were saving seats for us, but Ben would be furious if we missed anything.

After a few blocks he said, "The Bobbsey Twins were in today."

"Who?"

"From the Purple Parrot."

I imagined Anna and Sylvie sitting nervous but determined on the beige two-seater couch in his office, almost overwhelmed by the large painting behind them—a male and a female elk at a mountain stream. It was a painting by one of the province's artists, on loan from the province's art bank.

"How did it go?"

"They're earnest enough—misguided, but that's hardly a sin. Trying to turn this into a cultural issue isn't going to help them. Or Scales. They can write all the letters they want."

"Did you tell them that?"

"Of course not. They'll find out for themselves." He glanced over at me. "They went out of their way to point out that you weren't involved."

"That was nice of them." When he didn't say anything, I added, "Because I'm not."

He looked as though he were weighing this, then said, "You do work for Mark Scales."

"That's beside the point."

"Not entirely."

He drove into the school parking lot, drove around it. There were no parking spaces. I looked at the clock on the dashboard— we were now ten minutes late. He drove out of the parking lot and started slowly down the block. Down the next block. In the third, he found a spot.

I felt distant with Archie, oddly guilt-free. His arrogance tonight only added to my sense of separateness from him. But the mere thought of letting Ben down plunged me into near-panic, and I was ready to explode.

Archie turned off the engine and said, "I'm sure Scales is delighted to have you working for him."

"Don't start," I said. "We've got to get into the school."

"You need to think about these things."

Gripping the door handle, I said, "Are you suggesting he's employing me just to embarrass you?"

"I'm suggesting that's part of it."

I got out and slammed my door and started walking as fast as I could toward the school. I'd worn heels, and they slowed me down, and he quickly caught up with me. "That's the way politics are," he said. "I shouldn't have to explain it to you."

"You don't," I said.

The lobby of the school was deserted and the doors to the

auditorium closed. Two young ushers made us wait until a scene had ended before admitting us.

We stood against the wall until our eyes had adjusted to the dimness. There were about five hundred people in the audience, but finally I saw Millicent waving at us about two-thirds of the way back.

The production of *The Importance of Being Earnest* was hopelessly amateurish, even for a high school. There was a pause before almost every line from Lady Bracknell, during which the whisper of the prompter was faintly audible even from where we were sitting. The rest of the cast—I recognized two as friends of Ben's—either over-acted or under-acted, and most of them looked scared to death. We should have attended the second night rather than the first, let the kids get past their opening-night jitters. But Wednesday was the only night Archie was free all week.

I tried to concentrate on figuring out what the stage hands might be contributing to the production so that I could talk sensibly about it later with Ben, but it was hard to get my mind off my irritation with Archie. He was always so ready to see ulterior motives in everyone but himself.

At last the curtains closed for the intermission.

"Well," Millicent said as we stood up, "it's going much better now."

"Better than what?" I asked her.

I could hear Archie behind me. "Thank you." "Do my best." "Got a great team." At least five people had reached over to shake his hand and we hadn't even reached the aisle.

Millicent stopped and let Edward and Archie go past. In a quiet voice, she said, "Got off to a bit of a rocky start. Before the play began, Ben and one of the other fellows were out on the stage moving chairs around, when suddenly the curtains opened. You should have seen their faces." She laughed. "They took off like a shot, and they closed the curtains again so fast it took about five minutes for them to stop swinging."

"Poor Ben," I said.

"Good thing it's a comedy," she said. "Off on the right foot for that."

This was Ben's first year of senior high school but there were familiar faces in the lobby—parents we'd known from elementary and junior high. There were a lot of business people and professionals in this part of town, and several of them came over to talk to Archie—extending congratulations on his decision to run again, wishing him well, seeking his opinion. There were people who didn't know him who recognized him, too. You could see it in their eyes before they looked away—obviously turning to ask, "Why do I know that face?" then turning back for another look when the answer had been given. Edward stood beside him, enjoying the attention, too.

The lights dimmed to warn us that the production was about to resume, and I thought of the days when we would appear at events like this when Archie was still a teacher. The people who approached him then wanted to talk about their children's marks and to hear what fine individuals they were raising. It was often awkward, Archie fumbling around as he tried to connect the name of the parents with the sea of student faces in his memory bank.

Now he was in his element. He loved to be recognized, loved to be lionized, loved the cachet that came with public office.

The play finally ground to a halt after eleven, and Millicent and Edward went home immediately. Archie and I waited for Ben in the hallway, along with a bunch of enthusiastic young people—most of them carrying flowers—and a lot of other yawning parents.

Archie stood at the back of the crowd, leaning one shoulder against a creamy white stone wall, his overcoat over his arm. The first of the actors came out of a door to the left of the auditorium, still wearing make-up and looking shy and proud. A cheer went up.

"How much do you make there anyway?" he asked me. "Still minimum wage?"

"It's more than that," I said.

"Can't be much more."

"It's not the money."

"It's not?"

"It's the way I feel there," I said evenly. "It's the atmosphere." I'd told him this before.

Several more of the actors emerged from the door behind the stage and were welcomed with hugs and applause.

"Mark's got his reasons, you know. For being upset about

Bellamy and Cato."

"I thought you didn't talk about that kind of thing with him."

"He didn't raise it," I said. "I asked him about it."

"Why?"

"I was curious. It's not like him to go off the handle."

Archie shifted himself against the wall, crossing his arms. "And what did he say?"

I explained what Mark had told me about Bellamy & Cato and about their reputation. Archie seemed to be listening, so when I was finished, I said more gently, "Why can't you edge off on it? It's getting close to the election. Might buy you a few votes, show them that you're human."

He smiled. "That's one good reason why I can't." He took a deep breath, came up from the wall and put an arm around me. "Look, honey," he said seriously. "I know you like your little job, and I'm sure you think Mark Scales is great. But you're not looking at it objectively. He's bitter, and there's money involved here. You can't trust everything he says."

I bit back several things I might have said. "He had no reason to lie to me."

"I'm sure he knew you'd pass on to me whatever he said to you...."

"No. I'm the one...."

"And you fell for it." He shrugged. "That's natural. You don't need to blame yourself."

I closed my eyes and looked away.

"Just leave these things to me, okay? I know what I'm doing."

Ben had emerged into the lobby with a group of other students in blue jeans and T-shirts. Archie went over to shake his hand, and after a few moments, I followed.

"Great job, son," Archie said, patting Ben on the back.

"Did you see it all?" Ben asked.

"Sure. Why?"

"You're always late," Ben said.

Archie shook his head.

"We were late," I said. "Your father held us up."

Ben glanced at me. "You *were* late?"

"Just a few minutes," Archie said.

"Both of you?"

I nodded and said, "Sorry."

Ben let out an enormous sigh. "No," he said. "That's great." Archie looked puzzled for only an instant before he looked over at me with an expression that said, "You see?"

15

"**Y**ou've lost weight," Alana said, giving me a hug and sitting down across from me.

I shrugged. "A pound or two, I guess."

"What's happening?"

"Let's order first," I said. "You have to get back to work."

Her eyes wandered to her menu. After a moment, she looked up at me and said, "I read the other day that there are more than a hundred places to eat and drink in Old Watchford. Can you believe that? Just think about it, Maggie. Every place has a menu, and let's say an average of twelve lunch choices. That makes one thousand, two hundred decisions to make every day at noon." She closed her menu. "It's a good thing I can't afford to eat out every day. I'd go mad."

Our waiter appeared, and Alana asked for a half-order of cannelloni and a salad. I ordered the linguine. I wasn't hungry, but it would get complicated if I didn't order something.

"Okay," she said the moment he was gone. "Tell me what's going on."

"Basically, it's my job," I said. I didn't need to choose my words: I'd thought ahead of time of what I wanted to say to her, and how. I told her about Sylvie and Anna, and then backed up and explained about the Bellamy & Cato contract when she said she hadn't noticed anything about it in the news. I told her how Sylvie and Anna had met with Archie, about the meeting they were organizing for tomorrow, about Mark's suggestion that I take the day off.

"It's Archie's attitude that's getting under my skin," I said. "None of this is any kind of threat to him—he's said so himself—and Mark's going out of his way to keep me out of it." I was over-tired, and even talking about it made me feel like weeping. "Archie's always acted like the Purple Parrot was more of a hobby than a job—like it's not important. Now it's as though he's indulging me or something, 'letting me' stay on there." I sighed. "I don't know, Alana. It's my job. It's got nothing to do with him, but he's twisting things around, even trying to make it sound as though Mark's using me to get at him. It's not like that at all. I know Mark. Archie doesn't."

Alana had been fiddling with the large ring on her right hand, a piece of costume jewellery with numerous red and turquoise stones that matched her earrings, while she listened to me. Now she waited for the waiter to refill our mugs, and then she looked up and said, "You want to know what I think?"

I nodded.

"I think Archie has a point," she said, looking down at her ring again. She shrugged. "You said you wanted my opinion."

I decided I hadn't explained it properly, and tried again. "Look at your job," I said. "It's about you. Right? It's about who you are. You contribute something to Sanderson and Lebel. How would you feel if Vern suddenly started to make it sound like you were only there because he *let* you be there? Or imply that your job was disposable? After all the seniority and respect you've built up?"

"Unfortunately, my job isn't disposable," she said. "We need the money."

I looked away.

"Look at it from Archie's point of view, Maggie. Among other things, it could be embarrassing for him, couldn't it? No one likes to be embarrassed."

I looked back at her. "People try to embarrass politicians all the time. They deal with it. This isn't going to embarrass him."

Alana sighed. "I know what you're saying—and I know what you want me to say. It's your work, you have rights, all that stuff."

I wanted her to say more than that. I wanted her to say that Archie was being a jerk—that Archie was a jerk. That she didn't know why I stayed with him. That if I left him, Ben would be just fine. I wanted her to say those things, and other things, in that tone of absolute conviction of which only she was capable. But she didn't.

She leaned forward. "Look, Maggie. It's not like I agree with Archie on this contract you're telling me about. But if there was any possibility my job might compromise Vern, I'd quit. No questions asked." The waiter put down her salad and she picked up her fork. "He'd do the same for me."

"I'm not compromising Archie," I said thinly. As I watched her shrug and start in on her salad, I was thinking I should never have called her. My urges to share my problems came in spurts— usually over before I acted on them. But I'd been sure Alana would take my side. I hadn't been prepared for this.

I took a breath and tried another tack. "Even if my job doesn't contribute anything essential to the household income, it's important to me."

The pasta arrived. I watched Alana tuck in, and felt nauseated.

"You like what you're doing there," she said mildly. "You're fortunate that way."

I nodded. "The people at the Purple Parrot are interested in different things than the people I see with Archie. Their priorities are different. It's not about manipulating other people, and it's not about money. It's about creating things that last, that matter— about creating art, or trying to create it—and that makes for a whole different set of priorities. A whole different way of seeing the world." I looked up at her. "I think what they're doing is more valid, even if it doesn't pay as well."

"It's certainly more romantic."

She was being stubborn, determined not to understand no matter what I said. I looked at my watch.

"You haven't eaten anything," she said.

I shook my head. "Not hungry. Do you want some of mine?"

She ignored my question. "I'm sorry, Maggie," she said. "Don't get in a twist about all this. You look tired, and you're

108

losing weight. You've got to look after yourself—that's what's most important."

The waiter was as concerned by my untouched lunch as Alana had been, and I had to assure him that it had nothing to do with the food before he'd take my plate away. While we were waiting for the bill, I said, "You usually sound more gung-ho about your job than you do today. Is something the matter there?"

She leaned back and lifted her hair away from her face. "I'm getting sick of it," she said. "I told you about Swimmer."

"And the young woman lawyer? Yes."

She nodded. "Now Swimmer's wife's got some kind of growth on her ovary or somewhere. She had a biopsy more than a week ago, and she still hasn't got the results." She looked up. "She's been waiting for more than a *week.*"

I shook my head, thanking God for the millionth time that Archie wasn't Minister of Health. Not that it let him off the hook regarding the cutbacks as far as most people were concerned—including Alana, and including me as well sometimes—but it padded things a little.

"So she's scared to death. Who wouldn't be? She calls and calls, and it's getting under Swimmer's skin. You should see the way he rolls his eyes when Alice tells him Estie's on the line. It makes me sick. And in the meantime, he's keeping up with Marianna like there's nothing going on at home. One afternoon he got Alice to call Estie and tell her he had to go to a development appeal board meeting and it was likely to run late, which was an out-and-out lie. He hasn't been to the DAB in weeks. It was an excuse to disappear with Marianna. If I was Alice, I wouldn't do it, even if it meant my job. Of course Alice is a single parent, so she can't afford principles, and to make it more complicated I think she's hot on Swimmer herself." Alana sighed and shrugged. "I can hardly stand talking to him any more."

It sounded trite and shoddy. But who knew what it was like for them? Who knew what Swimmer's wife was like? What it was like between them? There was no way anyone could know for sure what was happening, except the people who were involved.

"You're a million miles away," Alana said.

It was true. That was the way it felt. As though she and I were moving farther and farther apart until we'd see one another as tiny, far-off specks.

"It's hard to know," I said. "That's all."

She looked at me for a long moment. "Don't tell me you're feeling sorry for Ken Swimmer?"

I shook my head. "I don't feel sorry for him."

She nodded. "Good. For a minute I thought you'd flipped your lid."

It was curious, I thought, the way Alana kept referring to Ken Swimmer by his last name, to Marianna by her first. Everything I noticed about Alana from this distance made me feel more alone, more anxious to be alone. But at the same time, I missed her, missed the closeness that was usual with us. Several times in the past few days I'd thought of things I wanted to tell Alana about Zeke before remembering that I couldn't.

I wished for someone I could talk to, about everything.

"Maggie," she said, pulling out her wallet to put her change away, "it's just a job, you know. What you're doing, what I'm doing, they're just jobs. What we do to earn a living has nothing to do with who we are."

"I know," I said. "I know."

It wasn't the way I felt, and it wasn't the way it should be, but I could see that there was no point in trying to explain that to her, either.

16

When I got into the car to leave the city on Friday morning, there was a gnawing feeling in my stomach that was more like nausea than appetite. It was born of nervousness and annoyance, weariness, fear of discovery, defiance. But as I drove, some of the layers lifted off. Along with eagerness at the prospect of seeing Zeke again there was an odd calm, as though I were going home rather than driving away from it.

It had rained again late the day before, and the rain had been followed by a freeze. The main highway was clear, but the secondary highway after the exit ramp at Osier was wet where the sun hit it, slick where it did not. The side road beyond Waldham was even worse, and by the time I reached the lane to Zeke's cabin, my car was coated in mud. I took the turn too slowly, and got stuck.

I knew that if I tried to move forward or back, I'd just sink myself in more deeply, but I'd brought no boots with me so I couldn't get out of the car. I leaned my hand against the horn—

once, twice—surprised at how close the tears were.

Finally Zeke appeared and the sight of him settled and reassured me. He was wearing rubber boots and pulling on a jacket. He assessed my situation with a long look, waved and disappeared again.

I had at least managed to get stuck in sunlight, which shone in the passenger window and warmed the car. I rolled my window down and took deep breaths of the sweet air.

When Zeke reappeared, he was carrying burlap sacks and a second pair of rubber boots, a set of dark blue coveralls over one arm. He came alongside the car.

"Hello," he said. "You're beautiful."

I nodded at his armful. "Looks like you were prepared for this."

He smiled. "Maybe not for this, exactly."

He put two burlap sacks down on the muck, stepped onto them, and handed me the boots through the open window. "Now you can get out."

I opened the door, pulled off my running shoes and drew on the boots, which were much too large for me. I joined him on an icy bank, and we considered the car.

"What we're going to do," he said after a moment, "is to get it back onto the side road and leave it there. It's only a few feet, and there's no point in trying to come any further in. You'd just get stuck again."

"I should have left it out there in the first place."

"True," he said, and handed me the coveralls. Hopping on one foot and then the other, I pulled them on. When I got them up over my jeans, I took my jacket off and slid my arms into their arms.

"A fine fit," he said, taking my jacket and tossing it neatly in through the open door of the car. "You look great in coveralls."

"Thank you," I said. "You look great, too."

He did, and I let my eyes linger on him for a moment longer until he drew me back to the problem at hand by asking if my car was front-wheel drive.

I told him I had no idea.

He crouched down and looked at its underside for several moments, then went back and put a burlap sack behind each of the back wheels. He came around to the driver's door and got in, first knocking off some—but not all—of the mud from his boots.

There was going to be a lot of cleaning up to do before I went home.

He started the car, put his left leg out on the ground and held the steering wheel. "Okay. You go to the front and push."

I did, and we managed to move the car back over the burlap. Zeke got out, tugged the sacks free, and then drew them around so that they were again behind the tires. After repeating this routine twice more, we finally got the car up onto the road. He pulled it off to the side, and turned the engine off.

I looked at my watch, thinking that we were always losing time.

I had difficulty walking in the oversized boots, and he took my hand to guide me along firm ground to the cabin.

"These can't be yours," I said. "They'd be too big even for you."

"Found 'em under the house. Last fall." He put an arm around me. "Did you see how well we worked together?"

"We did," I said. "That's true."

He said, "I've missed you."

I left the rubber boots on the verandah and, inside the door to the cabin, unbuttoned the coveralls and slipped them off. I looked up and saw him watching me.

"You have mud on your face," he said, taking the coveralls from me and hanging them on a wall hook near the door. "Little specks of mud." I put my hand up but he gently started brushing them away. His face near mine he said, "I've wanted you to be here."

His light touch made my legs feel weak.

"Me, too," I whispered, my mouth so close to his face that I could feel my own breath coming back at me. "I've imagined being here a hundred times since I saw you last."

"What did you imagine?"

"Well, not getting stuck," I said.

He smiled.

I shrugged and said, "Having time. As much time as we want." I kissed him, felt the longing rise.

His arms around me, he pulled me closer, said again, "Tell me. What did you imagine?"

"I imagined you working—I love it that you're a writer." I breathed his smell deep into me. "I imagined you up late, working, my coming here and finding you asleep."

"And then?" he said into my neck, a murmur.

I pushed my hands up between us and started unbuttoning his shirt. "Unbuttoning your shirt," I said.

He moved back, just enough to give my fingers space, his eyes on mine. "I don't wear a shirt to bed."

"Then I'd unbutton mine."

He started to do that, still keeping his eyes on me. "And then."

"Your belt."

"Like this."

"Like this. Yes."

"I don't wear a belt to bed." He leaned back to find the button on my jeans. Found it. Pulled the zipper down. Found my bare belly with the flat of his hand and slipped his hand inside. "After that," he said. "What about after that?"

I shook my head, hungry, sliding his jeans down over his hips, memory, the desire to talk, retreating.

We stayed in bed for a long time, discovering one another with fingers, tongues, the planes of skin on skin. He touched me with experience and close attention—he could almost read my longing better than I could.

Close together, we talked about the past. He prodded at my memory, urging me to recall with him parties, concerts, lectures—many of which I had not been at. I wanted to talk about that night he'd walked me home—it was becoming in my memory like a signal from then to now—but he wanted to move on, to find out what happened after he had left. It seemed to please him that the group had come apart without him. He was disappointed when I couldn't tell him what had happened to everyone we'd known.

I was surprised he hadn't stayed in touch with any of the others. "You were like the glue," I said. "You connected them to one other. Us to one another."

"Maybe I'll look a few of them up after I finish this book. Not now." He shrugged. "But I had to cut the ties. I was trying to re-invent my life."

He'd had a lot of different jobs—stocked grocery shelves when he was younger, worked in a department store—"In sporting goods," he laughed. "Can you believe it? I've never even owned a pair of skates."—waited tables off and on for years, delivered flyers for a winter. Everything he'd done had been directed at the writing: to feed and shelter himself was to feed and shelter the work. The women who distracted him, he left; the women who did not, left him. The consistent had been the fiction, not the people or the jobs.

"I'm a slow writer," he said, "and too easily distracted. It would take me a couple of years to do a book even if I could give it my full attention, but the way I've had to work it's always taken me four or five. There's the research, then the first draft. Then rewrites—the big work, where the actual writing happens. When I have to be away from it, it takes me days to get back into it. I didn't worry about time when I was younger, the loss of it. It irritated me, but I didn't worry. So much of what I've written has related to geology: just thinking about that stuff flattens out your sense of time. But a few years ago, it started scaring me. Time wasted. Time gone. Time left."

"You don't earn enough money from your books, to live on." It was a question.

He laughed briefly, then leaned over to get a cigarette from the pack on the orange crate beside the bed, dumping the ashtray into a coffee can on the floor beside it. "My writing's paid me enough to live on for one six-month period, and that's it." He lit the cigarette and leaned back on the pillows. "After *Catastrophics* was published, there was a small grant, some readings, a few royalties. Wasn't much, but it was enough for a while. I got hopeful." He shook his head, blowing out smoke in a tight stream. "When I get hopeful, it usually means that disaster is about to strike. Which it did. First *Kapstone* went out of print— for a second time, in fact—and this time the publisher didn't want to reprint it. Turned out he couldn't afford to reprint it, or print anything for that matter. He went bankrupt about six months later. Then *Bergmehl*, which was with another publisher, Ecandale, sold out too, and they decided not to reprint that. Another cash problem." He shrugged. "They did *Catastrophics*, too, which you can still get some places down east. But rumour has it now Ecandale's about to go belly up as well."

"Can't you get another publisher?" Head propped on my hand, I lay beside him, watching him talk about his work. I liked looking at him naked, at his leanness, loved the easy way he moved, the easy way he rested. Loved his hands, his toes, his fingers. The flat lobes of his ears. That tiny scar, the greying hair. "I need a new book for that, and even then who knows? I haven't exactly sold like hot-cakes, and these days publishers are into hot-cakes. Have to be: governments are squeezing them to death." He looked across my shoulder, toward the window. "But what I'm working on now is good. It's good. If it goes, takes off, then the earlier books might be reprinted." He shook his head ruefully, and laughed.

"What?"

He looked down at me and said, "There I go again. Getting my hopes up."

"Nobody'd ever do anything if they didn't hope."

He pulled me closer. "That's true, and that's wise, and you're right." He kissed the top of my head.

I smiled, moving a fingertip along the rise of his hipbone, watching him stub out his cigarette. "When did you decide to come back here?"

"My old man died and I had to come out to take care of a few things. There are times in life when you get a sign and you know what you have to do, and that was one of them. I'd gone back to waiting tables by then, about ready to give up—"

"Give up writing?"

"Give up period. I was out of money, I'd lost a book I'd been working on, lost the vision, and I felt like I'd lost everything. I began to see myself as a waiter who dabbled in writing instead of the other way around, and I started wondering how long they'd let me keep it up. I mean how many doddery old men do you see out there serving tables in restaurants?" He took a slow, long breath. "I started hearing my father's voice in my own head, wondering how I was going to live when I got old. I honestly thought I'd never write again. It was a pretty bleak time." He looked down at me. "And then," he said, "Kaboom. The old man kicks, and I get one more chance."

"Doesn't sound like you liked him very much."

"It was mutual. The last thing he intended with his will was to bail me out. In fact, he left every cent to the Foster Parents Plan—which actually impressed me. I'd never realized he was capable of irony. But with a little fancy footwork from a lawyer out here, I managed to salvage enough of the estate to buy a little writing time." He paused. "You want a cup of coffee?"

"Not if it means you have to move."

He smiled, but stood up, picked a towel up off the floor, and tied it at his waist.

"Is it enough to buy a book?" I asked.

He glanced down at me.

"It had better be," he said. "I don't have any more parents to kill off."

He went out to the kitchen and I tried to remember who had told me that his mother had died when he was small. That he lived with his father. That they didn't get along. Someone had, but the memory of who and when was gone.

The room was cooler than I'd realized—cooler without him beside me—and by the time he came back with two steaming mugs of coffee, I'd pulled the spread up over me.

He put the mugs on the orange crate and sat down on the edge of the bed.

"You know what you want," I said. "You've always known. I envy that."

He leaned toward me, ran his hand softly over my hair, along my face, just barely touching me. "I want you," he said.

I smiled and touched his face as well. I said, "I envy that you've done it, too. You've got four books.... That's huge."

He looked away. "Three. I've got three books. You don't have books until they're done. They're slippery creatures, not to be trusted until you've pinned them—nailed them—to the wall."

I smiled at the way he'd said it, but he seemed quite serious. "Okay, then," I said. "Almost four. And more to come after that. It'll work out, Zeke. I know it will. The financial part, I mean, and in the meantime you're doing something. Making something." I thought of Alana and moved my head at the truths she couldn't see, would never know.

He took a sip from one of the mugs of coffee, and lifted the other to me. I sat up to take it. Even before I put it to my lips I could smell the alcohol.

I looked at him, quizzical.

"Bit of brandy," he said, nodding. "To warm you."

"I haven't even had breakfast," I said, but it tasted good.

After a few sips I said, "It's more the determination I envy, the actual work, than the accomplishment. It's not only knowing what you want to do, it's also being bloody-minded about sitting down and doing it. I haven't even touched the stuff I've been working on since I met you."

He smiled. "Don't worry about it. You're new to it. Given time and patience, you'll be just as miserable as I am."

"I don't think I'm any good at it."

"You could let me have a look."

"You won't even talk about your work with me, much less show it."

"It's different," he said. "I've done a lot of writing. Maybe I could help."

I shook my head. "It's really nothing, just something I'm doing for myself. A memory."

The bed had no head- or footboard and we leaned against the wall, a beige quilt drawn up to our waists, sipping the coffee-brandy mixture. Almost absent-mindedly, he moved his fingers over the skin along my leg. I felt aroused and at the same time my eyes were heavy with the need to sleep. I thought of what it would be like to stay out here with him. To work quietly while he worked, to learn focus by example. To walk, to talk. It would be so simple. It would change me.

"I'm not trying to pry," he said. I tried to remember what we were talking about. The writing: that was it. He said, "If you really don't want me to see it...."

I moved my head back and forth, relaxed. "I don't know. I'll think about it. Maybe next time."

I wondered what he wanted from us, besides this. Maybe nothing more than this. He had his work.

He took my hand and moved it across the quilt until I felt the hardness of him beneath the covers. I increased the pressure and he took my coffee mug and lowered it with his to the floor. When he rolled back, he pulled me to him underneath the covers.

17

I stared glassy-eyed through a wall of windows as streams of hot water washed suds from a car—not mine, not yet—into the gutters. A boy sat on a stool beside me eating French fries. The smell of hot greasy food made my stomach turn and I moved back a little. It was crowded at the viewing windows; it a was Friday afternoon, it was spring, the car wash was busy. The press of people irritated me. I wanted to be back in the country, with Zeke. Or somewhere else, alone. Not here, and not where I was going next.

I also wanted to sleep. My head throbbed with the aftereffects of the brandy, my body was weary from lovemaking, my brain deadened from too many restless nights. On the way back into the city I'd rolled my window down, let the wind on my face keep me awake. If Zeke hadn't been so full of energy, I'd probably have fallen off to sleep beside him.

He'd been keen to get back to work, almost eager, I'd felt, for me to go. He said the brandy always helped to get the creative juices flowing. On the way back to the car, my having donned again the sloppy, oversized rubber boots and carrying my shoes, he'd talked with optimism about his work. "For the first time in my life, I've got it all together—time, a little money, and now you for inspiration. I really believe I can do it, Maggie—write a book that makes a difference."

"Of course you can," I said, happy for him, and envious of his purpose and his energy.

At the door of the car, our noses close together, he said, "Thank you."

"You're welcome," I said. "For what?"

"Recall. Focus. Enthusiasm. Support. Great sex." He grinned, then spun away, punching his fist into his palm. "Yes!" he shouted. "Yes!"

I laughed, overcome by affection, happy for him.

At last the Tempo came into view, moving slowly through the shooting water. It was ten after three. Ben would be home soon, dropping off his books, collecting a change of clothing for the after-party that was to follow the final performance of *Earnest*. From me, he needed a couple of sandwiches and a ride back to the school. He was staying at Josh's overnight, which meant that I could go to sleep as soon as I'd dropped him off and stay asleep until morning.

When I thought of putting my face against the pillow, my eyes closed of their own accord.

Four teenagers climbed into my car and started to mop the windows—working for minimum wage when they should be still in school. I willed them to hurry, then to be thorough: a lot to will of kids. As though it might egg them into working faster and more efficiently, I moved toward the window. The movement of my reflection in the glass caught my attention, held it.

I was wearing the grey wool jacket and a turtleneck sweater, black. Certain I must look a wreck, I raised my eyes to the reflection of my face. But in the glass, I was relieved of signs of weariness, smoothed of lines, and my hair looked soft and young. What a gift that was, I thought: the kind of gift Zeke gave me. A chance to do it over, a chance to get it right.

"Hello, Maggie," a voice said at my elbow, and I whirled, my heart pounding. It was Edna Lazenby, the woman from the nomination meeting.

"I've startled you," she said.

I felt my face go hot, as though I'd been caught naked, my thoughts written on the glass. I jammed my hands into my pockets so she wouldn't notice when they started shaking.

"Hello, Edna," I said.

"Is there something wrong?" she asked hopefully. "You really don't look well."

"Not at all," I said. "Everything is fine. I'm just a little tired."

She was standing too close, and I found myself looking down at the mole in the part line of her crimped reddish hair. I tried to gather my thoughts, to put myself back together. To be—to remember how to be—Archie Townsend's wife. I was suddenly horrified by the thought that the woman might be smelling brandy on my breath, or Zeke on my body despite my scrubbing. I began to edge away, but she came with me.

"You should be getting your rest," she said. "You'll need your health for the campaign." I could smell her breath. It was unpleasant, sharp.

Out of the corner of my eye I saw the teenagers clambering out of my car. Relieved, I said, "I've got to run, Edna. Ben's in a play. I've got to get him to the school." With a wave, I moved off.

"I'll see you tonight," she called.

Tonight? I paused and turned.

"At the Stovers. Lila said you two would be there."

Friday. The party at the Stovers. Jesus. Shit. Tonight.

I waved—"Of course!"—and left.

Outside, I took the receipt from the attendant and stood for a moment, deliberating. I should check the car closely, inside and out. Ben would notice mud anywhere: his eye was keen for deviations from the norm. But Edna wasn't far off, just through the glass doors behind me, and I felt her eyes on my back.

"Is there a problem?" the young man asked me, holding open the driver's door.

"Not at all," I said, turning to him with a warm smile that I intended Edna to see as well. "Everything looks fine."

Half way home, I'd stop. I'd check the exterior of the car for mud, and the floors and floor mats in the front, and while I was at it I'd check my own reflection in the rearview mirror to see what Edna Lazenby had seen.

18

By about ten thirty, having eaten a number of intricately constructed hors d'oeuvres and drunk two glasses of very expensive wine, a sardonic calm had settled over me that I failed to recognize as dangerous. I just knew I was feeling physically better than I had in days, and that the circumstances of my life had granted me an awareness that was superior to that of anyone else at the Stovers' party. I accepted a third glass from a roving waiter, bestowing on him a warm and empathetic smile. Who knew what creative talents might be concealed within the black-and-white uniform?

The evening had not started out so well. At the precise moment we were supposed to be arriving at the party, Archie had wakened me from a deep sleep in our darkened bedroom to ask the whereabouts of the grey shirt with the houndstooth pattern. With groggy irritation, I'd explained my attitude toward laundry generally, and toward his presumption that it was my responsibility to know where all his clothes were.

Then, dressing—after he'd found, without comment, the shirt

he was looking for in the closet where I'd left it—he announced that he'd told Victor about my connection to Mark Scales, and that Victor had said without hesitation, "We have to get her out of there."

"We?" I repeated, furious, incredulous. "What's Victor got to do with it?"

Archie took a breath and said, "He's being paid good money to make sure nothing goes wrong with my campaign. He's trouble-shooting, Maggie."

"My job has nothing to do with your campaign."

"He thinks it does. Could."

"And you? What do you think?"

"I listen to what he says."

"You didn't think it was a big deal until you talked to him. Have you stopped thinking for yourself completely?"

Even with my back to him—I was looking through the closet for something to wear to the Stovers—I felt his temper rising. I felt no urge to interfere with that, as I would normally have done. Mine was rising, too.

"It doesn't seem to matter to you whether I'm re-elected or not," he said, coolly, at last.

"Of course it matters," I said, turning. "But, Archie, the election hasn't even been called yet. This thing with Mark is petty. It'll blow over before the premier drops the writ."

"I hope so, for your sake."

"What's that supposed to mean?" I asked, flipping through dresses with more force than necessary.

He paused, grey-suited, fully dressed, on his way to the door to the hallway. "Think about it for a second," he said. "We're talking about a campaign to get me re-elected. Compare that to a part-time job in a gift shop. Which one's more important?"

"To whom?" I said angrily, locking my eyes on his.

"To us," he said with equal anger before he turned and left.

On the way over in the car, we'd uttered a few excuses for our irritation and apologies we didn't mean—conventions we'd established long ago for de-escalating our arguments when we were about to be with other people.

Lila Stover apparently mistook the vestiges of my anger for

vivaciousness, and told me I looked radiant. That released something in me, and I floated away from her, from my coat, from Archie, into the room. Solitary, radiant, me.

Now I stood a small distance from a group of women I didn't know and sipped my wine.

"...and then there's Eddy," said one of the women, who appeared to be in her mid-forties. "He's looking at a hockey scholarship,"

"A scholarship!" said another woman. "Wouldn't that be wonderful!"

"Not that we need the money," the first one added quickly.

"I didn't know you could get a hockey scholarship in Canada," the other one said.

"It's a college in the States."

"Don't athletic scholarships restrict your choices?" a third woman said mildly. "Academically, I mean. Jason could probably get one in lacrosse, but he's more interested in his long-term future."

The first woman laughed. "I didn't know they even *had* lacrosse at universities."

I imagined Zeke's expression if he were listening to this conversation and at that instant, the lacrosse mother rolled her eyes in my direction, just as I'd decided he would, but not for the same reason. She said archly, "Lacrosse was Canada's first national sport."

The hockey mother smiled. "No sport is more Canadian than hockey."

Archie was across the room, talking with a group of men and women, two of them fellow MLAs. The Stovers' house was a considerable size, and he was, in fact, quite a distance away from me. Still I could see that his face was slightly flushed, that he was intensely interested in whatever the group was talking about. A woman at his elbow was looking up at him as though transported.

"If it's so Canadian," the lacrosse mother said, "why does he have to go to the States to play it?"

"Economics," said the hockey mother.

He stood straight and tall. He seemed to be growing into himself, becoming more handsome as he got older, and he really was in his element in this world: self-confident and happy. He looked so different from the Archie Townsend who'd been a high-school teacher, even then a world away from the man I'd met at university.

He should be with someone else, I thought. Someone who wants to live like this. There are lots of them around, starting with the woman next to him. Or Dagmar, a woman like her. A man like Archie would never be alone for long.

"What about Ben?" the hockey mother suddenly said to me.

"Ben?" I repeated.

"Ben. Your son. What's he planning to do, after high school?"

I felt a flick of anger that she even knew I had a son, much less his name and age. When you're married to a public figure, people you've never met before know things about you that no stranger should. It always feels like an invasion, and I wanted to snap something at her to throw her off the track—maybe tell her Ben was considering theological school, that he'd decided to be a priest. That we were insisting the school be Canadian.

Fortunately—unsure that my tongue could skip around all those words—I decided not to do that. I glanced in Archie's direction and saw that Edna Lazenby was walking toward his group.

"He's only in grade ten," I said to the woman, and headed off to head off Edna.

Archie took my arm when I arrived, and Bill Tugwell, a short heavy man I didn't like, told me I was looking well.

"An amazing transformation," Edna agreed. She looked at Archie. "I ran into her this afternoon at the car wash. I thought that she was ill."

"Something I ate for lunch," I said. "I'm feeling much better now."

"You didn't tell me you weren't feeling well," Archie said, solicitous, with a glance at Edna.

I shrugged. Now he'd probably attribute my earlier anger to indigestion, and dismiss it.

"The point is," said a tall, thin grey-haired man who'd been looking impatient at the discussion of my health, "too many small businesses in this province have been feeding from the trough for far too long. It's a dog-eat-dog world out there. You stick to your guns on this printing business, Archie. You're doing exactly right. You, too, Bill. You keep up the pressure on those freeloaders out there."

"Oh, don't worry," Tugwell said. "I will. I will."

Susan Tugwell turned to me with a small hard smile. "So," she said, her voice oily. "How are things at work?"

Archie glanced in my direction, and I looked away from him. "They're wonderful," I said. Susan Tugwell "stayed at home with the children," who were now in university. She had a lot of time for research and conjecture. She would know about Mark and the Bellamy & Cato connection.

Susan's husband was one of the prime targets of Fiona's outrage with the government: Fiona could turn herself red at the mere mention of his name. Unlike most of his fellow assembly members, Tugwell regularly vocalized his belief that the province should abolish its entire program of grants to artists. The Opposition rose just as regularly in response, in order to remind the Speaker that these programs were considered enlightened by artists and critics across the nation and even provided the province with good press in other countries, and to cite figures and statistics on employment income generated by the arts.

Tugwell was undeterred. Grants, he said were a waste of time and money. They led, he said, to sloth. He happily trotted out examples of apparent insanities, reminding his colleagues of the visual artist who'd got five thousand dollars to create landscapes out of coloured sand, of the government-funded writer—"government-funded" being Tugwell's term for artists who got grants—whose book, when "finally" published, included the word "cunt" six times, "prick" fourteen, and "fuck" three hundred and twelve. The book—which I had read and loved, and which was, among other things, about two street kids who'd managed to beat the odds—had been nominated for at least one national and one international literary prize. That didn't matter to Tugwell.

I was certain that most government members privately concurred with Tugwell. They would dearly have loved to have seen the lottery monies that went to culture diverted to general revenues, to help pay down the debt. The problem they had with putting this desire into practice had, so far, proved a major stumbling block: due to the current system of grants distribution, if they diverted the funds now earmarked for culture, they'd have to divert funds for sports and recreation at the same time. That would lead to public outrage, and it wasn't really what they wanted anyway. There might be enough poetry and music in the world already, but nobody could argue about the benefit to a province of a professional football team, or baseball diamonds for the local kids.

I suspected that they gave Tugwell his way when it came to mouthing off about the arts in order to see how the public would react. Media surveys showed that in general, people agreed with him—a fact lamented in occasional newspaper editorials, and hotly disputed by the regulars at the Purple Parrot.

I went off to get another glass of wine.

Archie found me somewhat later in a wingback armchair in the Stovers' television room.

"You're drunk," he said in a sharp whisper.

"No, I'm not," I said, offended, measuring my words.

"I watched you walk in here," he said. "You were weaving."

"Room may tilt a little," I said, shrugging. "But not me."

He closed his eyes.

"I've just had a revelation," I said.

He opened his eyes and looked at me with something close to loathing. "What are you talking about?"

Aware that my mouth was a little numb, however clear my thoughts might be, I carefully started to explain. I waved my glass in the direction of the living room. "Figured out why so many of these people are insufferable."

"Insufferable?" he said, his voice flat and cold.

I nodded and sat up straighter. "Is because they've been appointed to their jobs. Don't you see? Appointed. Promoted. Elected. Not you—I don't mean you. But Tugwell and the others. They get their power from other people, and that makes them think they're doing something valuable. They're not, but they think they are. Power isn't coming from inside them—someone else has given it to them, and that's what makes them so...."

"I have no idea what you're talking about," he said, keeping his anger under control only with great effort. And then he said, "We're leaving," and turned and walked away.

When I stood up, I discovered that he'd been quite correct about the inebriation. It was hard to manoeuvre. I did my best to manage a normal gait, but I bumped against at least two people as I made my way to the front hall. I apologized elaborately, and they seemed more than happy to forgive me which, I felt at the time, exonerated me from any possible criticism from Archie, who was nowhere to be seen.

For the same reason, I made sure I thanked the Stovers properly for the party. "Is wonderful," I said, pulling on my coat. "Sbeen lovely." I looked around me. The dining-room table was set with dishes of hot and cold food. There were three magnificent centrepieces which appeared to be trees of jumbo shrimp. Well dressed men and women were making their ways around the table, chatting, laughing, filling plates. Pouring themselves cups of coffee—a good idea, but a little late for me. I nodded at Lila Stover and said I was happy to see that the recession hadn't hit them very hard.

"It was a pleasure to see you," Lila said somewhat thinly.

Roger Stover added, "Archie said to tell you he's waiting in the car."

"I bet he is," I said, nodding as I settled my coat more evenly on my shoulders and steadied myself with the assistance of the door frame. I thanked Lila for saying earlier that I looked radiant. "Archie doesn't notice any more," I told her sadly. "Husbands don't."

Lila looked away.

"It's such a waste," I said to Roger. "You should try harder. Before it's too late."

Roger looked away as well.

Sense got hold of me briefly at that point, and I left the house. There were many cars parked in the driveway. I used them to steady myself as I made my way toward the Blazer. It was running with its lights on—the beams of Archie's anger reaching out to me.

"What the hell do you think you're doing?" he asked when I opened the passenger door and began to get myself inside.

"Didn't have supper," I said. "Not real supper anyway. Hit me kind of hard. After being sick earlier...."

I got no sympathy from him. He said, "You embarrassed me in there," and he sounded surprised as well as hurt.

I was surprised, too. I turned carefully and looked at him, and shook my head. "Oh, no," I said. "I was very careful."

"It was obvious you were drunk."

I caught him in my gaze and stared hard at him. "Archie, it's a party. What do people do at parties? They're supposed to party at parties." I turned away. "Besides party, I mean. What are they supposed to do?"

"You see what I mean?" he said.

"Well, they should."

He looked away.

Making an effort, I said as slowly and clearly as I could, "It looked like you were doing fine. With Tugwell and those other people. They're behind you all the way."

He cast me a glance, a glare. "That's the last thing I need," he said.

"What is?"

"To be associated with Bill Tugwell."

"Why?"

"Well, he's hardly secure, is he?"

"He's not?" I said hopefully, thinking of Susan Tugwell.

"Tugwell walks on limbs. Limbs break. Maggie, do you have no idea how this system works?"

"I guess I don't," I said.

"I guess you don't," he said.

In the silence that followed, my mind came to rest on Zeke and I leaned back in the seat and closed my eyes, imagining his arms around me.

As we went around a corner, I opened my eyes to try to find the level, glancing briefly at Archie. "Some people have brandy in the morning," I said. "Is not the end of the world."

Jaw tight, he said, "Maggie, could you just hold off on your nervous breakdown or whatever it is you're having until this election's over?"

I smiled and said, "Exactly what I'm doing."

19

I reached up and depressed the sleep button, trying to figure out why I felt so terrible. It didn't take long to remember, and I pulled a pillow over my head—opening one eye to make sure Archie wasn't in the bed beside me. As images of myself at the party, of the drive home, came to the surface, I put a corner of the pillow into my mouth and bit down, sending a shooting pain through the pounding thickness in my head.

I didn't fall back to sleep. Couldn't. When I moved I felt sick, and I lay as still as I could for as long as I could, until the alarm went off again. Again I hit the sleep button. My head throbbed and my throat was dry. I told myself I should get up and get some water. I was dehydrated. But I couldn't bring myself to move.

Lila Stover's face rose up before me. Roger Stover's. Susan Tugwell's. Edna's. I remembered surprise and condescension on the face of Bill Baynes, a fellow MLA of Archie's into whom I'd staggered on my way to the Stovers' front door.

No one got drunk in that circle. What I'd done while I was in that state was less important than the fact of it: inebriation was, in and of itself, enough to make people talk. It had been self-indulgent. Thoughtless. While it had not been my intention to embarrass Archie, I had. I hadn't been thinking of him at all.

That was his milieu. I was the outsider, the visitor, and I'd drawn attention to him. Made his colleagues wonder about him, about me, about us. I'd been wrong when I'd said that the gathering at the Stovers' was supposed to be a party, where people relaxed and enjoyed themselves. It had looked like a party, but wasn't one. It was a deadly serious event, and I had broken rules I had no right to break because they had nothing to do with me. I shook my head. Winced. Lay still until the pounding slowed again a little.

But wandering through the guilt and the remorse, I found resentment. Not that I had any urge to repeat my performance. I was sure at that point that I would never drink again. But I resented the need for restraint, the need to behave myself for Archie's sake. Zeke's slug of brandy in a morning coffee would be a hanging offense in Archie's group. I tried to imagine Archie or the premier or even Bill Tugwell pouring a capful of something into his morning mug, but such images were too ludicrous to summon.

I didn't want people walking half-corked or even mellow around the Legislature Building: that was not the point. They had work to do, even if the value of most of it could be argued. They needed their faculties, their focus. What irritated me was the way they accepted a code of behaviour without question, from which deviations were seen as signs of instability. At a Stover-type party you couldn't admit that your kid might not even graduate from high school, much less get a scholarship, or that your new motor-home had turned out to be a lemon. You could never let on that you were bored by sermons and your husband's political speeches. You could never let anyone know anything that they might be able someday to use against you.

That was what Archie had been saying. That's what he had meant when he said I'd embarrassed him.

If only all those people knew what else I'd done yesterday.

I hugged the pillow over my face and moved my head slowly back and forth, loathing my surroundings, longing for the cabin, for Zeke, for the more honest life I felt he represented. Even a hangover, if I had to have one, would be easier to live with in the country. There would surely be less guilt.

I thought of the orange-crate bedroom in the woods and decided I was an orange-crate kind of person. One who felt, at the moment, ghastly awful.

Gingerly, I raised myself on my elbow and looked at the clock on the bedside table. Eight-thirty. I had to get ready for work.

I sat up to turn the alarm off and saw that behind the clock, where I wouldn't knock it over, Archie had carefully placed a tall glass of water and two headache tablets.

Life being what it is—or was—I shouldn't have been surprised that it was one of the busiest days in memory at the Purple Parrot. The phone rang and rang—calls for Fiona, messages for Mark. Fiona had disappeared into her back office with some artsy-looking friends who'd arrived with huge take-away cups of rich-smelling coffee, leaving Bill and me to cope with the customers, the window-shoppers, the curious. People I hadn't seen in months stopped by, people who hadn't been in for years.

Bill Bold, a tall, lanky third-year Arts student with long thin hair and a thin beard that was, perhaps, an unsuccessful attempt to hide his pimples, was normally a good, steady worker. But pressure rattled him, and today there was plenty of it. Every few minutes he was at my side, asking for advice, direction or assistance.

Around eleven, Sylvie and Anna showed up, wearing their matching T-shirts under their spring jackets. Anna was carrying a small grey plastic bag.

Rather than embarking on their normal tour of the shop to check on their watercolours and examine everyone else's work, they stood quietly near the sales counter. When I asked them if I could do anything to help, Anna said they were waiting to talk to Fiona. I went and told Fiona, and she rolled her eyes but said she'd be right out. Her office was full of people and laughter.

Despite the headache tablets and a tablespoon of bitters, my head was still pounding, my stomach still queasy, and my mind was rapidly transforming Zeke's cabin into a safe haven from the new sick feeling that came over me whenever I thought of Archie. Because we were so busy, I was also irritated with Fiona's continuing absence. The customers weren't just window shopping, and several times there'd been actual line-ups at the till, a phenomenon I'd seen before only once or twice near Christmas. We could really have used her help, and by now she'd kept Sylvie and Anna waiting for more than half an hour. I kept having to walk around them to get to the till, which I did each time with a shrug or an apology: "She's got people in there with her." "I'm sure she'll be out in a minute."

At about quarter to twelve, she finally burst out of her back office like she'd been sucking up energy in there. She was wearing black leotards and a black sweater and her index finger was hooked into a brown suede jacket she was carrying over her shoulder. Her friends came along behind her like an entourage. Her eyes sparkled, her long gold earrings glittered, even her hair seemed bigger than usual and shining. The sight of her made my headache feel worse and my energy level drop to zero.

"Lunch time," she said on her way past me to the door. "We're famished." She waved her hand around. "Don't worry about all this. I called Mark. He's going to come over and give us a hand this afternoon."

"Fiona –" Sylvie said.

Fiona turned to her. "Oh, God," she said. "I forgot you two were here."

"We're here to give you an update," Sylvie said.

"I don't have time –"

"And this," Anna said, holding out the small grey plastic bag.

Fiona took the bag, looked inside it and, smiling, pulled out a T-shirt that was exactly the same colour as the ones Anna and Sylvie were wearing. She held it up and shook it out, and I saw that on the back there was a remarkable likeness of a huge white parrot sitting on a perch, its beak half-open as though to speak. Above it in a semi-circle were the words, unevenly lettered and connected by dashes, "Save—the—Purple—Parrot." Below it, "Save—small—business."

Sylvie looked at me uneasily.

"Aren't these cute?" said Fiona, turning to show the T-shirt to her friends, holding so they could admire the parrot on the back. "Sylvie and Anna had a few of them made up. Designed it all by themselves."

She handed the T-shirt back to Anna.

"We were thinking you should wear it," Sylvie said evenly to her. Fiona laughed. "With what?"

Anna closed her eyes and Sylvie pressed her lips together. I felt embarrassed for them both.

An older male customer who'd been listening said, "I wouldn't mind having one." I thought he was also feeling sorry for Anna and Sylvie, until he added, "Maybe I'll take two. How much are they?"

Anna looked at Sylvie and then at the man. Fiona seized the opportunity to make her exit, taking her friends with her.

"Twenty dollars," said Sylvie, cheered. "No tax."

"We've only got four," Anna said uncertainly.

"We can order more," Sylvie said to Anna sharply, adding more gently to the man, "They could be done by Tuesday. In whatever size you want."

"You could order them from us," Anna said, getting into the swing of it. "That would make it easier for you."

"Of course he will," Sylvie said. "How else would he get one?"

"I'd like one, too," said a young woman with a baby in a stroller who was half-way across the shop.

"Me, too," said someone else.

A small line-up gradually formed beside the one leading to the till and Sylvie and Anna located pens and paper and started taking orders. They took off their jackets as they got to work, revealing T-shirts that were identical to the one they'd shown Fiona. Thus outfitted, they attracted the curiosity of several more customers—one or two of whom, I noticed, asked what the T-shirt meant only after they'd placed their orders.

Consumer buying habits confounded me. People who would spend hours dithering over some object that cost fifteen dollars, ask to have it put on hold while they went away and thought about it, would apparently line up to hand over twenty dollars for a T-shirt they didn't even understand. Maybe it's because none are available, I thought. Maybe all fads start with shortages. I couldn't imagine that it was the artwork that was attracting them.

Mark, who arrived half an hour later, was amused at the attention Sylvie and Anna had attracted, but he could also see that they were in my way. He suggested that they set up a table in the back of the shop and conduct their business there.

"We could make a sign," Anna said.

"And another one for the window," Sylvie said, delighted.

"You're naturals," Mark said to them, and I felt a swell of affection and gratitude toward him, even as I imagined how impressed Fiona was going to be when she found out what he'd done—her own fault, I decided, for taking a two-hour lunch break on a day like this.

On my own break, I went home to collect Ben and take him to a hockey practice. I ate a piece of toast he hadn't had time to finish, my first food of the day, and took another two headache tablets, and another tablespoon of bitters. They quickly warmed and settled me—partly the alcohol content, but it was also partly the association with Gran that always accompanied the spicy, sharp, slightly cinnamony taste.

It was the second time that day that a memory of Gran had nudged me: Anna's hand around the T-shirt when Fiona gave it back to her, the angle of light on the knots of arthritis in her hand, had brought back Gran's hands on her needlework. She was always knitting or crocheting or embroidering, and from the time I was small I'd pester her when she was at it to let me try it, too.

She'd finally put down her work, select a thin skein of remnant wool for me, put needles into my hands, and sit down close beside me. She'd hold my hands in hers and show me how to make the first loop from the wool, slide it down the needle, press the other needle through the loop, draw wool across the bridge, pull the new loop up and over.

"There," she'd say. "That's one. Now do one on your own."

And I would start, and she would coach in quiet, patient words: "No, draw it down there, Maggie. No, dear. Not here. Back there." She'd take my hands in hers again, and then again, as my irritation built at the slowness, at all the complicated steps I'd forget between one stitch and the next. Finally I'd throw down wool and needles and pound my hands into the couch, shouting and bouncing up and down with rage.

Gran would rise without a word, gather up the wool and needles, and put them on a shelf I couldn't reach—making me even angrier. And then she would take me—still shouting and kicking—and shut me in my room.

I never learned. I kept asking, receiving, losing. What kept me coming back was Gran herself, her steady work, the marvellous silky tablecloths and creamy doilies and neatly ribbed hats and gloves she was able to create without ever consulting an instruction sheet.

She grew increasingly disinclined to teach me, for which I can hardly blame her. But watching her work, seeing the serenity that attended that work and the wonderful pieces it produced, continued to make me hungry to know how. Hungry to try again. And, for years, made me endlessly irritated: how could an activity that seemed so peaceful be so frustrating?

When I was small, I thought that the calm and the success must be inherent in the work that she had chosen. I believed that she'd kept the best projects and materials for herself, and that the fault in what I did was not in me but in the discards that she'd assigned for me to use. Of course she'd never let me anywhere near what she was working on. "The tension wouldn't be the same," she'd say—an explanation she must have delivered with a good deal of private pleasure.

It was still busy at the shop when I got back and all four of us were tied up with customers when Anna and Sylvie returned. They were carrying an enormous piece of pale purple Bristol board and were anxious to show off their work.

Mark brought over a customer he'd been busy with to help him admire what they'd done. They'd tacked a T-shirt to the board, showing the parrot artwork on the back, and in the same lettering that was on the shirt had written, "Order your Purple Parrot T-shirt here!" along with the price. After the customer had left, Mark helped them put it up near their corner in the back, the three of them forming a knot of activity and enthusiasm.

Anna told him that several people had asked about "the protest," and Sylvie added that we'd make an excellent "action central" for the "demonstration."

"We've decided to use the proceeds to buy coffee and hot chocolate for the protesters," Anna said.

Wishing I hadn't heard even that much, I went to help a customer near the front.

When the day was finally over, Bill, Anna and Sylvie gone and the doors locked, Fiona looked at Mark and said, "What the hell do you think you're doing?"

I'd watched her grow increasingly surly as Sylvie and Anna entrenched themselves over the course of the afternoon.

"We'll talk about it over dinner," he said. "I'm going to take you out."

Fiona glanced at me. After a moment's thought, she nodded to herself and leaned back against the counter. She ran her hand through her hair, took a deep breath and said lightly, "I'm not sure I can handle success."

"It won't last," Mark reassured her.

With a shrug, she lifted herself away from the counter, said good night to me, and went into the back office.

"What demonstration?" I asked him quietly, pulling on my coat, when she was gone.

He sighed. "At the meeting yesterday, the group decided on a little gathering the Legislature Building. A few speeches, things like that." He sounded regretful.

"When?"

"April nineteenth." He glanced at the calendar. "Two weeks from today, in fact."

I looked at my feet. "And is... the protest... directed specifically at Archie?"

"No," he said, and I felt his hand brush the elbow of my jacket. "I admit that's where it started. But no. It's the whole government they're taking on."

"Oh, good," I said sarcastically, looking up into his face. "That's much better." Then I said, "Jesus." My headache was coming back. "You don't expect me to keep this to myself?"

"No," he said, a look I couldn't classify flicking across his face. "No," he said. "I don't."

20

"You've got to stay put," Edward said.

The moment my coat was off, he'd taken me into the living room, poured me a glass of sherry, and started talking about the article that had appeared in the morning's paper. It had been about the demonstration, and I'd been relieved to see it because it meant I didn't have to tell Archie what was going on at the Purple Parrot. It turned out Archie had known about it anyway.

He was now in a meeting which had started at ten that morning with Victor, Jack Armstrong and a few others, so Ben and I had come over early by ourselves. Millicent had taken Ben off to the basement for a game of darts, no doubt part of some master plan she and Edward had cooked up before I arrived so that Edward could be alone with me. I could smell the chicken roasting in the oven, occasionally hear it spitting.

I took another sip of sherry.

"Archie doesn't seem too concerned," I said, "or at least he didn't when I talked to him this morning."

"Then what's this big meeting all about?"

I shrugged. "Victor's getting nervous."

Edward clenched his teeth together at the mention of Victor's name. "No surprises there." He shook his head. "Maggie, if you quit now, it will look like an admission of guilt, or something even worse."

"I'm not planning to quit."

"It might be tough," he said. "Just be calm and friendly. Be yourself. Act like nothing's out of order."

"Nothing is out of order," I said. "They're not out to get Archie specifically: they're mad at the whole government."

"And that's ridiculous. This government had the courage to do what needed to be done, and anyone who doesn't see that is a fool. Most people do. I'm sure the whole protest won't attract more than a hundred, if that, if it's left to run it's course. Which is why I think you should stay exactly where you are. Appearances count for a lot, and even if these 'protesters' are fabricating issues out of thin air, they'll become real if Archie's team mismanages them." He'd leaned forward in his chair, and the light through the horizontal slats of the window blinds behind him made the silver in his hair shine. He shook his head and said, "I'm afraid that Maxwell's going to sink the ship. His instincts are all wrong."

I said to reassure him, "Archie seems happy with him. And Victor's never lost –"

"Arrogant and misguided is what he is," Edward said, still shaking his head. "They haven't managed this Bellamy and Cato protest well from the beginning, and I lay the blame on him."

"What should they have done?"

"At the first sign of noise, Archie should have reversed himself. It was too close to the election to be starting with that stuff anyway. It would have been a strong move if he'd retracted the decision at the first sign of trouble. Let people see that politicians listen." He looked up at me. "But it's too late for that now. Which means they're all holed up somewhere talking about how to manage a crisis that never should have happened in the first place."

"That wasn't Victor's fault, Edward. It was Archie's decision. He didn't want to reverse himself. He said he believed that what he did with the communications contract was the right thing to do, and he wasn't going to be influenced by pressure from Mark Scales or anyone else." I was beginning to feel much better. The sherry was doing its work, dissociating me. I wondered if I were becoming an alcoholic. "Besides, it's not a campaign issue anyway. It was a government decision. It would have to be the government that changed its mind."

"At this point, everything the government does is a campaign decision." Edward got up and poured himself a second scotch, and refilled my glass with sherry. "One of Bob Sanders' greatest strengths as a political organizer was that he was in touch with the average voter. He thought like them. Maxwell doesn't. He thinks like an over-aggressive businessman."

"A lot of voters are in business."

"More of them are not." He looked down at me. "Why are you defending him so strongly? Do you see something in him that I don't?"

I shook my head. "I don't like to see you worrying so much, that's all. Archie has confidence in Victor, and the Conservatives are sure of a majority. I don't think it would matter if Peter Rabbit were running his campaign. Archie will be fine."

"I certainly hope you're right," Edward said.

I did, too.

With a glance at the window, Edward said a little more cheerfully, "Well. Here's the candidate himself."

By the time they came to the table, Edward and Archie were talking about Archie's main opposition, the Liberal candidate Sharon St. James. When I'd asked Archie about her a week or two before, he'd dismissed her as an unknown member of a weak and disorganized party.

Edward, it turned out, had studied her more closely. "She's bright and down-to-earth," he said. "She says what she thinks, and what she says makes sense. You can't dismiss her, Archie."

"I'm not dismissing her," Archie said, taking a sip of wine and sitting down next to me. We had so far barely acknowledged one another's presence, which Millicent had probably noticed even if Edward hadn't. "Come off it, Dad," he said. "Don't be such a doom-sayer."

"I'm only being realistic," Edward said. "I've been involved in one hell of a lot more elections than you have. Nothing is ever certain, and I don't want you to forget that. Just because the polls put the Conservatives ahead doesn't mean every seat is secure. And as far as I'm concerned, you're running with one hand tied behind your back."

"I presume you're referring to my campaign manager," Archie said, starting to get angry.

Edward's expression said he was.

I was surprised to discover that I was actually getting defensive about Victor Maxwell myself. Edward's blanket condemnation of the man seemed to have more to do with loyalty to Bob Sanders than with Victor's actual shortcomings. I'd always considered Edward objective as well as politically astute, but this time he was letting his emotions get involved. He was afraid his son would lose. It was the first sign of weakness I'd ever seen in him, and I found myself taking his comments about Sharon St. James with a grain of salt as well.

Edward provided Archie with examples of St. James's directness and diplomacy. It appeared he'd even gone so far as to visit her campaign office.

"Oh, that's great, Dad," Archie snapped. "Good God. It's not like anybody recognizes you. I don't need spies wandering around on my behalf—especially not my father."

"I wasn't spying," Edward said sharply. "I was reconnoitering. I wasn't trying to pretend I was anyone besides exactly who I am."

"I don't need your help," Archie said. "Not that kind of help anyway. Why don't you come down to our campaign office? We could use a hand around there."

"I have been down. Three times," Edward said flatly. "I've never seen you there. I saw St. James at hers."

"I've been down to mine. I've been there." Archie brought his fist down firmly on the table. "I've also been busy at the Legislature Building. And in meetings. She doesn't have a seat to hold down—and she never will."

"Eat something," Millicent said. "Both of you. Calm down, please, and eat something."

I looked across at Ben. His head was down, his attention apparently focused on his plate. But he wasn't eating, wasn't moving, and I knew he was listening intently. He was emerging from adolescent awkwardness into the good looks of young adulthood, but he was both kid and adult inside. He'd taken off his cap for dinner, and his tufts of unsmoothed hair made me nostalgic for the days when I'd been able to scoop him up and hug him whenever I felt like it.

In response to Millicent's directive, Archie had pressed the tines of his fork into a carrot. Now he put the fork down, the carrot still impaled. "Do you have no confidence that I might win at all?" he asked his father.

"Of course I do," said Edward. "Of course I do. I feel a lot better about this Bellamy and Cato thing, now that I know the premier's involved."

"He is?" I said.

Ben's head came up too.

"Archie's going to talk to him tomorrow morning," Edward said proudly. "About managing the demonstration."

"That's good," Millicent said. She looked at Archie. "Isn't it?"

Archie shrugged. "We'll see."

Edward said, "I for one am glad to see he's getting some support."

"Who knows?" Archie said. "They could just cut me loose."

"They won't do that," Edward said. "You're one of their best candidates." There was a false heartiness to his voice: he really was concerned.

"Fiddle the demonstration," Millicent said in a similar tone. "I wouldn't worry about that at all. Nobody showed up when it was university students or even health-care workers. The last thing they're going to do is support a group of entrepreneurs. Protesters and business people are two entirely different breeds of cat."

"You can never be too careful," Edward said. "There's an election coming up."

"When is it?" Millicent asked Archie.

"The nineteenth," Archie said.

"The nineteenth?" Millicent asked, astonished. "That's only two weeks off."

"I think she meant the election," I said.

"The election," Archie said, nodding. "Right. We should hear about that soon."

"Maybe the premier will tell you tomorrow," Millicent said.

"No. He won't do that."

The phone rang and Millicent rose to answer it. It was Victor, for Archie. Ben took the opportunity to excuse himself, and I sighed and put my fork down.

"You look unwell," Millicent said to me when they were gone. "You're still not eating properly." She looked across at Edward, then back at me. "If you quit your job you'd have time to rest before the real campaigning starts."

So there was disagreement here as well about what course to take. I said nothing.

"She's not going to leave her job," Edward said. He sounded tired. "I'm not inventing this stuff, Millicent. He really does have a strike or two against him. He's got to be very careful, and so does Maggie."

Looking worried, Millicent said to me, "You'll do what you think is best."

I nodded, wondering what I did think was best—and then, briefly, how it might look to an outsider. If I kept working, did it look as though I were simply getting on with my life, secure about Archie's political future? Or would my resignation be a stronger indication of support?

I couldn't get my mind around it. I didn't care enough. There was a simpler life, and I knew where it was.

"Besides," Archie said, coming back to the table, looking more cheerful, "the voters don't agree with her politics. They agree with ours."

"St. James?" Edward shook his head. "She's a conservative Liberal. And like I said, she's smart. Not that you're not solid, but she'll give you a run. Especially if you're not careful."

"I told Maxwell what you'd been up to—penetrating enemy territory." Archie's conversation with Victor had obviously bolstered his confidence, and he picked up his dessert fork with far more enthusiasm than he had put it down when he went to get the phone.

"And…?" Edward said, jutting out his chin.

"He thought it was great," Archie said. "He thinks you should go back regularly. Keep us posted on what you see."

The last thing Edward wanted was to be used by Victor, and an internal battle was still occasionally playing across his face when I said it was time to go.

21

"Mark and Fiona sometimes had these little parties," I told Zeke, "after the shop was closed. She called them her 'salons,' which is typical Fiona. It was mostly the regulars, artists and customers, and they'd bring in wine and people would stay for hours talking about everything imaginable. I went a few times. It was great."

"And did you talk for hours?"

I moved my head. "Mostly listened. Watched and listened."

"True to character," he said, smiling.

"I never knew what to say."

"Not a criticism," he said. "Most people talk way too much at things like that—myself included. No doubt the free booze." He began to move fingertips in a circle in the small of my back.

"I don't know why they stopped having them," I said, my eyelids heavy with pleasure. "But they did, and by the time I started working there, the skid was underway. So it's never been the way I imagined it would be to work there—until now. Ironic, isn't it? But now it's packed again, people are hanging around to talk, and they're buying, too. We're busy, and they need me."

"And you need them."

I nodded, and said, "I think you'd like it there. A lot of it's junk—not real art, at least—but the ambiance is great."

"After my book's done," Zeke said. "Not going anywhere till then. Not seeing anyone till then."

"What do you call this?" I leaned to brush my lips against his shoulder.

"This?" he said. "This is serious business."

I laughed.

"I mean it," he said. "This is inspiration. The other is distraction. This feeds the soul. That drains it."

I smiled and rolled onto my back, stretching. "Well, you'd have to go on my day off anyway. It would knock me flat if you showed up at the Purple Parrot. I've got enough turmoil there as it is."

I told him about the Purple Parrot T-shirts and the little display Mark had helped Sylvie and Anna set up at the back of the shop. I told him how the day before the two women had added to Fiona's general irritation with the very existence of the display by showing up at ten o'clock with a sign for the front window and their lunches in neat paper bags, by rearranging everything in the window several times to accommodate the sign and a sample of the T-shirt, by requesting permission to use the office telephone—it was important Purple Parrot business, they insisted—and by suggesting (this was Sylvie, in an avuncular tone of voice) that Fiona would be doing her own business a favour, not to mention the campaign, if she would just pull on one of the Purple Parrot T-shirts. Over what she was wearing, if she liked.

Fiona, who at that point had been moving things in the window so that they were more or less back to where they'd been before Sylvie and Anna got to them, stood up suddenly, bumping her head against the low ceiling. Wincing, her hand on its way toward her forehead, she whirled.

"Look at what I've got on," she barked at Sylvie. "I am wearing a silk shirt. It cost me nearly a hundred dollars, and it's puce. Puce, Sylvie! I am not covering it up with a god-damned purple T-shirt."

"Purple goes with everything," Anna had said quietly behind me.

"It does not," Fiona said, straightening. "It absolutely does not."

Looking down into my face, Zeke said, his voice teasing, "I thought you hated scenes."

"I didn't enjoy it at the time," I said. "I don't mind telling it."

"You're a writer at heart," he said.

I didn't tell Zeke how the busyness at the Purple Parrot helped to keep at bay the constant low-grade tension I felt whenever I was there. I kept worrying about whether I should relay what I saw and heard to Archie—not that I'd learned anything that I thought would be specifically helpful to him, and I went out of my way not to hear as much as possible, but it was the principle. I didn't want to tell him anything, and that made it worse. Archie wasn't expecting me to be a spy, but I kept wondering what that ephemeral perfect politician's wife would do—a ridiculous as well as fruitless exercise.

The premier had told Archie he thought I should quit the Purple Parrot. Archie had repeated this to me, his face closed, his jaw hard, obviously on edge, as he sat eating his reheated dinner late on Monday night.

"What business is it of his?" I'd asked, folding my arms on the table and putting my forehead on them.

"It wasn't a command," Archie said. "He was just saying it might be a good idea."

"For whom?" I knew the answer: for Archie, for the Party.

"Solidarity extends to families," he said.

"Archie, I'm not trying to bring you down, or the government."

"I know you're not," Archie said, his voice weary. "And you aren't. That's not the point. Appearances are the point."

"Do you want me to quit?"

He shrugged. "I'm thinking about it."

I felt my own jaw tighten, but I kept my head down and said nothing.

"Victor's positive you should," he said, "and now the premier, too. But I'm not sure. Victor's concerned about the election— my election—and the premier's concerned about the Party as a whole." He sighed. "I think the election will be announced on Wednesday, by the way."

"In the middle of all this?"

He looked at me sharply. "The protest is hardly a major issue in the larger scheme of things." He balled up his serviette and dropped it on his plate, then pushed his chair back and stood up.

"Anyway," he said, "I think we should hold off for now. Dad's got a point. In terms of the big picture, if you were going to quit, you should have done it weeks ago. I don't want to look like I'm running scared. I'm not." He touched the top of my head on his way into his office, the way he often did with Ben. A reassuring pat. "There are a million other things I have to deal with at the moment. We'll give it another day or two."

I bit my tongue, the edges of my anger sanded down by guilt. My motives for keeping my job were growing darker and more selfish. Three years at the Purple Parrot had given me flexibility, invisibility. On my days off, I might be running about on errands or putting in extra hours at the shop. People had grown used to not knowing exactly where I was, and I didn't want to lose that. Especially not now.

It all seemed justified when I was here, but like a beckoning figure at the edge of a loose-lipped canyon, there was also the temptation to see myself as others would—Archie, the Tugwells, Millicent and Edward, Alana. I knew—and feared—what I would see if I tried to be objective. No one would ever understand what I felt when I was here. No one would want to try. And when it came to Ben.... But no. I could not bear to think of Ben.

Zeke ran his fingers up my spine. "I want you to stay here," he said. "To be here all the time."

"I can't," I said. "Not yet."

He sighed and rolled away.

I opened my eyes, watched him pull out another cigarette and light it.

"Come, on, Zeke," I said, pulling the sheet around me and sitting up. "It's not like all I need to do is to go and get my toothbrush. I have a whole life in the city." Running my hands back through my hair, I said, "There's the timing, too. The election. I can't do it now."

Looking at the tip of his cigarette, he said, "If you want something, you have to go for it. Sometimes the moment passes, the opportunity. And doesn't come again."

I watched him lift a shoulder.

"That sounded like a threat," I said, as lightly as I could.

"It wasn't meant to," he said, stubbing out the cigarette.

He stood up, walked around the bed and over to the window. The curtains were fitted on a flat rod, and he pulled one across at the top, using two hands to slide a gather into it to keep it open. My heart had begun to thud at distance that had come between us so unexpectedly, and I watched him, thinking how much I loved his body, how familiar it had become already.

After a long minute, he turned and said, "I'm not playing games here, Maggie. This isn't some little fling for me." Letting the curtain drop, he came back to sit on the bed beside me. "Yesterday afternoon I hit a wall. I couldn't work. Now that you're here, I'm ready to get back to it. That says it in a nutshell."

Surprised and moved, I took his hand in mine, looked up into his face.

"You reassure me in ways I don't understand at all," he said. "It started with the writing, but it's become much more than that." He looked away. "I have to admit it scares me." He looked back at me. "It's made me afraid of losing you."

I shook my head. "It's not a fling for me, either, Zeke. Just because I can't come out right now doesn't mean I don't intend to come at all. To be with you, I mean."

He kept his eyes on me, but he'd gone thoughtful—his mind already somewhere else. I wanted to know what he'd meant when he said it had started with the writing—wanted to know how it had started, period. I took a long slow breath. "Zeke," I said, raising his knuckles against my lips then lowering them, "Why did you come to the nomination meeting?"

He looked at me, then over my head toward the living room. Considered. Looked back at me and said, "I engineered it for a reason."

"What reason?"

"When I first came out here," he said, "the writing went just great. It was what I'd always dreamed of: no distractions, a place where I could write. I was doing five pages a day—as many as ten sometimes. And it was good stuff, great stuff for a first draft. Then—almost overnight—I hit a wall." He shook his head. "Me." He moved his head again. "I could never understand other writers when they said that they got blocks. I thought it was sheer laziness—I used to envy them the luxury of time to even *have* a block. But it's not laziness. When it hits, you absolutely cannot work. It gnaws at your gut. You can't think about anything but the writing, and you can't do anything else. No matter what you try to do, it's all you can think about. All you can do is *not* write. It's mental paralysis. You're convinced it will never end, and that you'll never write again." He closed his eyes. "I never want to feel that way again."

I pressed his fingers, but he withdrew his hand. He stood up and walked back over to the window. "In the middle of all that, I found this magazine—an old one, in a cupboard. Some redneck rag, but I flipped through it—anything to distract myself. There was an article in it, about provincial politics." He turned. "Your picture was in it. You were standing next to your husband. I knew you right away."

I remembered the photo, and the event where it was taken: the opening of a new park in Archie's riding.

He shrugged. "It was a sign." He turned back to the window again, said flatly, "The book's about us, Maggie. It's about back then." He paused. "Not *us* precisely. But based there, based back then. At least that's where it starts."

I closed my eyes. After a long time, I said, "Before, you said there was a dream."

He came back to the bed, sat down and took my hand. "The dream came after. A few days later. My subconscious telling me, I think, that I would ignore that photo at my peril." He touched my forehead. "You on the walk that night. You in the photo. You in the dream." He shrugged. "My subconscious was right, and now I don't want to lose you."

I put my arms around him and held him close.

"You won't lose me," I said.

Later, when I came out of the shower, he'd pulled on his jeans and was standing, bare-chested, looking through some papers on his desk, a beer can in his hand. I had his bathrobe wrapped around me and I walked over close beside him, feeling warm and clean and deeply tired.

He put his face into the place between my neck and shoulder and inhaled.

"I brought my notebook with me," I said. "Do you want to see it?"

"Of course I do," he said.

He watched me as I went over and got my handbag. I dug out the bulging notebook, the scraps of writing held inside it by two elastic bands.

"It's about my grandmother," I said. "It's nothing like you do. It's only bits and pieces at this point, but there's something about her that attracts me. Something about her I'd like to be myself. I don't know what it is." I held it out to him. "I guess I'm looking for it here."

He took the notebook as though I'd offered him something of great value. He ran his hand over its surface, over the elastics. He drew me close to him, the book in his hand between us.

"It's going to be all right," he said. He held me close for several minutes and then moved his head back and said, "We're going to be all right."

"I know," I said. "I know."

22

"I want you to imagine a line that extends from here to here to here," Fiona said to Sylvie and Anna on Wednesday afternoon. The tip of a perfectly manicured fingertip moved through the air, conscribing a space of about five square metres in the back of the Purple Parrot, about the same area that was illuminated by the halogen floor lamp Mark had brought over from his printing company. Within it was contained Anna and Sylvie's table, now covered with lists and schedules and order forms, and the two chairs in which they had taken up residence. It also encompassed the sign on the wall behind them that had the T-shirt pinned to it.

"This is your space," Fiona said, "and I want you to stay inside it. We still have a business to run here, and I don't want our customers to be hounded. Do you understand that?"

"We are hardly 'hounding' them," Sylvie said defensively.

"We aren't hounding them at all," Anna said at the same time.

"Whatever you're doing then. However you want to describe it."

"We're just explaining—"

"A lot of them don't know—"

"I don't care!" Fiona snapped, her fierceness somewhat undermined by the energetic concerto that was dancing through the shop. "I want them left alone. If they want to talk to you, they can come back here to do it. Do you understand that?"

Sylvie and Anna said they did, looking hurt but not repentant. It was true that they tended to drift from their display when things got a little slow back there, to chat up the customers out front. They were hardly pushy, but they were committed, and they wanted everyone to know, at least, about the demonstration and to consider, at least, the purchase of a T-shirt or a small donation to help defray costs for coffee and hot chocolate. "It's only April," they warned. "It could be quite chilly." "It might even snow."

The customers didn't seem to mind. In fact, most of them seemed quite happy to talk with Sylvie and Anna, which added to Fiona's irritation. It was in Fiona's best interests to support the protest, and she knew it—and she was doing it—but she resented the control she needed to give up as a result. She also seemed to resent the pivotal roles Sylvie and Anna had assumed in the organization of the demonstration. On both counts, her anger had more to do with territory than with economics or philosophy.

This morning she had finally succumbed to pressure from someone—more likely Mark than Sylvie or Anna—and worn a Purple Parrot T-shirt to work, and that seemed to have pushed her level of resentment to new heights. She'd managed to make herself look fashionable in spite of it—she'd worn it over shiny mustard leotards and a long-sleeved pink shirt, and had added a printed scarf that drew the mustard, the purple and the pink together. But she didn't look happy. She'd gone almost rigid when Sylvie and Anna had reacted to her attire with expressions of satisfaction and strings of compliments.

Now, after extracting one more assurance that Sylvie and Anna understood what she was asking, Fiona turned on her heel, threw her head back, and walked off toward her office.

The line Fiona had drawn with her fingertip was almost identical to the one I'd drawn in my head in order to appease my conscience. I'd told myself that if I stayed away from the T-shirt table and helped only legitimate Purple Parrot customers—referring all inquiries about the protest to Sylvie, Anna or

Fiona—I would be in the clear. If I did that, I would be doing the work I'd been hired to do and nothing more—working to rule, as it were. It was a thin line—you couldn't get much thinner than imaginary—but so far I'd managed to stay on the side of it I could live with, and the others seemed to respect that. No one had suggested I wear a Purple Parrot T-shirt.

I was too busy to get involved with the protest even if I'd wanted to—which obviously I did not, although the spirit of excitement and enthusiasm it was generating was contagious. Fiona, busier than usual herself, had asked me to assume full responsibility for keeping track of stock—contacting the artists whose work we'd sold, getting them to bring in replacement pieces, receiving and cataloguing the new work, putting it out for sale. That kind of work, in addition to the increased volume of customers, had me running off my feet. Unlike Bill Bold, who seemed to get more confused the busier we got, and whose errors I was trying to cover up so Fiona wouldn't fire him, I was thriving on the busyness, and I was beginning to think my talents had been wasted until this crisis came along. The thought of trading the activity at the Purple Parrot for envelope-stuffing at the campaign office was difficult to contemplate.

I might have kept myself away from direct involvement with what Sylvie and Anna were doing, but I wasn't deaf, and I heard the rumours that made them so excited—that a sizable group of health-care workers would be at the Legislature on the nine-teenth, that students and professors at the university were urging one another to be there, that a Harley Davidson owners' group was planning to attend—with motorcycles—although with them no one was sure exactly why. Sylvie and Anna had received calls from seniors' groups, from an association of parents of children with learning disabilities, and from someone Anna was sure was connected with a union. One customer suggested that this was the last big chance before the election for a lot of people to voice their anger about all the years of cutbacks and lost jobs: he'd heard some big labour organizers were about to get involved.

Certain that Mark's prediction of five hundred was low, Sylvie and Anna argued endlessly about how many coffee cups and boxes of sugar they should buy, how many tables they'd need to rent, and how many people would need to be there early in order to set things up.

The premier had been busy too, in recent days. First he'd announced the arrival in the provincial coffers of several million dollars—revenues that were, he said, the result of the government's solid fiscal policies over the past four years and a coincidental increase in the price of oil. The government would, he said, inject a good proportion of these new monies into health care and education. And then he'd announced the election.

No one could have been happier about the good economic news than I was: it looked less and less as though the protest could have any effect on the vote. Fiona, on the other hand, had greeted the premier's announcement with scorn and outrage, Sylvie and Anna—I thought—with disappointment.

"Wouldn't be so busy in the Purple Parrot if not for us," Anna said quietly, standing carefully on her side of Fiona's invisible line. I glanced at the office door Fiona had closed behind her and nodded noncommittally. Then I said, "She knows that. She's just tense and busy."

Anna had just vocalized the one truth that fuzzed my own imaginary line, and clouded any clear spots remaining in my conscience. When a customer had purchased an Anna Perry watercolour—an oddly proportioned mountain ash that had been hanging in the shop for a very long time—the woman had told me she was buying it because she was impressed with Anna's energy and all the work she was doing "for the people of the province." As I was processing the sale, I thought that things were not as clean as I'd have liked.

I'd managed to get out for a few moments the night before to call Zeke from the pay phone at the convenience store. He'd been working steadily, he'd said, and he'd sounded almost elated at how well the work was going. The only downside was that he hadn't yet had a chance to start reading through my notebook. He hoped I would understand.

I was disappointed—I'd become eager to know what he thought of what I'd done—but his enthusiasm for his work infected me as well, and the disappointment didn't last for long. After what he'd told me the last time I was out, I felt an almost proprietary interest in his novel.

By about two in the afternoon, there were nearly a dozen people milling about the Purple Parrot proper, and a half-dozen more talking with Sylvie and Anna over behind The Line. I was helping a customer near the front when the street door opened, and I looked up at the sudden coolness in the air.

A camera flash exploded.

Instinctively I put one hand up to protect my face as another flash went off and Fiona, who was at the till, said, "What the hell is that about?"

A young-looking man who was with the photographer went over to Fiona, identified himself as a reporter from *The Daily Press*, and asked who he should talk to about the protest. I watched, my insides feeling cold and tight and scared, as Fiona escorted them over to Anna and Sylvie's table, introduced them, then disappeared in the direction of her office. I'd considered a retreat to the washroom in the back, but I was now the only employee left in the shop and I could hardly disappear. A moment later, Fiona came out of her office, her hair combed and her lipstick newly reapplied, and—smiling cheerfully—went over to join Sylvie, Anna, the reporter and the photographer.

I kept my head down, which wasn't hard because a customer wanted a pair of salt-and-pepper-shaker pigs gift-wrapped, stealing a glance only when the camera started going off again and I was sure it wasn't pointed in my direction. By then, the three women had arranged themselves beneath the T-shirt sign to have their picture taken. Anna and Sylvie, grinning, had each thrown an arm around the other's shoulders; Fiona, who, with that angle to her head, her shoulders, and her hips, wouldn't have looked out of place in a fashion shoot, stood a little apart from them.

The next time I looked over, Sylvie and Anna were alone at their table, whispering to one another, and the photographer was packing up. I breathed a sigh of relief—I'd made it—when a voice right behind me said, "Mrs. Townsend?"

I closed my eyes. Opened them and turned. He was standing not two feet away from me, right behind the counter. Up close, he was older than he'd looked from a distance—almost forty, I thought. His face was flat and smooth, the skin an unhealthy grey. He smelled of stale cigarettes.

"Arnie Keenan, with *The Press*. I wonder if I could ask you a few questions."

"I don't think so," I said. "I'm busy."

"Maybe I could buy you coffee. On your break?"

I looked around for Fiona; she was talking with a older man at the far side of the shop and she didn't look over. Several customers, however, were looking with interest at the reporter's interest in me—as were Anna and Sylvie, although they were pretending not to.

"I don't take breaks," I said softly. My heart was pounding, and I was sure my face was flushed. "I have nothing to say to you."

"Nothing to say about what?"

"About anything," I said, increasingly uncomfortable. "About anything," I said again.

"All right," he said, flipping a notebook open. Nodding in the direction of Sylvie and Anna, he said, "This protest seems to be gathering some momentum. There's still a lot of bitterness out there, and it seems to have struck a chord. I'm curious how you feel about it... as an employee of the Purple Parrot."

I wondered for a brief, hopeful moment if it was possible he didn't know. Decided not. I shook my head. "No comment."

"How long have you worked here?"

"No comment." I was still nervous, but I was getting annoyed with his persistence.

He took a deep breath. "You're in rather an uncomfortable position, aren't you Mrs. Townsend?"

I said, "No comment," and thought about how much more comfortable I would have been without him in my face.

"Are you planning to continue working here?"

"No comment," I said. The sound of my voice was getting stronger.

"And how do you feel about the Bellamy and Cato contract?"

The customers had wandered off; we were essentially alone. I looked him directly in the eye and said, "That has nothing to do with me, Mr. Keenan. Now get the hell out of here and leave me alone to do my work."

To my amazement, he backed off, said he was sorry to have disturbed me, and departed.

When he left I felt empty, shaken. A customer came over and handed me a scarf, and I avoided her eyes as I began to ring it in. Almost immediately, Fiona joined me at the till. I thought she might offer some sympathy or commiseration, although I wouldn't have been surprised if she'd just shared her amusement at my predicament. Instead, she turned her back to the shop and said in a voice barely more than a whisper, "You should have heard those two. You'd think they *owned* the shop. And they took every bit of credit for the protest. Who do you think is making all of this possible for them? I swear they drive me nuts."

"For God's sake, Fiona," I snapped, still irritated with the reporter, still dizzy that he'd released me, "they're having a good time. What does it matter who gets the 'credit'?"

She gave me a sharp look, and she continued to look at me as I put the customer's purchase in a bag, forced a smile and handed the bag and her change to her. The smile I got back looked equally forced.

When I turned back to Fiona, she was leaning against the counter, her arms crossed.

"You're not yourself," she said.

"The reporter…," I said. "Sorry if I snapped."

"I mean generally. Something's different about you."

"Like what?"

"I can't put my finger on it. You're less wimpy or something."

I laughed. "Less *wimpy*?"

"Yeah," she said. "Less wimpy. It's a definite improvement. When you first came in here, I had no idea what Mark saw in you. Model mom from the middle-class ghetto, scared of your own shadow if you weren't pushing a grocery cart and holding a shopping list. Now you're loosening up. You look more comfortable in your own skin." She smiled, a genuine smile. "I think this place is good for you."

Flustered, but pleased, I said, "Now look who's taking credit."

"Touché," she said, and laughed. And nodded. "There. That's exactly what I mean." She started off, then turned and said, "Don't worry, though. The other Maggie isn't lost."

"What are you talking about?"

She shrugged. "I'm writing a story about her."

23

Zeke insisted we go out for a walk. "I've got to get out of here," he said. "Do something. Move. I've been inside that computer for too long."

He'd seemed distracted when I arrived, his mind somewhere far away from me, but I could tell he was excited by whatever was going on inside his head. At first, my spirits dampened by his distance, I'd reflected on how easily one got used to being the centre of attention, but I'd reminded myself that his distractedness was positive, that it meant he was getting on with his work—which was what he wanted to do, and what I wanted him to do. Living with a writer would be like this sometimes, I told myself, but there would be my writing, too, to think of. I loved to imagine the two of us working under the same roof, separate but together.

His work schedule explained why the cabin looked the way it did. The kitchen was a mess, its counters cluttered with cereal boxes, a package of bread, empty beer cans and a liquor bottle or two, the sink piled high with dishes, pots and pans. In the bedroom, the floor was strewn with clothes and towels and open books. I wondered if the earlier tidiness had been created for my sake.

I was reluctant to go out, warm and comfortable in the cabin, and it seemed an unlikely day for a walk. A wind had come up after I'd left the city, and I'd nearly frozen on the short dash from the car. But when I saw he could not be persuaded to stay in, I asked to borrow a warm jacket and a toque. At the door, he handed me what I'd asked for, along with a pair of work gloves.

By the time I'd pulled them on he was outside, dancing around on the gravel in front of the cabin, punching the chill air.

I'd come out of the city feeling good as well. Archie was so happy about the announcements from the premier that his eyes were shining, and I felt that he would be all right. Even Ben had seemed abnormally well-adjusted in the past few days. Everything appeared to be do-able—everything that I wanted, and everything Zeke wanted, suddenly seemed within reach. I felt that all of it could be accomplished with a minimum of disruption and a minimum of pain if I just waited until the election was over before making any moves. Timing was everything, I repeated to myself. With patience, everything was possible.

Now we headed up the lane way, Zeke ahead of me, still lost in thought and walking fast. I ran a few steps to catch up with him.

"Slow down," I said, laughing, when we were almost at the secondary road where I'd left my car. "I can't keep up with you."

He turned and looked at me as I came up beside him, then put his arms around me. "Sorry, Maggie," he said. "I might as well be on another planet."

I put my arm around his waist and we walked close together, and headed off onto the otherwise deserted road. "Does it feel good?" I asked. "To feel the way you're feeling?"

"Obsessed?" He nodded. "It's the only way. But it makes me terrible company."

"Maybe I shouldn't have come," I said. "I've interrupted you."

"Oh, no," he said. "I want you here. My mind may be someplace else, but it's like it's being refuelled when you're here. You make me calmer. Whole." He grinned at me. "And happy. And content."

"Anything else?"

"Let me think. Yes. Sane! I wouldn't have thought of coming out here if it weren't for you, and I really needed some fresh air."

"I'm glad it's going well," I said.

"It's going great," he said. "If I can keep this up through the first draft, this level of concentration, I will have it. I will have something.... I will blow them away. Blow them right out of the water. It's good, Maggie. It's great stuff."

I smiled, caught again by his enthusiasm. "And they'll publish a million copies, and you'll win awards and be rich and famous, and you'll live happily ever after."

He looked at me oddly. "Jesus," he said. "That would be nice, wouldn't it?" He gave me a squeeze. "And *we'll* live happily ever after."

I asked him what he'd do if he had a million dollars.

He laughed. "I have no idea." After thinking for a while, he said, "I guess I'd buy a place. Pay cash for it—no mortgages or anything like that. So I'd always have a place where I could go to write. After that, I'd travel. Peru. Egypt. Katmandu." He was silent for a few moments, then he added thoughtfully, "I guess the freedom would be the best part. To be able to work whenever I wanted to, for as long as I wanted to. Not having to worry about money. That would be the best part."

"People who win lotteries usually want to *quit* working, Zeke."

"This isn't a job," he said. "That's the point. I'd never need to have a job again."

"But it is work. What you're doing."

"It's more than that." He shook his head as though shaking off a bug. "Anyway, that kind of money's not going to show up from this book. But some will. It will be a start."

His fourth book—a start. I felt tired on his behalf.

"Maybe I should buy a lottery ticket too," he said, grinning at me. "Insurance."

"Did you call about the grant?" I asked. I'd suggested he apply for one the last time I was out. If the book fulfilled its promise, I'd have a dozen copies of it delivered anonymously to Bill Tugwell.

He shook his head. "I've been working every waking minute since I saw you last—aside from throwing together the occasional sandwich, and attending to other necessary bodily functions. And this morning I took a shower."

"For which I'm grateful. But you should call. You could use the money."

"I should call," he said, suddenly sounding edgy. "I should go and get some food. I should pay the bills and answer a letter or two." He shook his head. "When it's coming, it's coming, and you can't afford to ignore it."

I thought about how many things you would have to ignore in order to write a whole book.

"I don't think I could ever write that way," I said. "I'm so used to fitting things in when I have the time—around all the other stuff."

"Jesus," he said.

"What?"

"Your writing. That's another thing I wanted to do and haven't. As soon as we get back."

"I'll have to go when we get back."

"Can you leave it one more time? Please?"

"Sure," I said, suppressing another wave of disappointment. I'd seen my notebook sitting at the end of his table when I came in, and I'd assumed he'd looked at it. I'd been waiting ever since for him to mention it, to tell me what he'd thought of it. "It's not like I need it or anything," I said, "and I haven't had time even to think about adding to it."

"I'm sorry, Maggie."

"It's okay," I said. "Your work's more important. You've got to get it done." I was glad Alana wasn't there to hear me say that—but in this case, it was true. We were talking about literature, not politics.

"Looks like you've written a lot," he said. "Is it all about your grandmother?"

I nodded.

"She must have been quite a woman."

"She was. Very strong willed. Not aggressive or pushy. Just determined. Used to getting her own way."

"She raised you?"

"My parents—my mother was her daughter—were killed in a car crash during a holiday in England. They'd left me with her, and I just stayed. I think the accident must have been my father's fault. She never mentioned it directly, but the way she talked about him sometimes...."

"How old were you?"

"Three."

"Do you remember your parents?"

"Very little. I remember the funeral for some reason—or at least the party after it, or whatever you call it. I don't think I was at the service itself. Gran wasn't into entertaining, but the house was packed that day. Maybe that's why I remember it."

"Brothers and sisters?"

"Nope. I'm the only one."

A little farther on he said, "She didn't get her way that time, did she?"

I smiled. "No, I guess she didn't. But I never got the feeling she resented it. The way she talked, you'd think it was perfectly normal, people dying and leaving their kids to be raised by grandparents. It worked out pretty well until almost the end of high school. After that she went downhill, and I resented it. I didn't handle being the parent as well as she had."

He kicked a small stone with the toe of his boot, moving it along with us a little way. "Lots of kids are raised by one person," he said. "They turn out all right."

I wondered if he meant himself.

I said, "Tell me about your son."

He kicked another small stone off toward the shoulder of the road. "His name's Marcus. He's eight, and he lives in Scarborough with his mother."

I glanced over at him. High on his jaw a spot was moving, tensing, then releasing. He looked over at me and said, "He's a nice kid. Does well in school. Plays soccer. The usual stuff."

"But you never see him."

Zeke shook his head. "I did when I was down east. Sometimes." He looked away. "Deborah's remarried. She and Howard have a kid: He's five now." He shrugged. "It's like Marcus is theirs, belongs to them. They make me feel like I'm a distant relative, an uncle or something, rather than his father."

"How old was Marcus when you two—?"

"We lived together for a while before she got pregnant, but it came apart even before he was born." He took a deep breath. "She started sounding like my father—wanting me to get a job, settle down, 'give up the writing nonsense.' She'd been enamoured enough with the idea of my being a writer when we met. It hadn't been 'nonsense' before." He looked over at me. "Maternal instinct, I guess. Does funny things. Anyway, she got what she wanted. For her and for him. A nice middle-class existence." He shrugged. "It's probably better for Marcus in the long run."

"Doesn't sound like you believe that."

"I'm not such a bad person. Such a bad influence. And I miss him. I thought it would be easier if I was way out here, but it's not."

I took his hand and squeezed it, and he squeezed back. Looking up the road ahead of us, he said, "He's *my* son. He's turning into Howard."

The wind had reddened patches of skin on his cheeks. I could feel it doing the same to mine. I hoped we'd go back soon.

In the distance, a car appeared, the first we'd seen since we'd been out. It was moving towards us quickly, the dust it raised blowing off to the side behind it. Almost without thinking, I dropped his hand and moved away from him, crossing behind him and walking down along the shoulder. I kept my face averted as the car approached, went past.

"What was that about?" he asked as I came back up to his side.

I shrugged. "People I don't even know, know who I am. I never know where they'll turn up."

He walked along, saying nothing, his hands stuffed in his pockets.

"You ready to go back?"

"Yeah," he said and turned abruptly. Again I had to run a few steps to catch up to him.

"Please slow down," I said, more testily than I had earlier.

"It's not like he's the prime minister, or even the premier."

"I'm just being careful, Zeke," I said.

"You're not him," he said.

"That's true," I said. "But you never know. Honestly, people I've never met before come up to me in the grocery store and greet me by name. At the moment, for his sake, I have to be really careful."

I slowed, letting him go ahead.

We were almost back at my car. When he realized I wasn't with him, he stopped and turned.

"I have to go," I said, more for dramatic than practical reasons: my jacket was still inside the cabin.

He sighed, and came and took me by the hand. We walked past my car and started down the lane. "I resent that other life of yours," he said. "And I know it isn't good for you. I want you out here with me."

I suddenly felt like crying. "I've told you," I said. "It's not as simple as you think. Other people are involved."

I almost added, 'I have a son as well, you know,' but I wasn't yet ready to get into that with him, to impress on him how much I'd still need to be a mother, even when I was with him. I'd started to think about it myself—how we'd need to be in the city, in a place with room for Ben—but raising such matters with Zeke would wait until his first draft was finished. Until after the election.

He put his arms around me.

I looked up at the trees to hold back the tears, and saw the branches here and there were tinged with green. "Look, " I said, taking a deep breath and pointing the index finger of his work glove. "Spring. At last."

"Bloody cold for spring," he said, looking up at the trees, looking around at the countryside, looking back at me. "Which is not, in itself, entirely bad. It suggests a shot of brandy."

On the way back to the city I had one of those flashes of Gran that I would once have written down at my first opportunity. She was standing at the bedroom door saying, "Don't do it then, if it's so hard," and both of us were looking at the math book I'd just thrown across the room. It had hit with a smack against the wall, bringing Gran to see what was the matter.

I was at my desk, nearly rigid with frustration and anger.

"But I have to do it," I said as the tears came. "It's due tomorrow morning."

"No you don't," Gran said. "Skip the assignment. Take the consequences."

"I can't!"

"Of course you can. You have other choices, too. You can phone someone for help. You can give up completely. You can take that other math course—the easier one. You could get through that." It sounded as though she were saying, "Even you could get through that," and her tone made me even angrier.

"I need this one for university!"

"Maggie, it's your decision. If you choose to do this assignment, then do it. If you don't, then don't." She turned and went away.

"That's no help," I shouted after her. "You're no help at all."

Gran's voice came down the corridor. "I'm not trying to help. I'm trying to read my book. In peace. That's all I want to do."

Peace at any cost. I shook my head. The trick was that she'd pulled it off—when it came to peace, Gran had it. And what I wanted to know was how.

24

When I'd called Ben from the grocery store, where I'd gone to fuzz up time, there'd been no answer. I'd considered that an unexpected bit of good luck, allowing me to hone my excuses while I pressed through the aisles at Safeway, but now when I called his name from the back door and there was still no answer, I began to get concerned.

In the back hall, I put down plastic bags full of cans and lettuce and milk, took off my shoes and came up into the kitchen. The message light on the telephone was flashing. I went to the bottom of the hall staircase and called Ben's name again before I went back to the phone.

The first message was from Archie. His voice near whisper-level, he'd demanded at five to ten that morning to know what in the name of God I thought I was doing talking to reporters without telling him about it. I wheeled guiltily, feeling my stomach turn. *The News* was open on the kitchen table where I'd left it. I hadn't even thought about picking up a copy of *The Press*, which Archie got at work but we didn't take at home. What had Keenan written?

Then at three thirty, Ben had called: "Mom. Where are you? We're going to be late!"

My eyes shot to the calendar. Nothing there. Late for what? My mind was blank, and increasingly fogged by apprehension.

Now Archie again, a few moments after Ben: "Where the hell are you, Maggie? I'm in the middle of a meeting, and Ben just called about some hockey picture."

Then my own voice, astonishingly calm compared to theirs, compared to how I felt at the moment: "Hi, Ben. It's me. Got held up at the mall. I'm getting groceries. Make yourself a snack. I'll see you soon."

As I erased the messages, memory started to return. Sometime late the week before, Ben had handed me a piece of paper he'd brought home from a game which told me the time, location and cost of the photos that were to be taken of his team. I'd been irritated because we'd have to go all the way across town and back in rush hour, and now I remembered saying I'd have to pick him up from school, that we'd never make it otherwise. Remembered Ben shrugging, answering, "Don't blame me."

It was the kind of note I always transferred to the calendar, but April 10 was an empty square. Nothing. I glanced back at the newspaper.

I was getting sloppy. Dangerously sloppy.

I stepped over bags of groceries and went down to the basement. His hockey equipment was gone from the furnace room; his school bag was there on the floor. Someone had got him home from school and got him off again. Archie. He'd be livid.

I had to find that newspaper.

Apprehension and guilt gave way to nausea when I pulled the tabloid from the stack at the convenience store and saw the bait on the top corner of the front page—"MLA's wife employed by protest leader. Story, photo, B3." I rolled it under my arm, and paid for it that way.

At home I put *The Press* on the table on top of *The News* and slowly unpacked the groceries. When there was nothing left to put away, I sat down to it, my eyes closed. I took a deep breath. I opened my eyes. I opened the paper. I turned to B3.

There I was, in black and white—my expression merely curious at that point to know who'd opened the door of the

Purple Parrot and let in the cool air. They must have seen me—identified me—through the window, drawn their bead before they even opened the door, because I was smack dab in the centre of the photo. Over my shoulder was Fiona, at the counter, her mouth open slightly in surprise.

The caption read, "'Nothing to do with me,' says Margaret Townsend, centre. The Purple Parrot, where Townsend works, has organized a protest against her husband, MLA Archie Townsend. As many as a thousand people are expected to show up."

I read the article.

> Margaret Townsend, wife of Conservative MLA Archie Townsend, declined to comment yesterday on her involvement in an upcoming demonstration targeted at her husband.
>
> Mrs. Townsend works as a salesclerk at the Purple Parrot, an arts and crafts shop in Old Watchford. Organizers of the demonstration, to be held at the Legislature Building a week from Saturday, say that while the shop is planning headquarters for the one-day protest, Margaret Townsend is not connected with the demonstration.
>
> At issue is a contract awarded to the communications firm of Bellamy & Cato by the Department of Public Works, the portfolio for which Archie Townsend is minister responsible. The contract is likely to result in the loss of fifteen government jobs, and local printing companies have charged that it could also lead to financial shortfalls for contractors who formerly supplied services to the government.
>
> When asked about the contract, Margaret Townsend said, "That has nothing to do with me."
>
> According to local artists who display at the Purple Parrot, the idea for the public protest originated at the shop. "It was our idea," artist Anna Perry said. "Sylvie [Monod] and I came down and got the mailing list and started phoning people. It just kind of grew from there."
>
> Monod, who is coordinating requests for information about the demonstration through the Purple Parrot, said yesterday, "It looks like Bellamy and Cato's the last straw for a lot of people. We're getting a lot of calls." Monod and Perry predicted that as many as a thousand people could show up on April 19 to express their anger with the government.

Monod and Perry insist that Margaret Townsend has not been involved in the planning of the protest. "She works for the Purple Parrot," Perry said. "She stays on that side of the line, and we're on this one."

Mrs. Townsend has worked at the Purple Parrot for three years. Her employer is Purple Parrot owner Mark Scales, who is also president of Scales Printing and Graphics. Scales, who has been vocal in his criticism of the government's move to privatize communications, declined to comment on Mrs. Townsend's employment at the Purple Parrot.

I stood in the shower and let the water pound over me until it started to turn cold. Just before I'd turned the water on, I'd heard a downstairs door slam: they were home. It was nearly six, and I didn't even have dinner ready to distract them from their various forms of outrage. There would be questions, too—about the article, about my absence.

"Just let me out of this one," I mouthed into the water, "and I'll be a perfect wife and mother until the election's over. I won't even go out to the cabin. I promise. I promise. I swear."

When I came out of our bedroom, fortified with bitters but still apprehensive, it was oddly silent in the house. Ben's door, which had been ajar when I came up earlier, was closed. I took a deep breath, went down the hall, and knocked.

There was no response.

I knocked again. "Ben?"

"Go away," he said.

"Look," I said, "I'm sorry. I forgot to write it on the calendar. I just forgot."

No answer.

"Did you get there okay?"

No answer.

I gave up and went cautiously downstairs. There was no sign of Archie anywhere, but on the kitchen table on top of the newspapers was a receipt from Your Team Photos Inc., for thirty dollars and some cents. Bread crumbs were scattered across the counter, the milk was out, a knife still thick with peanut butter was lying in the sink. I wouldn't be able to use food to tempt him out.

I went back upstairs. "Ben," I said at his door, "Where's your dad?"

Silence.

"Ben, please," I said. "Don't be ridiculous."

"Leave me alone."

"Did he go back to the office?"

There was another silence and then he said, his voice hard and mean, "How should I know where he is?"

"Wasn't he with you?"

"Maybe you'd know where he was if you weren't so busy talking to reporters."

I leaned my head against the door frame. After a minute I took a breath and said, "You want to talk about that?"

"No," he said.

"It's nothing. Really. Did you read the article?"

"Go away," he said.

"It's nothing."

Silence.

Guilt screwed into me. The kitchen was a mess. The whole house was a mess. Despite my shower, I felt sullied, despicable. I'd pushed my luck too far.

I did not want to see Archie. Or Ben. Every instinct told me to run, to hide, to sleep—to disappear beneath the covers and hope that tomorrow would restore control and perhaps even self-respect. Tonight obviously would not.

But how would I sleep, in this state?

I thought of Zeke, and a small light went on.

I took the last clean glass from the cupboard in the kitchen, tiptoed into the family room and opened the liquor cabinet. I poured a finger or two of brandy, closed the cabinet, and tiptoed to the bottom of the stairs. I put one foot on the first step.

Heard Ben's door open, saw light slant across the landing.

"Ben?"

His door closed, shutting off the light.

I shook my head, relieved. He'd made a move; he'd make another. He wanted to be angry, and for me to know it, but he also wanted it to be over. I just had to be available.

Sighing, I went back to the family room and carefully poured the brandy back into the bottle. I went to the kitchen and gathered up the newspapers, and took them downstairs to the recycle bin. In the furnace room, I caught Ben's book bag by the strap and carried it back up with me. I left it outside his door and told him it was there, collected the laundry hamper from the bathroom, carried it down to the basement, and started a dark wash. Then I went to the kitchen, took sausages out of the fridge, wiped the counter, and started to peel potatoes.

When Archie came in, the house smelled of the food I was keeping warm in the oven for all three of us, and from downstairs came the comforting sounds of the washer and dryer in operation—making things clean and usable again. I was unloading the dishwasher, putting away still-warm plates and knives and forks. A semblance of order was gradually returning to the house. At some point, Ben's book bag had disappeared from the hall, although I still hadn't seen him.

Archie glanced at the dining room table, which I'd set. He said, "I got a sandwich and a salad at the club."

"That's okay," I said quickly. "It's only sausages."

In the past year alone, I had probably asked Archie half a dozen times in irritation to let me know when he wasn't coming home for supper. I could see him notice that I didn't blow up this time, but he didn't seem surprised. He went to hang up his coat, and I continued to put away the clean dishes. The feeling of nausea had returned and my mind went to the bottles of bitters in the cabinet upstairs. Maybe I should keep one in the kitchen, too.

Archie was standing in the hall, looking at me.

"Archie," I said as evenly, as normally, as I could, my heart beginning to thump. "About the article? I'm sorry."

"Come here," he said.

"What?"

"Come here, I said," he said.

I did. He put his arms around me.

"You managed it just fine," he said into my hair. "Just fine."

My eyes went to the spot on the table where the newspapers had been before I started to clean up. My face was against his shirt: he smelled clean, newly showered. "I was very careful," I said. "The guy made a big deal out of nothing."

"That's what they do," he said. "Don't worry, pet." He ran his big hands up and down my back. My back prickled and felt cold— there was something ominous in his calm. "You're just inexperienced," he said. "You don't know how to manipulate people."

Should I feel relief or apprehension? Believe his words, or the feeling in my gut? I didn't know. I felt tearful, isolated from him within the circle of his arms.

"As Victor says," he said, "problems are achievements in the making." He was still running his hands up and down my back, and the repetitive motion was beginning to irritate the skin on my back. I wanted to move away. I had the feeling that he knew his hands were rough instead of comforting, but it was only a shade of difference and I could not be sure.

"Good old Victor," I said stiffly.

"Victor has some ideas," he said, and his hands stopped moving.

I straightened. "Ideas?"

I stepped back far enough to see his face. "Damage control," he said. "He wants to put you to work."

"Can't we just let it go? Forget about it?"

He turned away. "What happened is not completely insignificant, you know. Not without its power to do harm. We'll need to turn it around and make it work for us." He said it as though it were obvious. "I've asked Victor to drop by."

"Tonight?"

"Were you planning something?"

"Sleep. I was planning to sleep." I felt my temper rising and drew away from him. "It's already almost nine."

"It's only eight thirty. This won't take long. We've already come up with several approaches we could take—" He began to pace. "We've agreed that the basic, most important thing is to make you more visible. Out there, with me. That shores us up. You're independent, but you're right with me. We need to think it through, the details, but that's the gist of it."

"You're beginning to think like him, to act like him."

"Like Victor?"

I nodded.

"And you don't mean that as a compliment."

"No, I don't. I don't talk to you any more, I just talk to him through you. You're treating me like a puppet, Archie. How can you call me independent, and do this?"

His face went harder. "Your 'independence' is plain stupid, Maggie. Pig-headed. It's running me into problems I don't need. We're trying to put the best face on it, and I'd appreciate your help."

I looked at him for a long minute, then closed my eyes. Opened them again. Walked out of the kitchen, into the family room. Looked at the liquor cabinet. Went into the living room. Looked up at the family of dolts in the painting. Closed my eyes again, took a long deep breath. Just three more weeks and I'd be rid of all of it.

Archie had followed me as far as the arched doorway to the dining room. He was watching me, and waiting. He no longer seemed angry.

I thought of Zeke, the pink spots on his cheek bones. The touch of his hip on mine as we walked. The green haze the buds had given to the trees.

Three weeks and three days. I could do this. I could do it.

I turned. "Okay," I said. "Okay."

"That's my girl," he said, immediately restored. His expression said he'd known I'd come around.

He came across and took me in his arms again. I put my head against his shoulder.

"Just remember we're doing this for us," he said. I felt his lips on my hair.

I moved my head.

"Another few weeks," he said.

Three, I thought. Three, and three. Twenty-four days.

"After that," he said, "we should go away. Just the two of us."

I nodded.

After a pause, he said, "Where's Ben?"

"Probably at the top of the stairs, listening."

"You got him to that picture thing okay?"

I let this digest for a moment before I said, "He got there."

So which mother had he imposed on? I was surprised. Impressed. Ben had organized it on his own.

25

"We'll get her up for five minutes at the opening on Saturday," Victor said suddenly. "That makes her not just visible, but involved."

"You mean Maggie?" Archie said, sounding surprised.

"You mean me?" I said. I hated public speaking, and I was sure that Victor knew that. But unlike Archie, I was not surprised: since he'd arrived for this little meeting, Victor had let me know in a variety of ways that my talking to a reporter was a transgression great enough that I owed him whatever punishment he decided to mete out.

I'd made coffee and put out small plates and a cake with chocolate icing I'd found in the downstairs freezer. Ben had scooped four pieces of the cake onto a plate and taken them into the family room, where he was now doing his homework in front of the television set.

"You want Maggie to speak?" Archie asked.

"Nothing big," Victor said, nodding. "No big deal. Five minutes max."

He was wearing an expensive-looking navy-blue cashmere sweater, Levi's and, as usual, a lot of gold. Even at this hour, and by now it was nearly ten, he was wired, leaning forward one moment, sitting back the next in the wingback chair he'd claimed when he came in.

Archie glanced in my direction. "Would she say anything about the protest?"

Victor looked at me as well. "The best scenario would be if she'd get up there and announce she was no longer working for Mark Scales."

She. He'd been referring to me as "she" all evening.

I didn't move.

Victor continued to look at me. "Short of that, I don't think she should even mention the Purple Parrot, or the reporter, or anything connected with the demonstration. There will be other times and places for that. This will be a straight-out gesture of support for the candidate, her husband. Intended to show 'em exactly where her loyalties lie." Now he was looking at me as though he were trying to ascertain where, in fact, my loyalties did lie.

Archie examined his fingernails and thought about it for a minute, then he looked up at Victor. "Is that the best place?" he asked. "I mean, how big an audience is it going to reach? It's just the opening of the campaign office—not likely to get a lot of media attention. If we're going to use her, maybe we should hold our fire."

'Use her.' Nice expression.

"I've thought about that, too," Victor said. "But don't worry about the opening—the media will be there."

"More coffee?" I asked evenly, to remind them I was there.

"Sure," Archie said, holding out his mug.

"Victor?"

Victor was looking up at the painting over the fireplace. "Doesn't flatter you," he said.

"It doesn't do any of us justice," I said, topping up Archie's coffee from the insulated pitcher. I moved it toward Victor's mug and waited for him to indicate whether or not he wanted more.

"I see what you mean," he said, looking back at me. "It's not good of you, either, is it? Or your son, now that I look at it."

"It was a present from my parents," Archie said, raising his mug to his lips and blowing softly before he sipped, a habitual gesture.

Victor smiled. "Then I guess you're stuck with it."

"Actually," Archie said, "I like it."

"Coffee?" I asked Victor again.

"Shouldn't have any more," he said. "Keeps me awake at night."

"It's decaffeinated," I said.

We'd had a similar conversation when I poured him the first cup, but he didn't seem to have any recollection of it. He held out his mug, and I poured. He had one leg over the other at the knee, and his foot was moving up and down. When the mug was full enough for him, he nodded.

I started for the kitchen, intending to plug the kettle in again, but I stopped and turned when Victor said, "Now, about her addressing the issue directly...."

Archie looked over at him, his finger on one of the documents he'd spread out to examine on the ottoman. He said, "What do you want her to do?"

"I want another article. But with *The News* this time."

"Oh, no," I said.

Ben looked up at me, depressing the mute button.

"That woman columnist," Victor said, looking over at me. "You know the one I mean. Vandameer? Whatever it is."

"Vandermeer," I said.

"She can talk about how independent she is," Victor said to Archie. "Make it a real statement. It'd be a sympathetic story with that woman writing it, and Maggie would just need to make sure she got across how supportive she is of you as well."

"Maggie's not very good at directing interviews," Archie said.

"She doesn't have to be," Victor said. "That's the beauty of it. This is just the kind of shit this Vandameer woman goes for. Pardon my French. Really, Archie, it's perfect. She'll write exactly what we want."

Ellen Vandermeer was widely read. She was a good writer with a strong affection for human beings in general, and particularly for those who were trying to pull their weight in the face of disadvantages. Her columns focused on people whose lives raised subjects that normally tended to be thought of as the property of the left—the effects of two-income families on kids, teen-aged pregnancy, respite for parents of disabled children, day-care for seniors—but she treated these subjects with moderation. She didn't see socialism as the solution to the world's problems, and neither did most of the people she interviewed. They just wanted a fair shake.

I had no interest in meeting her.

"No way." I shook my head. "I'll do something at the opening if you insist. But no more interviews. I hate them. I never know what I'm supposed to say."

"Don't judge them all on the basis of that scumbag from *The Press*," Archie said.

"No," I said again, even more firmly. I went over and put my hand on Ben's shoulder. "I promised Ben half an hour ago I'd never embarrass him in public again if I could help it. This time I can help it."

Ben looked up at me skeptically.

"Maggie…" Archie started –

"No," I said.

"Come off it, Dad," Ben said, turning his attention toward his father. "It's bad enough you're on TV all the time."

Archie looked from Ben to me to Victor. Shrugged and said, "Maybe if she doesn't want…."

Victor shrugged too. "Okay. Let's start with the speech for Saturday afternoon."

"Not speech," I said. "Something short. A minute or two. That's all."

"Fine. Whatever," he said, beginning to sound irritated. "Whatever it is, however long it is, we need to go over what you're going to say."

Ben lost interest at that point and turned the volume back up on the television set.

"Just give me a minute," I said to Victor and Archie over a cackle from Roseanne, and I went into the kitchen. There I remembered the Purple Parrot and instead of plugging in the kettle I went through the kitchen, down the hall and back out to the living room. "Did you say Saturday *afternoon?*"

"The office opening," Archie said.

"I thought that was Saturday night."

"Two p.m. on the dot," Victor said. "Cake and coffee and dancing bears. It's the place to be."

"I work Saturdays," I said. "You know that, Archie. I always work on Saturdays."

Archie looked at me. Victor drained his mug and looked at me, too. Then he looked back at his coffee mug.

"Is this decaffeinated?" he said.

I nodded.

"I knew it. I can always tell."

"I'm glad to see you here," said Edward, appearing at my left side.

"I thought you worked Saturdays," Millicent said cheerfully, taking me by the elbow on the right.

"I'm taking a late lunch."

Fiona had restrained herself from looking disgusted when I'd explained why I'd have to be gone for an hour or so. I suspected that she felt badly about the article. She'd mentioned it just once—she'd been unhappy with the photograph, or at least the part that included her—but probably she, like Sylvie and Anna, was disappointed that the reporter hadn't focused on the Purple Parrot and the demonstration instead of focusing on me. I was disappointed about that myself.

"Not enough media people here," Edward said, looking around the room. "But at least they've finally got Sanders back on board. That's a relief to me."

Bob Sanders, a man in his late sixties with a balding head, was standing across the room near the door of Archie's office. He raised a hand and smiled when he caught sight of the three of us. We all waved back.

The campaign office was in a strip mall, in a space occupied until recently by a video store that had gone under when a larger one opened a couple of blocks away. Today, the place was packed with supporters, and I felt my heart beat faster when I thought about having to say something in front of all of them. But I wasn't going to back out of it. I would do whatever I could to help get Archie re-elected.

When I allowed myself to think about what was going to happen after that, my forehead tightened and my stomach started knotting. There were so many details, all of them trailing untidy threads—How long after the election, exactly, would I wait? Would I go directly to Zeke, or choose a neutral location, an apartment or something, first?

And what would I take with me? 'Nothing' seemed the best answer for someone who wanted to start fresh, start over, start again, but it also seemed impractical. For the same reason, I'd need to keep my job at the Purple Parrot. Zeke was broke and I would be as well. And then, if Ben –

And there my mind went blank. It always came down to Ben, and it always went blank when it did.

"Where's Ben?" Millicent asked, as though reading my mind.

"Hockey," I said, feeling a flush start up my face. These two would really hate it when I left. They'd never understand, not in a million years. They would hate me. They'd have every right. A lot of people would hate me—I'd have to learn to live with that.

If we lived out of town, it would be easier. But I had to be near Ben.

Stop it, I told myself.

"Must be getting close to playoffs," Edward said.

In the middle of the room, Dagmar and Victor were helping Archie climb up onto a table.

"He's in a tournament," I said. "I should be there, too."

"You're doing the right thing," Edward said.

"Shh," Millicent said. "They're about to start."

A young man I didn't know—he looked to be about eighteen—had also been helped up onto the table, and he called for silence. He talked for a few minutes about how the Young Conservatives in the area were contributing to Archie's campaign, and then he introduced Archie. There were whistles and applause. When the noise died down again, Archie welcomed everyone to the official opening of the campaign office, and then announced some of the goals of the Party for the next term— which had been revised since I last heard them, because of all the new money.

My sense that the government would be returned with an overwhelming majority grew stronger every day. It wasn't just from listening in places like this where supporters would support, almost no matter what, it was also in the papers and on the radio and it was what people were saying on street corners while they waited for the light to change. I was worried about a lot of things, but the success of the Party as a whole was no longer one of them.

Archie went on to talk about small business, in much the same way as he had at the fund-raising dinner. Watching him, so confident up there, you could have no doubts about his prospects, either.

"And speaking of small business," he said, "one issue seems to be attracting more than its fair share of attention—a small communications contract recently awarded by my office." He paused and looked around the room. "I'd like to address that issue. Once and for all."

There was applause, an unexpected amount of it. These really were supporters.

"Bellamy and Cato is only one of thousands of items of business to which the hard-working staff at Public Works has attended in the past few months," Archie said, "but it's the one that seems to have caught the public eye. To my mind, it's less a 'needle in a haystack' than a 'hay stock in a haystack'."

That brought laughter, and he waited before he spoke again. He was learning Victor's lessons well. Then he said, "I want to address this issue in order to put it to rest, in order put it behind us, ladies and gentlemen, so we can get on with the campaign."

There was more applause as he took a paper from the inside pocket of his jacket. He looked at it, looked up. "I have a document here," he said, "that lists the companies—small companies—in this province that are employed—are working perhaps at this very moment—on government work, thanks to Bellamy and Cato. I would like to read you this list of companies."

There were at least ten of them, and he read them slowly—indicating the city in which each company was based. Then he turned the paper around and held it up, moving it back and forth, sharing its contents with everyone.

"No matter what anyone does, grousers will complain," he said. "This is proof, ladies and gentlemen. Proof. We have saved this government, and the people of this province, thousands of dollars with this move, and those thousands are going right back into small business—where they belong."

There was huge applause. Millicent, beside me, clapped enthusiastically and even began to stamp her feet. Edward was more subdued, but he clapped, too.

A camera flash went off, which reminded me that Victor had

promised a good media turnout. But when I looked over, I saw that it was Dagmar who held the camera. There was one guy who looked like he might be a reporter leaning against a wall, but that was it. Hardly an inundation. Edward was right.

Archie clenched his teeth slightly, a sign that he was pleased with his performance, then moved off the subject of Bellamy & Cato and onto the excitement he felt at the prospect of another term of office.

Suddenly he stopped and turned in our direction.

My heart began to beat faster.

"Just a moment here," he said. "Here I'm talking as though I could do all of this on my own." He waved his hand at me, beckoning. "Maggie," he said, "come over here."

The crowd of clapping people made way for me to get through, and I started forward, as we had planned.

"Ladies and gentlemen," Archie said, "many of you know her, but I want to formally introduce you to the person on whom I rely the most for advice and good judgement...." (That'd be Victor, I thought.) "My very strongest supporter...." (Edward, I thought.) "My wife, Maggie Townsend."

He reached down to help me up beside him, and I took his hand.

My heart thumping with nervousness, I stepped up onto the chair and then the table, then looked around me as the applause grew. The walls were plastered with posters and signs and balloons, and nearly fifty people stood around the tables or leaned against the walls. About half of them were wearing plastic name-tags on strings around their necks to designate them as campaign workers.

I took a breath and held up my hand, as we had planned. "I'd like to say something," I said.

People hushed one another until it was quiet. "I want to say something," I said again. I put out my hand and touched Archie's shoulder. "Many of you know this man. But I know him better."

As I waited for the laughter to die, an almost icy calm came over me. I had to do nothing but repeat the words that Victor had told me to say, and I didn't even have to repeat them accurately. They'd laugh when I wanted them to laugh, and they'd applaud no matter what I said. None of this was real, and I didn't need to worry about it. I didn't need to like it, but I didn't need to worry about it either.

"Archie Townsend is a sincere and honest man," I said, thinking suddenly of the sermon in church the week before, about the man, Peter, who'd denied that he was friends with Jesus when things started to get rough. This was sort of the reverse. "He's a wonderful father and a great husband—at least when he's at home." Again I waited for quiet, admiring the sound of my conviction. Taking my time, I told them how dedicated he was, even in private, to his constituents, to the Party, to the great city and province where we lived. I turned and smiled at him, then turned and smiled at the audience. "I'm proud of him," I said. "I'd vote for him even if we weren't married."

That brought the house down. As we had planned.

I turned and hugged Archie and he whispered in my ear, "You did great." Then he added, "Thanks."

I had to get back to work, but—relieved to be alone and away from the crowd—I took my time about leaving the small bathroom at the back of the campaign office. As I opened my handbag to pull out my hairbrush, I heard two male voices, hard with anger, through the wall. At first I thought it was people in an adjacent shop, but then I recognized Victor's voice, and then the less familiar voice: Bob Sanders'. I moved closer to the wall. Their words were audible despite the din from the main room behind me.

"It's dead in the water," Victor was saying.

"That's where you're wrong," Bob Sanders said. "It's still a volatile issue, Maxwell. It's going to blow up in your face."

"Look, Sanders," Victor said as though he were talking to a child, "I let the media know that Archie was going to talk about Bellamy and Cato today, and none of them showed up. That's proof. It's dead, I tell you. Dead. I know what I'm doing, Sanders."

"If you did, you'd know there isn't—"

I opened the bathroom door and stepped out, closing the door carefully behind me. In the main room, the chatter was still loud: it was unlikely Victor and Bob could be heard by anyone out there. I knocked on the inner office door to warn them to shut up, then opened it and went in, quietly closing that door behind me, too.

"Maggie!" Bob Sanders said, coming over to me. "It's wonderful to see you." His face was still flushed from anger. "You did a great job out there."

"Thanks," I said lightly, affectionately. He'd always made time to stop and talk with me when he ran Archie's campaigns—even asked my advice from time to time.

"Little departure from the text, there, Maggie," Victor said, pulling at his cuffs, trying to regain his composure.

"I felt inspired," I said, keeping the sarcasm out of my voice. I'd changed only a few words.

"Never mind," Victor said. "It turned out all right. Not that there was much point since the media didn't show."

"The people matter too," Sanders said sharply.

"Don't get holy with me," Victor said. "I know what I'm doing."

I said, "Did you know that from the bathroom you can hear every single word you say in here?"

Bob looked over at the offending wall.

Victor, who had leaned back against the desk and crossed his arms, examined his fingertips.

Bob looked at Victor and said in a hard voice, "That should have been checked, Maxwell. This office should be soundproof."

Victor glared at Bob and stood up. "Jesus, Sanders. It is none of your—"

"It's absolutely basic, Maxwell. Essential. You've got to know—"

"It's Dagmar's responsibility to—"

"Don't try to slough it off on Dagmar."

"Stop it," I said, surprising myself with the evenness of my voice. "Just stop it. You can fight with each other after the election. If you're here to help Archie, help him. Forget about everything else."

26

Real spring arrived at last, on Tuesday the fifteenth of April. By nine in the morning the air was spongy warm and drying in the sun. The sky was clear of clouds for the first time in days, and the trees had gone from haze-of-green to new-leaf green almost overnight. Here and there the last icy remnants of snow banks, still being shovelled high less than two months ago, remained in the shadows of fences, trees. Today perhaps they would go away for good.

I backed out of the driveway, drove through puddles down the lane, out into sand-mucky streets and headed for bare highway. I felt overwhelmed at my release, at my good fortune: I had somewhere to go on such a day as this, someone I loved, someone who loved me back, to be with. Spring was delivering on its promise. As I drove, my throat tightened with anticipation.

It had been gray and sleeting rain for four days straight, normally the kind of weather that got me down, immobilized me, but I'd been as doggedly consistent as the weather, amazing myself with my ability to focus on what I had to do. The determination that had taken hold of me at Archie's campaign office had persisted, and since then I'd worked my shifts at the Purple Parrot, done volunteer duty at tournament hockey games, gone to church with Archie and back to the campaign office with him, and fed everyone three balanced meals a day—including one Sunday night that included Millicent and Edward—and through it all felt calm and purposeful.

I had earned this break, this weather.

I stopped at a delicatessen on the way out of town and bought rye bread and wedges of Edam and cheddar, thinly sliced smoked salmon, capers, an almost artificially bright yellow lemon. At a wine shop next door I found a dry German that I'd tasted before, and liked.

I was eager to see Zeke, and eager to know what he thought of my little bits about Gran. My fantasies for the future increasingly involved some writing of my own. Surely by now he'd have had a chance to look at it.

I found him bent over the engine of his truck. Shielded by the open hood and a banged up radio-cassette player that was set on the bumper playing a Tom Waits song, he didn't notice my arrival until I was almost at the cabin.

"Something the matter with the truck?" I asked him.

He looked up and pleasure spread across his face. He looked down at the engine and said, "Been running rough. But mainly I'm just sorting out some thoughts. Sometimes it helps to get away from the computer."

He rubbed his hands on a rag, slammed down the hood and came over and took me in his arms.

"It's so beautiful today," I said, inhaling. "Even better out here."

He mumbled agreement into my neck and then, his hands encountering the bags I was carrying, said, "What's this?"

"Lunch," I said.

"Lunch," he said. "You're lovely. Put it down."

I leaned forward and put the bags on the hood against the windshield.

He pulled down the zipper of my jacket and began to unbutton my jeans. Aroused already by the day, I moved against him.

"Wanna go inside?" I said.

"Mm mm," his voice said. "Stay out here."

I looked over his shoulder in the direction of the roadway, up at the sky. His hand was up inside my shirt and I could feel the air on my belly.

"It's kind of cool out here," I said.

He moved his head against me, having none of that, pressed me up against the truck and pulled my shirt up, bending to put his lips on my breasts, to suck my nipples. I put my head back and let the feeling in, let the feel of the air on my skin increase my pleasure until I was eager when he began to pull my jeans down, off, and to get his down too, and he pressed me up against the truck and lifted me and took me.

Afterward, he rested his head against my half-covered breasts and I put my arms around him, my face in his hair, holding him close, both of us breathing hard.

"God, I love you," I said, my heart lifting, rising at the feel of him against me, the smell of him so close.

"You, too," he said. He yawned. "Want to have a nap?"

I laughed. "It's too beautiful for a nap." I started to pull my clothes together. "Let's sit out here for a while."

He nodded and yawned again, zipping up his jeans. "Sorry. Didn't sleep a lot last night."

"How come?"

He shrugged. "Just one of those nights. They happen."

I breathed deeply, admiring the look of him.

"When we're together," I said, "I'm going to spend whole hours just looking at you."

"We'll do nothing but stare at one other," he agreed.

"I guess I should go in. Tidy up a bit." I looked down at myself, checking tucks and zips, then looked up at him again. "I've never done that before."

"Never done what?"

I nodded in the direction of the truck. "Outside, I mean."

He looked almost incredulous. "My dear," he said, "you do have a lot of room for growth."

I smiled at him and said, "I know."

We sat outside and drank coffee until it was nearly noon, and then I went in and extracted a few plates and knives and glasses from the pile of dirty dishes in the sink and washed them. I noticed my notebook sitting on the table in front of the couch, half covered by papers and magazines and books. The disappointment was acute, and I decided this time I would take it back with me. If he hadn't looked at it by now, he never would.

As always, my irritation passed quickly. He'd been working. There was time. And it was so beautiful out here.

We ate lunch on the verandah, our backs against the posts— the sun on us so warm by then that I took my jacket off and let the light begin to heal my face and arms of winter.

I watched him bite eagerly into the smoked salmon and rye.

"You've been working hard," I said, thinking of the notebook again, and of the mess in the kitchen. I wondered if he drank while he wrote—there were four or five empty scotch bottles around now, a couple on the counter, several under the sink.

He rubbed his eyes with one hand, ran the hand up over his hair, down the back of his head. "Ran into another little impasse yesterday. Scared me, but I'll get through it. I feel better now. This is helping." He took a sip of wine and raised the glass at me. "Thanks."

"Did you call about the grant?"

It sounded so parent-like, nagging, I wished I hadn't said it. But he didn't seem to take offense. "Today," he said. "I promise."

He steered me back to the conversation we'd been having before I went in for the food. He'd been mining my memory again for details, encouraging me to recall again the hours I'd spent listening and admiring him and the others before Nola and Katherine invited me to join them. He nudged me with comments and questions into retelling it from different angles, prodded me to comb my memories. "What do you imagine Nola thought of that?" Or, "So Katherine went for women. Would have been even harder, then." Or, "Andrew was odd. Talked like a professor, deep and serious, that pipe pressed against his lip, but he never made any sense. Do you remember that?"

"They were your friends," I said, sleepy from sun and sex and wine and finally growing tired of going over it all again, again. "You knew them better than I did."

He told me about a summer day when he and Kevin Pine and several of the others and some I didn't know had driven out to

Waldham Village and spent the afternoon performing Hamlet on the beach, reading from their heavily annotated high-school playbooks, dressed in brightly coloured scarves and hats, and drooping threadbare dresses and suits they'd gathered from basements and attics and closets that belonged to mothers and sisters and great-uncles. Drinking beer and smoking dope.

"It's a miracle the RCMP didn't come sniffing around," he said, smiling at the memory, "that nobody called them out." He shook his head, looking around him. "We came to Waldham a few times, don't remember why that place particularly. I like living near it now. It helps to take me back."

Finally, curled down onto the pillow I'd wedged between my back and the verandah post, I could no longer keep my eyes open. "Don't let me go to sleep," I said, but I did, and when I awoke again—my hip sore from the hard wood planking—he was sitting not far off, my notebook open on his lap.

"What time is it?" I asked, scared. I could see that the sun had moved.

"Just after one thirty," he said, smiling and looking over at me, stretching. He'd finished the wine and was sipping on a beer. "I was just going to wake you up."

I sat up slowly, rubbing my leg.

"You've got a lot of good stuff here," he said.

I looked at him closely, but he seemed to mean it.

"I've only looked at a few pages," he said, closing the notebook and putting it down on the step. "I'll read the rest this afternoon, give it back to you next time."

"What about your own work? Don't you need to get back to that?"

A flicker of something crossed his eyes. "I'll get back to it," he said. "I need a little break."

I nodded. "It's that kind of day."

He nodded, too.

"You really think it's okay?" I asked him, looking down at the notebook.

He gave it a little pat. "I do. First draft's the big thing. You get it all down first, all of it, in some kind of order. Not necessarily chronological—better if it's not, in some ways. Later we'll worry about what to do with it." He edged over to me, put his arm around me, pulled me close. "Your perceptions are good. You have an eye." He took a breath. "Bit of a relief."

"I'll say," I said, laughing, more awake.

The embrace was awkward and we moved so we were sitting side by side on the step. I took a deep breath of the warm spring air, and thought that at this moment, life made perfect sense. The pieces fit, and the course ahead was obvious. It hadn't been Archie's fault, and I would tell him that. I'd met him before I'd known who I was, before I'd even had time to think about it. The appeal of Zeke's group should have been a signpost, but I hadn't seen it. I'd feared unfamiliar options, then. After Gran died, security was what I'd thought I needed.

But now, through Zeke, I'd seen it was immoral to allow the one life I had to get swallowed up in other people's dreams. To stand by and watch others grow, fulfil themselves—Archie, Ben, Fiona, even Alana when I thought of it. To watch, and not to do.

One of his hands was resting open, palm down, across my notebook—as though he were protecting it.

He said, "Your grandmother was something."

"She was." I took a breath. "There was a quality about her that I can't put my finger on, that I'm trying to find by writing about her. Something that gave her peace." I sat a little straighter. "Something I want for myself." I looked down at the notebook with new fondness, and with something more: anxiety to get back at it. To spend whole days of work on it. It was a longing of a kind, a depth I'd never felt before. The book was her, was me. I wanted to be in it.

"Twenty days," I said aloud.

"Pardon?"

"Till the election." I sighed. "Till I can begin to move." I looked down at the notebook and thought, twenty days till I can get to that.

"Twenty days. Seems like a long time."

I sighed and nodded. "And even after it...." I looked up at him. "I know what I want—just not how to get there."

He nodded slowly. "We'll work it out," he said.

I leaned against him and we sat, not talking, until it was time for me to go back. I recognized that afternoon for what it was— the point of deceptive calm before the rapids, where there's time only to draw breath. Even my sense of clarity and purpose—the shape of my small craft—was likely to be altered by everything that lay ahead. So for the moment, I was still. I felt his breath and mine rise together. I felt the sun on my skin, and knew how it felt on his.

27

I'd taken Ben's after-school basketball practice into consideration when I'd calculated my departure time from the cabin, and this time there were no crises awaiting me when I got home. I was going out door-knocking with Archie at seven, but I was home by four and I felt so full of energy that I washed windows while I was making dinner.

Alana called while Ben and I were eating.

"Hi, Kid," she said. "How's it going?"

"Alana!" I said. "How are you?"

I felt a curious combination of emotions. I was genuinely happy to hear her voice—I'd missed her—but at the same time, I'd been avoiding her, and I didn't want to talk to her now. She'd called once before, left a message on the machine that I had not returned. If she asked about it, I was prepared to sound surprised, to say that someone must have erased it accidentally.

"I'm fine," she said. "How about you?"

"Busy as hell," I said. "Campaign. You know what it's like."

"How's that going?"

"It's going well," I said. "Archie's feeling optimistic. So am I."

"You sound a little rushed," Alana said. "You want to call me back?"

"Good idea," I said. "We're just eating dinner." I knew she meant I should call her back in fifteen minutes—it was time to arrange a lunch—but I said, "I'll give you a call when things let up a bit," and she let it go with that.

"You never let me talk to my friends during dinner," Ben said when I came back to the table, looking up from the *Hockey News* that was open in front of him.

I apologized, but a few of the words I'd said to Alana had been intended for his ears, too. I needed for him to believe that everything was stable between Archie and me, that everything was all right.

"So, what's new in your life?" I asked him when I'd sat down again.

He shrugged. "Got an English assignment back."

"And?"

"I got an A."

"Ben!" I said. "I'm really proud of you."

He looked proud, too, moving his head a little side to side, his eyes back on the newspaper. It was so typical of him these days to keep that kind of information to himself until I asked—a year ago, he'd have told me the instant he was in the door.

"What was it about?"

"Some short story." He shrugged.

"You wrote a short story?"

He looked up at me as though I were daft. "No. I read one. Wrote about it."

"Well," I said. "Ben, that's so great. Most people couldn't… I mean, with all the campaign uproar…. All the stress? It makes it hard to keep your marks up."

He looked up at me, met my eyes directly. "I hate the election."

"I know," I said, and looked away. "It'll be over soon."

"No, it won't," he said.

I met Archie at the campaign office. Along with the two canvassers who'd been assigned to come with us, we set off on the short drive to the middle-class neighbourhood that had been targeted for the evening's door knocking. Everyone was polite, some even happy to see us. The closest we got to a negative comment was from a middle-aged man who complained about the cost of holding an election when it was obvious the Conservatives were going to win nearly every seat, but the man's wife quickly, almost superstitiously, sent up a prayer of thanks into the warm sky that we lived in a country where it was possible to vote at all. Archie added a few reverential words in support of the democratic process, and the man, disgusted with all the piety, went back to raking snow mould from his lawn.

That was the closest we came to discord. No one mentioned Bellamy & Cato. It was a nice Canadian neighbourhood, and everyone was in a good mood because of the weather.

When we went back to the campaign office, Victor came hurrying up to us, looking like he was about to burst. It turned out to be self-congratulation that made him look so full— somehow he'd got in touch with Ellen Vandermeer.

"She wants to do a story," he said, smiling smugly at Archie. "She'll call Maggie." He glanced at me with the briefest expression of discomfort, then recovered. "No hassle!"

Vandermeer was the last person I'd have thought would have been susceptible to Victor's electioneering tactics, and I was almost as disappointed as I was surprised.

Archie said, "Great," at the same time I asked Victor curtly, "How did you manage it?"

"Well, by the greatest stroke of good luck," he said with a little shrug, "it turns out she's the friend of a friend. This friend suggested you might make an interesting article. That's all there was to it."

"At your suggestion, I imagine?" I said.

He shrugged as if to say, We do what we have to do. He was looking at Archie, not at me.

I was sure that Victor had had this completely planned when he mentioned Vandermeer on Tuesday night, and that he'd gone ahead even though I'd said I didn't want him to. Much as I disliked them, I suspected that his tactics were exactly what was necessary for the management of a political campaign. So I overlooked the way I'd been manipulated and decided I'd talk to Ellen Vandermeer if she called. I'd resolved to stick it out for the campaign, and maybe this would help.

I thought about Victor's friend, and about the amazing power an intermediary could have to change the direction of an idea—like a lightbeam hitting water, or—more appropriately in this instance—a money-laundering device.

On the way home, Archie thanked me for the way I was pitching in—at last, his voice suggested, but the gratitude sounded sincere.

"Don't thank me," I said, meaning it more than he knew. "I haven't done very much."

"It helps when I don't feel like I'm dragging you along."

"It took me a while to get started. You know how I hate campaigns."

He looked over at me. "We're different that way."

"Yeah," I said. "We are."

"Maybe that's a good thing," he said, looking back at the road.

"Maybe," I said. I wondered what he'd meant.

A few blocks later, I ventured to ask him how he and Victor were feeling about the protest. "It seems to be building steam."

"You'd know more about that than I do," he said, glancing at me. Then, looking back at the road, he said, "I'll be glad when it's over, but I don't think it's going to change anything."

"You going to go to it?" The question made my heart thump, and I was relieved when he said "No."

"Victor's got his ear to the ground," he said. "He says the focus has shifted—it's not about the Bellamy and Cato contract any more. It's more general than that."

His voice came up in a little question at the end, and he waited. After a moment I said, "It seems that way to me."

Visibly relieved, he said, "Anyway, the best approach is to ignore it. Let it work itself out. Sure, there are still people out there who are unhappy about the cuts, but mostly it's the ones who were directly affected. It's a relatively small proportion. The average voter's just happy about the results—balanced budget, more money for the next term." He shrugged. "Victor doesn't think they'll get more than a few hundred out."

"Makes sense," I said.

"St. James will probably be there. But I'm going to let it go."

It was worrying him. I could tell that more from his tone than his words. But he'd placed his faith in Victor Maxwell and he had to go with that.

With only three days left until the protest, I was surprised to find the level of tension and excitement at the Purple Parrot considerably diminished when I got in on Wednesday morning. Anna and Sylvie spent an hour or so huddled at their table, checking things off lists and making new ones, and then they both went home. "We have to get some rest," Anna said, as though she needed an excuse to leave. "Saturday will be tiring."

It was fairly quiet as far as customers as well. At one point, alone in the shop, I found myself looking over my work at Anna and Sylvie's vacated corner, at the battered table they'd cleared of everything but a coffee mug before they left, at the boxes under it, at the poster and the T-shirts stuck on the wall above. Sylvie had left her dark blue cardigan hanging on the back of one of the chairs.

I thought about what Archie had said the night before and about the poll results that had been released that morning, and the protest suddenly seemed so amateur, so pedestrian, an energy-sucking but ultimately pointless attempt even to alter public opinion, much less to change the way things were. It reminded me of university—of Archie at university, with all his causes. What good had protests done back then? What good would they do now?

The poll predicted a landslide, and the accompanying illustration in the paper showed the Conservative election machine as a steam roller, flattening everything in its path. There was no alternative, and everybody knew it—even the opposition parties were no more than half-hearted in their campaign promises. They'd be lucky to get four seats among them.

Ellen Vandermeer called just after one, and with a calm born of fatigue, I agreed to meet her for coffee at ten the following morning.

As I hung up, the door chimes tinkled. I looked up, expecting it to be Fiona but, to my surprise, it was Alana's husband, Vern.

"Hi," I said, coming around the counter to meet him.

Vern Drummond is a mild-mannered, soft-looking man with a greying beard and mid-length greying hair, given to wearing corduroy pants, cabled pullover sweaters, loafers. He's the kind of man you trust on sight.

"I'm absolutely stumped," he said. "I figured you could help."

"Sure," I said, waiting for him to explain.

He looked around the shop.

"Something she'd like, I don't know, maybe fifty dollars or so."

Suddenly my brain clicked in. Alana's birthday. April 19—Saturday.

"Of course," I said, embarrassed, looking around the shop. I had no idea what to suggest, and I couldn't get my mind on it because I was thinking about Alana's phone call: she'd called to nudge my memory, and failed. All this talk about the protest—April 19, April 19, April 19—the day had been the focus of so many of my thoughts. How could I have forgotten that it was also Alana's birthday?

"She always appreciates your gifts so much," he said. "I thought maybe you could help."

We settled on a heavy, round-bellied teapot with six little matching cups, grey earthenware, hand-painted with tall green leaves. The minute he was gone, I called Alana at her office and suggested lunch on Friday.

"I thought you couldn't get away," she said, amused.

"Okay, I admit it, Alana. I forgot."

"We could do it another time. After the election."

"I'm not letting a tradition get away on us because of an election," I said—already wondering how I'd fit it in, what I would say to her.

28

I woke up the next morning feeling weary and disinclined to go anywhere or do anything at all. Given half a chance, I might have slept all day. But this was the day of my meeting with Ellen Vandermeer, and I'd told Zeke I'd be out to see him as well. For the first time, the trip to the cabin felt like an obligation. It wasn't that I didn't want to see him—I did. I just didn't want to have to go all that way to do it.

Ellen had suggested when she called me that we meet at a greasy spoon downtown, not too far from the newspaper building where she worked. The Star Café is well known in the city, distinctive because it has undergone no renovations since it opened in the Fifties. The waitress who saw me to Ellen's booth and filled my pale green mug with coffee was of an age and looked so weary that she might have been one of the originals—wearing the same frilled apron over the same salmon-coloured uniform she'd started in forty years ago.

The booth had an Arborite counter and bench seats of soft red plastic, cracking here and there. On the table in front of Ellen there was a small tape recorder, and a steno pad was open at her elbow. She was slim and healthy-looking, with short dark hair and intelligent brown eyes that were just beginning to show lines at the corners. I'd guessed from her column that she was younger than I was because she sometimes wrote about her pre-teen children, but she wasn't that much younger.

Her smile was warm, her greeting genuine, and I liked her immediately. Knowing we'd both been set up for this—and knowing that she didn't know we had—made me feel terrible. I didn't want to stay long, maybe twenty minutes at the most. I just wanted to get it over with and done.

Nervous, and dull from weariness, I reminded myself to keep my distance—to sit up straight and focus only on the reason I was there. In answer to her various questions, I told her how supportive I was of Archie and his campaign, how impressed I was with all the good things Mark Scales had done and was doing for the city's cultural community, how much my job meant to me, how much my husband meant to me, and how I was trying to keep my two lives separate and somehow preserve them both.

"Their politics are very different," she said, just when I was thinking we were finished. "Your husband's and Mark Scales'."

I nodded. "That's the problem, all right."

She looked up at me quizzically. "You're not taking sides?"

I thought carefully before I answered. Finally I said, "My husband is a very good politician. I support him without reservation."

"But support for culture is a political issue, too. Not one your husband's party is particularly well noted for."

My throat began to tighten. I shook my head and said, "Archie is the MLA, not me. I can't say anything about that."

She sighed and put her pen down. "We still have a long way to go, don't we?"

For a moment I thought she was talking about the interview, and my heart sank. Then I realized that she meant women, that she was trying to get to the heart of it, my employment problem, my political dilemma, everything.

A waitress came by with a full pot of coffee. Ellen nodded at the offer of a refill. I put my hand over my cup and shook my head. I had to get out of there.

"We always get cornered by what other people need," she said,

stirring milk into her coffee, looking at me evenly, sympatheti-
cally. "Do you think your husband would quit his job if you were
running for office?"

"He might," I lied, thinking how right she was, remembering
what Archie had said about that—what Alana had said as well. I
took a breath. "It would depend on the job, I guess. This thing
at the Purple Parrot's only part time," I pointed out. "It's hardly
a career."

The expression on her face said she knew how much I loved
the job, knew exactly how I felt. Why did the one person I might
so easily have opened up to have a pen, a tape recorder, and a
column? I reached for my handbag, and said, "It's more about the
principle."

"Independence," she said, picking up her pen again and
jotting.

"I suppose so. Yes." I started to put my jacket on.

"You have a son as well, don't you?" she asked.

Ben's face leapt into my mind. "Please don't mention him,
Ellen," I said. "He hates this public stuff."

She wrote something else in her notebook, looked up at me
again. The article she was writing would still be around, would
still be lying around somewhere, after I'd gone to be with Zeke.
I thought about how it would look, how utterly false and twisted
it would look. To Ben and all the others.

"And how about you, Maggie?" Ellen said softly. "How do you
feel about the 'public stuff'? It can't be easy for you either."

To my horror, tears welled up in my eyes and I shook my head,
unable to speak. She waited for several moments, then reached
into her handbag and pulled out a small Kleenex packet.

I took it from her, pulled out a tissue and dabbed my eyes.
Then I shook my head again. Took another tissue. Nothing was
going to stop these tears.

She'd turned off the tape recorder, and put down her pen. She
waved the waitress over, got me a glass of water.

I took a sip or two.

It was several more minutes before I was able to begin to
control my breathing. I was embarrassed, grateful that the café
was nearly empty.

"Look," I said finally, breathing carefully around the words.
"To tell the truth, I don't... want... you to write... anything

about me." I looked up at her, then quickly away again when I saw her sympathy and felt the onset of more tears. "It's more complicated...." I shook my head. "Stressful. I shouldn't have come here." I slid out of the booth and stood up. "I beg you," I said. "Don't write anything at all."

I grabbed my bag and left.

Every time I thought of the interview or Ben I was off again, and I didn't really stop crying until I was past Osier. By the time I got to the cabin, I'd regained some control, but I could see from the rearview mirror that my eyes were red and puffy. I was almost relieved when I realized that Zeke's truck wasn't at the cabin: I would have a few minutes to pull myself together.

I pulled in beside where he usually parked and turned the car off. I fixed up my face a bit and then just sat there. It was almost noon. I was much later than usual, but I'd called him on my way to the Star Café to tell him about my meeting.

After a while I got out of the car and went up to the cabin and knocked on the door. No answer. I opened the door and went in, called for him once or twice. The bed was a tumble of sheets and blankets, the living area and kitchen a worse mess than the last time I'd been out. The cabin smelled stale, of cigarettes, but the shower had been used that morning and the coffee was still warm on a low burner. I poured myself a cup, and then took off my jacket and hung it over a chair.

There were two or three good-sized stacks of manuscript pages on the table. It looked as though they'd been heavily edited—there were dark thick pencil marks through passages, notes scribbled in the margins. I wondered if that meant he was getting ahead with it. I hoped so.

I tried sitting on the couch, standing on the porch, but I couldn't bear the thought that inactivity brought on, so I started to clean up the kitchen. I found a towel and tied it around my waist to protect the skirt of my suit, and tucked the neckties of my green and white shirt inside my collar. It felt odd to be out here in stockings, odd to be working in the kitchen. Odd to be alone.

It took me quite a while to do even a cursory job—put a few things away, wash the dishes, wipe the counters. Through the back window I could see a stack of beer cases near the back steps of the verandah, and I put the empty liquor bottles and the beer cans out there with them. Outside, I looked out at the trees, down at the circle of stones that formed a fire pit near the bottom of the stairs—inhaling spring and country, and starting to feel better.

By the time I'd finished with the kitchen it was quarter to one, and there was still no sign of him. I'd made a new pot of coffee, and I poured myself a cup and wandered around a bit. I didn't know whether to feel worried or irritated at his absence: in fact, I was feeling neither.

As always, the area around his computer looked neat and tidy—it seemed to grow neater and tidier as the rest of the place got more and more disorderly, but that might have been an optical illusion. My notebook was lying on top of a pile of magazines and papers on the coffee table. I sat down on the couch, curled my legs back under me, and began to leaf through it.

It seemed impossible that it should ever turn into any kind of cohesive whole—into a book or even pieces of a book. It was a collection of impressions, of memories, of incidents embellished. As I read passages here and there I caught glimpses of it from the outside—sentences and phrases that appealed to me, others that did not—saw it the way that Zeke perhaps had seen it, that others outside my experience might see it. But I was not outside of it, and reading it pulled me not so much into it, as into Gran—into my time with her.

Holding the notebook, turning its pages, lifting out the scraps of paper and replacing them again, I saw that I'd done far more than I'd realized, but it was like daubing in spots of colour—there was so much left to do before the picture would be complete. My eagerness to work on the project had more to do with the individual daubs than it did with completing anything, and the new, larger perspective Zeke had given me just added to my weariness. I slipped the elastic bands back around the notebook and put it back down on the coffee table.

There was a thump and then a tap at the window behind me, and I jumped, twisting around to look. I'd heard no engine, nothing to indicate anyone was approaching.

Zeke grinned at me through the glass, then ran down the verandah and pulled the door open. Inside, he stopped on the doormat, threw his arms wide and said, "Maggie, my love. You're here."

I stood up cautiously. "I've been here for a while," I said.

"I've got it," he said, happily. "I've really got it nailed."

He came over to me, took me in his arms, hugged me, drawing himself and me tall with a long intake of breath. I felt the roughness of a day or two's growth of beard against my cheek, smelled fresh air on his flannel jacket.

"What have you got nailed?" I asked.

"Sit down," he said. "I'll tell you."

I wanted to know what had happened to his truck, where he'd been all this time, but I sat, and watched him pace, and waited.

"Okay," he said. "Okay." His eyes were bright with enthusiasm, but they also looked red and tired. "I told you that this novel starts where we started. At university, right?"

I nodded.

"Where we started with the group."

"Yes."

"Okay. So, the main character—Jeremiah. That's his name. He's the one we follow from that place, that group, into adulthood. And the point of the novel is that no matter where he goes and what he does, he can't leave that group behind, you see? He tries to break away from it—he makes the big break, never sees any of them again. But all of them are in him, and he can't run away from that."

"Sounds great," I said cautiously, unsure how I was intended to respond.

"It is," he said, intense. "But I realized that just telling Jeremiah's story from the inside's not enough. I've got to show him, too. It's been driving me mad for days. I don't want the distance of a third-person narrator, but we've got to see him from the outside. Out there…" he pointed in the direction of the window, "out there, I got it. I know what I have to do."

He paused.

I waited. Finally I said, "What?"

"A second narrator," he said. "A second first-person narrator."

"A second narrator," I said, still not comprehending the reason for his joy.

"Not all the way through. Just now and then. A chapter here and there. Weaving in and out like a braid. You see? He becomes the counterpoint to Jeremiah, this other guy. He shows us what we need to see."

He shook his head, looking far away. He was caught inside his work, caught inside himself.

He stopped, looking down at the papers on his work table, and shook his head. Turning, he leaned back against the table and closed his eyes. He put his hand up, rubbed the bridge of his nose, lowered his hand again. "There's a lot more I have to think about, but I know what I have to do." He opened his eyes and looked at me. "This is so… releasing. It is such a huge relief."

"Sounds like a huge novel, too," I said.

He shrugged. "I heard his voice out there. The other one. It's what I have to do." He came over, went down on his knees and put his arms around me. "Maggie, it's so good to be able to talk to you this way. About my work."

"Because I'm part of then—the place it started?"

"No, no. They're not real people any more, Maggie. Jeremiah isn't me, and the others aren't anyone you know. They've been transmuted by the writing." He put his head against my knee. "I was so glad to see your car when I came back."

Moved, I touched his head.

He looked up at me and rising, pulled his cigarettes from an inside pocket. He said quietly in a different voice, "Jeremiah's a great character, a great man. He's full of life. He looks to other people like he's done nothing, lived season to season and that's it. This other guy can show us what he's really done."

"Which is?"

He shook his head, put his fingers to his lips.

"Well, it all sounds very good," I said. "I can't wait to read it."

He found a lighter in the pocket of his jeans. As he lit his cigarette, he looked over at his computer and something flickered in his eyes: wariness or something.

I took a breath. "Zeke," I said softly, "I have to go."

His eyes lingered on the computer, then seemed to force themselves in my direction. "What?"

"I have to go," I said.

He looked up at me, looked around the cabin, out the window at my car. "Jesus. What time is it?"

"It's one thirty."

He stubbed out his cigarette and reached out a hand, pulled me up toward him. "Maggie. God, I'm sorry. You said you'd be late.… I just went out for a little walk."

I smiled. "You must have been gone for hours."

"I must have been." He shook his head.

"I thought you'd driven someplace. Your truck's not here."

He was looking at me as though actually seeing me at last. "You're all dressed up," he said.

"The interview. I told you."

"Oh, Jesus. Right. How was that?"

"Fine," I said, and nodded. If he'd been here when I got here, my control would have cracked at a touch, a look, a word. It might have been better. But I couldn't start that now: it was too late.

"Where's your truck?" I asked him.

He shrugged. "I couldn't fix it. Drove it into Waldham—when? Last night, I guess. Or the night before. No, last night. Thumbed my way back out." He looked out the window. "It's probably ready by now."

"Maybe they left a message."

He looked over at the phone and shook his head sadly. "No phone."

"What?"

"They cut it off. This morning."

"But I called you this morning."

He pulled me close to him. "You made it under the wire. Because you're magic."

"But, Zeke. You have to have a phone. What happened?"

I felt him shrug. "It's just a little mix-up. I'll attend to it when I go in to get the truck."

I stood back and looked at him. "Why don't I give you a ride?"

He looked at the computer, looked at me, shook his head. "I'll be okay," he said, and stuck a thumb out. "I'll get in the way I got out."

"But I'm going that way anyway."

"I'm not going now," he said. The softness had gone out of his face, and he said, "Don't try to organize me, Maggie. It won't work if you do that."

That statement or command or whatever it had been kept coming back to me as I drove, weary, back into the city. Outside at the car, he'd taken my hand in his, touched the tips of my fingernails with his fingertip and then his lips, looked up into my face and told me he was sorry. Sorry he'd snapped, sorry he'd squandered our time, sorry about the phone.

"It's okay," I'd said.

"I need you," he'd said.

"I need you, too," I'd told him.

Driving back, though, I still felt distanced from him. As I thought about how he'd let himself get lost inside his book, lost track of time, I resented and envied the permission he gave himself to float, to think and to imagine. Then, realizing that I'd left the notebook behind yet again, I wondered what that kind of freedom—time—would do to my writing about Gran. I tried to imagine having three days straight—or even more—when I didn't have anything to do but think about her—think about what I wanted to say about her, and how I wanted to say it.

I saw that you would enter another world in that length of time. Really enter it, as Zeke had done with Jeremiah. No wonder he didn't want to go and get his truck.

Time, and permission to let go. That was what I needed. Zeke would show me how to do it.

The phone was ringing when I got home, but I missed it and I leaned against the counter, unbuttoning my jacket, and waited for the message light to begin to flash. Instead, the phone rang again, and I picked it up. It was Bob Sanders.

"Maggie," he said, talking fast, sounding worried. "Thank God I've reached you. Archie's in some meeting and I'm sure as hell not calling the campaign office. You've got to get in touch with him right away—they'll put you through. They wouldn't me, and he's going to have to...."

"Slow down, Bob," I said. "What's happened?"

"It's the demonstration, Maggie," he said. "I've kept my ear to the ground. I still have contacts despite what Maxwell thinks. Contacts he'll never have in a million years."

"Bob...."

"Okay. All right. They've gone to another printer so it was tricky, but I found them out. I have people...."

"What was tricky?" I asked, impatient. "What other printer? What are you talking about?" I wished that he and Maxwell would sort out their own problems—or that Archie would—that they'd leave me out of it. I just wanted to be alone, to sleep.

"This thing is getting huge. There are organizers everywhere. You have to call Archie and tell him I've just found out that there are thousands of posters sitting in a warehouse with slogans on them—'enough's enough,' 'send a message,' ready for the demonstration –"

"And?"

"And they all have these little white parrots on them, Maggie. And under the little white parrots are little white letters."

"Letters?"

"A—B—T. Anybody But Townsend."

My heart stopped. "They can't do that," I said.

"Oh yes they can. They did."

29

I said I'd try to get in touch with Archie, but I didn't. How could I call Archie? I felt sick. Horrified and sick. I stood at the living room window for a long time, trying to think what I could do to stop this thing from happening. How many of them knew? Mark, certainly, he must have engineered it, and Fiona. Sylvie and Anna, too? How many of the others who'd been dropping into the Purple Parrot lately? Chatting with me, smiling at me, wondering inwardly at my stupidity. Blindness. Naïveté. My utter disregard for Archie's future.

The phone rang at some point, and I let it ring. Stood listening to it ring. Not moving.

Ben burst through the back door, excited—"Mom, Mom?" until I went to meet him in the kitchen. "Can I go to the hockey game on Saturday?" I looked at him for several moments trying to figure out what he meant—trying to imagine what he meant. All the tournaments were over.

"Please say I can go," he said, ten years old again. "Josh has tickets. Please?"

"What are you talking about?"

"The hockey game. The playoffs."

Not his team, the NHL.

Why not? No alarm bells. I nodded. "Sure," I said. "Why not?"

Elated, he was gone, pounding up the stairs to the phone, dragging his backpack with him.

I told myself to start on supper, but instead I wandered back to the living room, looked out at the cars arriving home from work, at children in the street on tricycles, with marbles, at two women chatting at the foot of a driveway. Normal lives. No answers there.

Ben yelled that his dad was on the phone and I didn't respond, didn't move, until he came to the top of the stairs and yelled again.

"Mom?!"

I went reluctantly to the receiver in the family room and picked it up.

"Hi, Archie."

"Bye, parents," Ben said cheerfully, and put the receiver down upstairs.

Archie said, "I won't be there for dinner." I heard in his voice that he knew, and that he was angry.

"Bob Sanders just called here," I said, my voice feeling thin and sounding sick. "Did he get hold of you?"

"He didn't have to. Victor got a call."

"I'm sorry," I said quietly. "I honestly didn't know."

"Maybe you should have," he said, and for the first time in many years, he hung up on me.

I replaced the receiver and looked at it. He meant that if I'd been so determined to keep working at the Purple Parrot, I could at least have done some good for him.

I'd been deliberately avoiding knowing anything there. I'd thought I was protecting him that way.

Protecting myself, more likely. Maybe he was right.

He was right.

I poured myself a drink and, like a zombie, went into the kitchen and tried to think what I could cook for Ben, tried to remember how long ago it had been since I'd last made him Kraft Dinner, couldn't, tried to calculate the damage I was doing to his physical well being with all these slap-dash meals, couldn't, poured myself another drink and put the water on to boil.

By the time the macaroni was cooked and I'd peeled a couple of carrots to go with it, I was feeling a little drunk. But I couldn't stomach even the thought of food, so I told Ben his supper was on the table and that I was going upstairs to change.

"Aren't you eating with me?"

"I had a big lunch," I said.

He knew something was the matter. When I came down again and plugged in the kettle for a cup of coffee, he started talking and he kept on talking, one eye on me, while he ate and even after he was finished. He talked about the hockey game, the team, some complicated three-way trade he thought they should have been involved in, never taking his eyes off me. He didn't ask me any questions. He knew I wasn't listening.

I made a second cup of instant coffee and went into the family room. He followed me in there as well, still talking hockey, flicking on the television set.

"*Simpsons*," he said. "Watch it with me."

"Not now," I said. "I need to do the dishes."

I felt sick and sad for him—sad because he knew something was the matter and was afraid to ask, and I wasn't helping him at all.

Finally I told him I was going for a walk.

"You want me to come with you?"

"No," I said, too quickly, astonished at his offer.

His face was wide open, begging to be let in.

I shook my head. "I just need to be alone for a bit, Ben," I said. "Think things through a bit."

"Is it the election?"

I shook my head again. "Everything is fine."

"Where's dad?"

"He's at work. In a meeting. With Mr. Maxwell."

I drew a deep breath to prevent myself from weeping. Ben, alone, hurt, aware but not aware—I wanted to protect him, comfort him. Saturday afternoon, the protest. Saturday night, the hockey game he was so excited about. I knew, as he did not, that he'd be preoccupied as he watched the game, his mind on his father's humiliation. How could I warn him of that?

Behind the couch, I bent and put my arms around him. "I love you, Ben," I said.

"I love you, too," he said.

"I'll just be a few minutes."

I pulled on my running shoes, pulled on a warm jacket, and went out into the night. I needed to talk to Zeke, not about this, but to talk to him, to hear his voice, to let his voice remind me that betraying people was not the only thing I did. I walked the three blocks to the convenience store, went in for change, then waited by the phone for ten minutes while a group of teenage girls made stupid faces and sounds into the receiver and looked at me with hostility. Finally they went away, and I stepped up, dropped my quarter into the slot, and dialled.

But Zeke's phone wasn't working any more. He'd told me that already.

Archie came in late and angry still, and I knew that he knew I was awake but neither of us let on, and he got in on his side of the bed and lay very close to the edge of the bed, not a word to me, not a touch, and was snoring steadily in five minutes.

I think I was awake all night.

When morning finally came, he left as silently as he'd arrived—me feigning sleep again for both our sakes. I had bitters and headache tablets for breakfast, got dressed, and started off for the Purple Parrot.

I intended to go in, pick up a few of my things, and tell Fiona I was leaving. I wanted her to know that I was furious—I wanted her to see that her betrayal of me, hers and Mark's, had forced me to betray Archie—but as I drove into Old Watchford, I knew I couldn't do it. I felt splintered, nauseated. Because of the lack of sleep, perhaps, I found I was more afraid than angry. One haughty look from her and I would collapse into myself.

Perhaps it had been intentional. The ultimate gash at a politician she didn't like, at a party she didn't want to be re-elected. So what if I'd been damaged too? If Ben had been? The accomplishment of her purpose was in sight: that was all that mattered.

And what of Sylvie and Anna? I'd thought of them a lot in the dark hours when I'd lain as still as possible next to Archie. Where had I got it in my head that just because they were older, they were kind? That just because they were awkward, they were guileless?

How long had this been planned? How long had I been making a fool of myself? I thought back to the day that reporter had come in, back to so many small incidents where I had smiled and wrapped parcels for those who would carry signs against my husband, and I closed my eyes in shame.

I turned out of Old Watchford and drove without direction for a long time. It was after ten: they'd be wondering where I was. Or they'd be coming to the awareness that I knew. How would they feel? Relieved that they didn't need to dissemble any more? The days when I hadn't been in must have been such a relief for them, allowing them to be free and open in their talk. I must have been a burden, not a help.

I thought back to the time before all this had started, to the curious little shop with its store of wonderful treasures and surprises, its gifts, its unexpected bits of art amid the kitsch and the plainly awful—back to the way I'd felt when I was working there, as though I had a toe-hold on something I wanted to be a part of. A world where meaning mattered more than appearance, where there was honesty, direction, joy.

At a coffee shop in an industrial area on the eastern edge of town, I asked for a phone book and looked up the address of Scales Printing and Graphics. I had never been there before, had no idea where it was, but I found I was within a few blocks of it, as though I'd intended to go there all along.

I'd always imagined that Mark's printing company would look a little like the Purple Parrot—dark, dusty, worn, with men in shirtsleeves, green plastic visors banded to their heads, pouring over sheets of newsprint under bald lightbulbs. Instead, I found Scales Printing and Graphics housed in its own building, a respectable looking brown brick structure surrounded by well groomed lawns, flowerbeds, young birch and aspen carefully planted, a few wooden picnic tables.

The day was warm and windy, blowing away the winter's dust, and I made my way past a slap-flapping Canadian flag on a tall pole to the entrance of the building. Its front, south facing, was brick and high glass windows. Inside, a wide staircase, stairs richly carpeted in blue, led to a mezzanine reception area where a young blond woman smiled at me and asked if she could help.

I'd called here often enough that I knew her voice and I felt disjointed at the contrast between the way I had imagined her—a vision that had involved dim light, another hanging lamp—and her reality, her brightness, the huge half-circle of a dark wood desk surrounding her—with phones, a computer monitor and keyboard, and neat stacks of paper in its smooth, cream-coloured well.

"I want to see Mark Scales," I said.

"I believe Mr. Scales is out at a meeting," she said. "Can someone else help you?"

I shook my head. "I need to speak to him. I'll wait."

I went to sit in one of the padded blue armchairs across from her. Looking a little unsettled, she asked my name and then called someone—Mark's secretary, perhaps—and told her I was there.

"He'll see you when he gets back," she said when she hung up, turning her attention to other matters.

Feeling grim, I settled in to wait.

The sun shone on my back through the high tinted windows behind me, and I gradually took in other details—tree-sized plants, real, well tended, two corridors leading off in opposite directions, one marked "Graphics" by a small rectangular silver sign with blue lettering, the other "Printing." Through glass doors I saw people coming out of offices, going into other offices. Well dressed. Young, most of them. Not one plastic visor, green or otherwise. The production rooms were out of sight, but I doubted there were visors there, either. Now I imagined them as they probably really were—huge computerized printing machines running smoothly, slickly, night and day.

The Purple Parrot wasn't going to pull this place down. No matter what happened: he wouldn't let it.

It must have been so much fun for him at the start—nice little hobby, a diversion of the kind the well-heeled seek when they take up painting, sit on boards, when their success is so well organized that they have time left over. Take on a sinking arts-and-crafts shop, right Mark? Hobnob with the creative community—better yet, be seen as its benefactor, while sharing none of its realities. This place is what counts, what pays the bills. Make sure the machinery runs smoothly, the furniture matches, the employees are happy. Different kind of people, these: they expect more out of life than artists. Expect benefits, pensions. Job security.

I took my coat off. I was getting hot—it must be close to noon, I thought—and suddenly I remembered Alana. I leapt up and told the blond woman I had to have a phone. She pointed at the one on the table right next to where I'd been sitting, but I shook my head.

"I need privacy," I said. "It's personal."

She nodded and stood up, came around her desk. Having dressed for the Purple Parrot, I felt out of place here as I followed her trim, short-skirted self down the "Graphics" corridor. She showed me into a small conference room with a round table and a phone, and graciously left me to it.

I sat down and dialled the number to Sanderson and Lebel. It was eleven thirty: we were supposed to be meeting in half an hour.

"Alana," I said when she came on the line, forcing a gruffness into my voice. "I feel terrible."

"You're sick?"

"Just came over me," I said. "I was going to come down anyway...."

"No, darling: absolutely not. I don't want you breathing germs on me. You sound terrible."

It occurred to me that her phone might be the kind that showed the number of the caller. "I was shopping—it just hit me. Maybe food poisoning, though I don't know what...."

"You go home and rest. We'll do this next week sometime. I'll be forty three for a whole year: there's certainly no rush."

"God," I said. "I'm sorry. Thanks. I'll call you."

I hung up the phone, stood, and turned.

Mark Scales was in the doorway, cool, handsome, richly, softly dressed as usual. I could see how his Old Watchford tastes suited him here at work.

He'd obviously heard at least part of the conversation, and he was looking at me with concern.

It all welled up at once—the posh surroundings, my slightly shoddy clothes, his having caught me in a lie and—at the sight of him—an overwhelming sadness at having lost the Purple Parrot.

"You bastard," I said.

"What are you doing here, Maggie?"

"You bastard," I said again, tears rising. I fought them down.

He furrowed his brow a little. "I'm not sure what...."

"Of course you are," I said, barely keeping hysteria from my voice. "Of course you know. You have a whole warehouse full of signs that are intended to sink my husband. To defeat him. To destroy him."

He didn't deny it.

"Why didn't you tell me, Mark? Why did you put me in this position?"

"What position are you in?"

"Oh, for God's sake. Don't be disingenuous with me."

He took a breath. "You didn't want to know. You told me...."

"You said it was a general demonstration, Mark. Nothing to do with him. You made me think...."

"It was. It was. This is a late development—since the weekend—we didn't tell anyone. It just became clear how we should approach it.... It had nothing to do with you."

"You could have called me, warned me."

"I sure as hell could not do that. It had nothing to do with you. If there hadn't been a leak somewhere, it would never have gotten out at all."

"Until Saturday."

He nodded.

"I've worked for you for three years. Mark, I trusted you."

"That's immaterial, Maggie," he said. "This is politics. It's a political issue—we're making a political point. One that needs to be made. And politics has nothing to do with people—as you of all people should know."

I looked away.

His voice softened. "It's a terrible thing when people get hurt, but they do. It's part of life."

I turned and hit him, hard, across the face. He didn't let himself react but I saw his cheek grow red.

I saw it grow red with pleasure.

"That's part of life, too," I said.

I didn't mean just the slap. I meant the way I felt about it: momentarily cheered.

30

The protest had been called for noon. Archie had gone out early without saying anything, and when I'd heard the front door close, I'd gone to the bedroom window to watch him leave. Victor had picked him up, and he'd taken his gym bag with him. I had no idea whether he intended to go to the Legislature and speak to the protesters or not. I hoped he wouldn't. I hoped that he and Victor would spend the whole day working out. Or hiding.

I'd told him I'd quit the Purple Parrot. There'd been no change in his expression, nor had I expected one. That was all we'd said to one another since Thursday afternoon.

Ben went out early, too, that day. Maybe he knew about the protest. Maybe he was just hoping that going to Josh's place would make the hockey game start earlier, or at least make the wait for it less long. Maybe he was trying to get away from his tense and silent mother. I didn't know. I didn't ask.

I wandered through the empty house, loathe to do anything but wander. In the rooms we occupied, things ticked and hummed;

in the deeper reaches of the house, a motor started, stopped. I felt disconnected from it all. The house might have belonged to someone else—and it seemed to me that it had belonged to someone else, once, that someone else had occupied my place in it before.

I allowed the reality that Archie might lose his seat. If he did, the defeat would not be only at the polls. Archie himself would be defeated: there was nothing he wanted to do except what he was doing now. But he had no say in the matter, and neither did Victor, and neither did I. His future was in the hands of other people, strangers. They might be wooed, even convinced—by either side—but they would make their own decisions, pass judgement, hand out sentences, on their own.

I told myself that whatever was happening at the Legislature Building at that moment was not my fault. The demonstration would have happened if I'd worked for the Purple Parrot or if I hadn't, and in exactly the same way. Whether two hundred people had come out or two thousand, they had nothing to do with me. But I had to take the blame for what had happened to this house. I was the one who had emptied it this way.

I felt sick for Archie. Having discovered what he'd wanted out of life, and having made it happen, he'd done his best with it. In so many other careers, the time and effort he'd invested would have given him seniority and tenure. Most people never even discover what they want to do with their lives, much less get a chance to live it. Archie had. If he lost, that would make it worse.

Archie's vocations and Zeke's were so entirely different. No one could take Zeke's writing away from him. No matter what he lost, he would still have the work he loved to do, because it came from within him. Archie stood constantly at the edge, dependent on the vagaries of others for the opportunity to do the work he loved.

And I bumbled around in the dark, turning over things and breaking them. I'd thought it was the woman beside him at the social gatherings, at the podium, that Archie needed, but I saw that it was the woman who would be waiting here when he came back alone. I hadn't seen that he might need my help. I had not considered that he might fail.

I had been prepared to leave him in victory; I had not been prepared for defeat.

It was nearly one o'clock when I turned on the television set—expecting, hoping to find golf and reassurance. I did not. All three local stations had abandoned regular programming to cover the protest. Never, a commentator said, in the history of the province had so many people gathered at the Legislature Building—as many as ten thousand, according to one estimate she'd heard. Behind her I saw faces, chanting, cheering faces, and a sea of signs—St. James signs, signs for other Liberal candidates and signs for New Democrats as well, but mostly the signs Sanders had told me about. They were dark purple, with white letters and a little white figure at the bottom right corner of each one—hard to make out on the screen. I knew what the figure was. I knew the letters beneath it.

I changed channels and found a helicopter view of the crowds that surrounded the Legislature Building, spilled out into the streets and down the bank toward the river. This reporter said that the scheduled speeches had just ended, that the protesters were now apparently waiting for someone to come out of the Legislature Building and answer them.

"There's a festive atmosphere down here," he said, "but it could get nasty if no one shows from government."

"It could get nasty if someone does," said another reporter's voice.

There was a tiny pause and then the first one said, "I guess that's true."

I flicked again. A political commentator from the university had been brought into a television studio and was being interviewed at the news desk; behind him, a large screen showed moving snapshots of the protest. The professor was explaining how Bellamy & Cato had galvanized right and left—bringing together business, unions, cultural activists and others. "Strange bedfellows," he said, "and an unusual phenomenon to be sure. But Bellamy and Cato seems to have been the final straw. There are people down there who have lost their jobs in recent years, whose husbands and wives and children have lost their jobs. People whose businesses have closed. And there are also a lot of people who support what the government has done, but want a new direction now. They're ready for better times."

"What are the protesters trying to tell the government?" the interviewer asked.

The professor nodded as though the question hadn't been as stupid as it sounded. "They want to send a message to the government—they want to say, No more cuts. And it looks as though they want to make Archie Townsend the bearer of that message."

"A scapegoat," the interviewer said.

"That's right. The government's going to bring in a huge majority—there seems no doubt of that. If they can defeat one candidate in one riding, they'll have made a statement."

On the screen behind him, a hand lifted the spigot on a coffee urn to produce a dribble for the Styrofoam cup that had been held out by someone else's hand to catch it. The camera panned back to show the people attached to the hands: Anna and Sylvie, grinning, shrugged, their hair ruffled lightly by a wind.

"How will the government react to that?" the interviewer asked.

"I imagine the Conservatives will distance themselves from Townsend as much as possible during the election. It'll be subtle, but you'll see it if you're looking. That way, they can say 'We hear you' to the voters without really losing anything."

The interviewer looked at the camera and said, "Now we go back live to the Legislature Building, where Liberal candidate Sharon St. James is about to speak."

I turned the television off. Behind Sylvie and Anna, I'd noticed a dark cloud climbing up the sky. It was the only hopeful sign I'd seen.

I put on a jacket and went out. I intended just to walk as far as the convenience store and try to get hold of Zeke. But his line was still disconnected and despite the black cloud in the south, which was growing bigger by the minute, I kept going.

I walked for half an hour before the sky broke open, soaking me almost instantly. I ducked into a small, nearly deserted bar to wait for it to pass. I sat by the window, my back to the television set, ordered a beer, and watched the rain pelt the streets. The sky was still heavy, a deep grey purple—this would keep up for a while.

I remembered a day like this when I was small, only it had been a thunderstorm that time, and I'd been hiding in the house, terrified of the approaching storm, the light and sound, desperate for Gran to come inside and be with me. Finally I'd crept to the window to look for her.

I was stricken by such darkness in the middle of the day, by the wiring white light in the distance. Gran was standing on her small stool, taking clothing off the line. Her newly laundered dresses—summer, light—and mine were whipped by wind—pale lengths of fabric beaten high against the blackness of the sky. Steadily, one by one she pulled these tossing ghosts to her, grasped and tamed them, then folded them into the wicker basket at her feet. In my memory she stands, pale herself against the blackness of the day, stands solitary and determined and untouched by the wind.

31

The Sunday edition of *The News* might well have been described as "The Townsend Edition." Half of the first section was devoted to the demonstration: it included reports and reviews of the speeches by Mark, several other "community leaders," and members of the opposition, interviews with protesters and political analysts, op-ed pieces, and eight or nine photos—including side-by-side shots of two wily entrepreneurs, one of whom had set up a hamburger stand at the demonstration and done a lively business, the other a busker in a top hat and short pants who'd made use of his trumpet to stir up enthusiasm and attract a little spending money—in addition to the half-page, full-colour photo on the front of the paper that showed thousands and thousands of people waving signs in front of the Legislature Building.

Archie's name was everywhere in the paper, but nowhere was the context positive for him. The consensus seemed to be that his political days were over, that he'd be cut loose by the governing party steamship, like some dead fish it had inadvertently snagged.

The rainstorm on Saturday afternoon had scattered the protesters before any government representatives could appear, and there had still been no official reaction—from the government, or from the Party. *The News* was highly critical of this silence—and in particular of Archie's silence. It was not as though he had not been given an opportunity to speak, they pointed out. Attempts had been made to reach him at his office in the Legislature Building, at home, at his campaign office, but he seemed to have disappeared.

I knew about those attempts to reach him—the phone had rung almost constantly from the time I got home from my walk until after midnight. At about eleven-thirty I'd started answering it again because I thought it must be Ben. It wasn't. Time after time after time it was a newspaper reporter or a television reporter or a radio reporter—not only ones from the local media, but from national ones as well—and all of them wanted a reaction. All of them wanted Archie.

Archie wasn't home, I told them truthfully enough, attempting to keep the hysteria out of my voice. I knew where Archie was—he and Maxwell were hiding ("meeting," he had called it) in the apartment of some friend of Maxwell's. He hadn't given me the number, so I was unable to call him to tell him that our son had disappeared.

I had assumed that Josh's parents would bring Ben straight back home after the hockey game, and when there was no sign of him by eleven, I turned on the television set to see whether the game had gone into overtime. It was twenty after eleven before the sports came on and they gave the wrap-up: it had been a standard three period game. It had started at seven, and that made Ben very late.

I called Josh's house and got no answer, and for ninety minutes after that I paced, my stomach in knots, my imagination spewing forth images of accidents, my heart coming to a standstill every few minutes at the sound of the phone—would it be Ben? Josh's parents? ("We're terribly sorry, but....") A hospital official? ("We're sorry that your son....")—screwing up all my courage before I lifted the receiver, only to find another reporter at the other end of the line. I wanted to scream at them that there was a personal emergency here, to shout at them to leave me alone, but I was afraid to do that, afraid to say it aloud, afraid to stir things up any more than they already were. I was frantic, helpless and terrified. And then they did stop calling, the reporters, about twelve thirty, and the silence was worse.

At quarter after one, Ben sauntered in the front door as though he hadn't a problem in the world. I threw my arms around him, and burst into tears.

"What's the matter?" he asked, drawing back to look at me.

I shook my head, trying to catch my breath.

"Is it Dad?" he asked. "Has something happened?"

"Your dad?" I wept at him, my voice suddenly released. "Your dad? It's you, Ben. Where the hell have you been?"

"Jeez, Mom," he said, his shoulders dropping in relief. "We got a pizza and went to Josh's place. He and his dad just drove me home."

"For three hours?" I asked. "A pizza for three hours? It's nearly two o'clock."

He shrugged, an edge hardening his voice. "There was a movie on TV. What the hell's the matter with you?"

"I've been sitting here since...." I shook my head as the tears started up again. He hated tears. I tried to stop, but couldn't.

He was looking at the stairs. "Where is Dad?" he asked.

"He's out," I said, gulping, fighting for control. "With Maxwell."

"Is he okay?" he said.

"I think so."

He put his hand on my shoulder. "I'm sorry," he said. "I was going to phone, but by the time I thought of it, I figured you'd be asleep."

The touch of his hand had set me off again, and I went to find the tissues in the family room.

"Look, Mom," he said. "You're tired. I think you should get some rest."

I nodded, then shook my head. Then laughed. "No. Wait a minute," I said, pressing tissues against my nose. "I'm still the parent here. *You* get some rest. Go to bed. And next time, phone—no matter what. You won't wake me up."

Archie came in at two.

"Hi, Maggie," he said, closing the door behind him. He looked exhausted and almost apologetic.

"Where the hell have you been?" I asked for the second time in an hour, but this time I wasn't crying.

"You know where I was."

"But I couldn't reach you there, could I? Our son's been missing and half the reporters in the country have been trying to get hold of you—and I can't even reach you."

"What do you mean Ben's missing?" he said, peeling off his coat.

"He was," I said. "He's home now. But he was."

He looked at the half-empty glass of scotch and water beside the armchair, looked up at my face.

"I thought Ben went to the hockey game," he said.

"He did," I said. "But he didn't get home until after one, and I've been worried sick, and the phone's been ringing off the hook with reporters. And you were—nowhere."

He looked at the glass again, then gave me a look of disgust and started up the stairs.

"Where the hell are you going?" I said.

"To bed."

"We need to talk about this, Archie."

"Lower your voice," he said. "You'll wake up Ben."

"Ben's not asleep—he just got out of the shower."

"You're drinking. I don't want to talk."

"He's not deaf, either, thank you very much," I said in a louder voice. I went to the bottom of the stairs. "I'm not 'drinking,' Archie: You make it sound so disgusting. I've been worried to death, and I'm having a drink. For God's sake, have you no concept of what you put me through tonight?"

He kept going up the stairs. At the top, he turned and said in a quiet voice, "Have you any idea what I'm going through?"

If I hadn't had the drink, I probably would have got in the car and driven out to Zeke and stayed with him forever.

Archie wasn't the only Townsend in the paper Sunday morning. Ellen Vandermeer's column was on the front page of the second section. It was everything Maxwell might have once dreamed it could be. She'd been fair and sympathetic, and she hadn't mentioned my tears or in fact that I'd talked to her at all. She'd used my situation as a springboard to a meditation on the dilemmas that could face spouses of politicians—she was careful to avoid the word 'wife'—reflecting that an individual's decision to step into the public eye was not without its unexpected repercussions. She came down firmly on my side when it came to sticking with my job—which seemed worse than ironic to me now—and then she shifted out of the specific again to explore how difficult it is to evaluate our obligations to our partners when they make decisions that affect our lives.

It was a beautifully written, if contentious, column—there was no doubt that the conservative element would disagree with her completely—but I still had the urge to find every newspaper in the city and tear it out before anyone could see it. I imagined the editor gleefully rubbing his hands together when he realized that Vandermeer's column—undoubtedly submitted before the protest—was about Archie Townsend's wife. What timing.

Archie spent most of the morning in his office on the phone—foregoing church for the first time in months, which amazed and relieved me. I couldn't have gone there with him that day—and then came out and announced that the two of us were going to the campaign office for the afternoon, and that I should tell Ben to get up and get ready because we were going to drop him off at Millicent and Edward's.

"They'll keep him for dinner, too," he said. "I don't want him here alone."

"We're all supposed to be eating there," I said, taking my cool tone from his: we were obviously not going to resume the animosity of the night before, but it wasn't over, either.

"I have to meet with Maxwell tonight, and I thought you might want to join me for that. You can go over there if you prefer."

Archie looked grey and exhausted.

"I'll stay with you," I said.

There were five reporters waiting for us outside the campaign office; aside from that, the place was like a mausoleum. While Archie talked to the reporters in his private office at the back, I made coffee and then looked through papers until I found the lists of people who'd volunteered to show up that afternoon for sign distribution, door knocking, to stuff envelopes with campaign literature. Rats from a sinking ship, I thought.

When the last reporter had left, Archie came out into the main office and sat down beside me.

"What did you tell them?" I asked him, standing up to get him some coffee.

"That the people had exercised their democratic right. That I wasn't concerned about losing my seat. The usual." He sounded gruff and tired.

"What about Bellamy and Cato?"

He sighed. "I'll get to that tomorrow. Victor and I have a few kinks to work out yet."

"Victor and you? What about the Party?"

He shrugged. "This is my little problem," he said.

"Are the papers right? Are they abandoning you?"

"They're doing what they have to do—we are doing together what we need to do. The most important part is the re-election of the Party. I'm just one candidate."

"But, Archie, the premier could...."

"Could what?" He looked up at me. "Get mixed up in this mess, too? I've talked to him. The problem is contained—and if I can resolve it myself, for myself, so be it. Otherwise...." He leaned back in his chair and closed his eyes.

"But it's your seat—your future."

He shrugged. "Maggie. It wasn't him who said that. It was me. If I go down, I'm not taking anyone with me."

"What if you reversed on the Bellamy and Cato thing? Maybe that would help. It would show you had listened to them. That you'd heard what the protesters were saying. Show that the Party had heard. You can do that, can't you, without their permission?"

He rubbed his eyes and stood up. "That's Victor's position, too. I still disagree with it. A principle's a principle."

I stood up, too. "Archie, you're being an idiot."

He turned away. After a long moment he said, "Thank you very much."

"I didn't mean that." I came around the table to face him. "Archie. Please. You're putting your neck in the noose—or at least not taking it out. This is your future. You want to be a politician more than anything in the world." I grasped the sleeves of his sweater in my hands and shook them. "Archie. If you aren't going to save yourself, who can?"

He stepped away, pulling himself free of my grip. "The

Bellamy and Cato contract was a sound government decision. I stick by it. I stick by my principles. If I lose as a result... I lose." He shrugged.

At that moment the front door of the office opened and an elderly couple came in, loyal campaign workers. Looking as though they were at a funeral, they came slowly up to Archie and shook his hand. They didn't say a word. The woman went back to the front door and flicked a switch, bathing the office in fluorescent light—I hadn't realized how dark it was.

"It'll be fine," the elderly man said to Archie when the lights were on. "It'll be fine, you mark my words. There's still lots of time till the election. Still two whole weeks. The memories of voters are short."

"Thank you," Archie said, and looked at me.

And so I thanked him, too.

Archie excused himself, saying he had some reading to do, and went into his office and closed the door. The older couple and I stuffed envelopes for an hour, talking about the weather, gardening, bird-watching—anything but politics. No one else showed up. I could see Archie through the glass window to his office. He was sitting at his desk, his head bent as though he were reading, but he didn't turn a page.

Victor Maxwell sauntered in—looking much the way Ben had done the night before, carefree and cheerful—just as Archie's official "Open Office" hours were coming to an end. He said he'd been out cycling and felt great. This started the older gentleman off on story of a cycling tour group he'd belonged to in England when he was young, and Victor wandered off toward Archie's office.

Archie looked up at him when he came in, and I at them: the one worn, the other full of vigour.

We boxed the envelopes and the older couple left, and then Victor and Archie and I went to find something to eat. I'd been thinking while I'd been working and chatting with the couple that if Archie weren't going to save himself, the rest of us were going to have to do it for him. But his spirits seemed to improve while we were eating. Victor—who reminded us twice that he'd never lost one yet—impressed me with his dogged good humour and determination, and when he finally backed off on trying to persuade Archie to reverse himself on Bellamy & Cato, we began to make some headway.

We decided to knock on every door we could possibly hit in the final two weeks—including a number of neighbourhoods we'd done already. Victor pointed out that the demonstration had made Archie a hot commodity, and that there'd be no problem getting him lots of local air time.

"You'll deal with it, then move on to other subjects. They'll hear you, your commitment and dedication, and they'll forget about the demonstration. Two weeks is forever in a political campaign. Trust me."

While Archie paid the bill, I went back to the campaign office to make sure the coffee pot was unplugged, and to pick up some papers I thought I could work on at home. Alone at last, my mind suddenly filled with Zeke. I missed him. I longed to see him, even for just a few hours. And I needed to get away from this insane, shifting sea, to breathe for a little while. He'd be expecting me on Tuesday, and I still couldn't reach him by phone. He didn't even know I'd quit my job.

I needed to tell him why I couldn't come out again until the election was over—explain what was at risk, how much I needed to help to fend it off—and I needed, for my sake as much as his, to show him how much I was going to miss him until I could be there again. He would understand; he had his book to work on. We would have time later.

I thought about Ellen Vandermeer's column. I was never going to go through anything like this again: when it came to obligations, I had reached my limit.

Tomorrow. Just for a few hours. I'd go out there one more time, just one.

32

Zeke was the only bright spot moving anywhere in my mind. From the moment I woke up on Monday morning, I was edging over obstacles, around them, through them, to the cabin. One final deep breath before the last long sprint.

Ben said he was sick and refused to go to school. I knew he was ashamed, not sick. I knew I should stay home with him, but I could not: I would be back soon. Just these few hours, and then I would be solid on my course. Solid for him, and Archie.

"Where are you going?" he asked me, looking over the back of the couch at me as I gathered up my handbag and my jacket. He looked thin and pale in his pyjamas, wrapped in two blankets in front of the television set. He was watching Mr. Dressup, and I remembered all those years, all those years ago, when Mr. Dressup had afforded me one small break each weekday morning. If only Ben were that small again, and I could hold him close.

"I have to go out," I said. "Just a few hours, Ben."

I'd made him chicken-noodle soup and left a sandwich in the

fridge, piggybacking on his charade to help myself out the door. But looking at his tousled hair, I could not ignore what I was doing.

"Grandma said you quit your job."

I came over and sat down beside him, tucking, smoothing blankets. "I did," I said. "I was afraid of what I was doing to the campaign by working there."

"Because of the protest."

I nodded. He knew more than I'd thought. What else had his grandparents told him?

I wanted to say that I just needed a little break, a few hours to myself, but I was afraid he'd take it personally, feel abandoned and rejected. So I took a breath and said, "I'm going to see Alana. She's having a few problems. She wants to talk to me."

"What kind of problems?"

I shrugged and looked away. "Adult problems."

"How long will you be?"

"I don't know." I calculated. "Two. I'll be back by two." I squeezed his foot, leaned forward and gave him a brief hug. "I'll bring you some Popsicles."

He nodded and I stood up, ashamed.

I will never lie to you again, I told him in my mind.

On the way out to the cabin, I justified. Ben was almost an adult. There were things he didn't tell me. He was safe and fed and well loved. I needed space as well. I wasn't just a mother. I was a human being. It was just for a few hours.

But I couldn't buy it, and the farther I got from the city, the worse it got. What if he really was sick? What if he started throwing up without me there? Such focused fears were woven into a tapestry of general unease, and when I reached the cabin, I parked out on the road—afraid, although the ground was dry and the sky clear, of getting stuck if I went into the lane.

When I reached the final bend in the lane, I saw that his truck wasn't there again. I felt relief—I could go back to the city right away, go right back to Ben—then, disappointment. I had to see him. I had to talk to him. I needed his arms around me. I needed to be with him. And then I realized the truck was probably still in Waldham.

Calling his name, I started up onto the verandah, but got no answer. I knocked on the door and called again. Pushed open the door, and called, and stepped inside.

The air in the cabin was close and heavy with stale smoke and the smell of days-old greasy cooking, and the cabin looked as though it had been ransacked. Books had been pulled from bookshelves to the floor, left open where they fell, the rugs were bunched and twisted, a chair near the kitchen counter had been overturned. There were empty beer cans everywhere, cold cups of coffee, saucers overflowing with the twisted ends of half-smoked cigarettes.

"Zeke?" I called, alarmed.

I heard a soft groan from the bedroom.

Half-expecting to find him bleeding in his bed, I pushed the door to his room wider with trepidation, and stepped in.

The thick smoke stink was even worse in there. Zeke was lying on his belly in a tangle of sheets and blankets, both hands pulling the pillows down over his head. An ashtray on the bedside crate was overflowing, and on the floor next to him was an uncapped, half-empty bottle of scotch.

He mumbled something I couldn't hear.

"What?"

"Close the fucking curtain," he said, moving his head just enough to let the words out.

I went to the window, stepping around books that seemed to have been scooped rather than moved from their bookshelves.

He rolled onto his back, still holding a pillow over his face, and groaned. He looked pale and child-like, lying there naked and in pain. Worse than Ben by far.

"Looks like you had quite the party," I said, coming around the bed and sitting on the edge of it. The smell of scotch lifted off his skin into my nostrils and I turned my head away.

He moved his head. "Can't talk," he said through the pillow. "Am sick."

"I see that," I said. I sighed and stood. "I'll get you some water."

I washed a glass in the kitchen sink and while I was waiting for the tap water to run cold, I went into the bathroom and looked in the cabinet for headache pills. I couldn't find any, so I rooted around in my handbag for the small packet I carried with me.

When I went back into the bedroom he was resting on one elbow, rolling himself a joint. I waited while he took a deep drag of the smoke and held it. He offered it to me. I shook my head.

The sweet smell took me back and back—I remembered seeing him through someone's kitchen doorway many years before, watching him take a toke mid-sentence, and then lean tall and straight against the counter before he let out the rest of his idea with the smoke.

Now he reached and took the two tablets from me and put them in his mouth, then took the water, downed it, and handed back the glass. He had another toke and then leaned back against the pillow and closed his eyes. After a minute or two he said slowly, "Better."

"You smell terrible," I said. I looked around the room. "This whole place smells terrible."

"I know," he said.

"What happened?"

Eyes still closed, he moved his head slowly back and forth.

I had to talk to him—to him, not to this zombie. I had to make him understand why I couldn't come back for a while. Even though I knew it wouldn't have mattered much to him if I left without saying anything, if I'd never arrived at all, I persisted. I got up and went over to the window again, pulled back the curtain and opened the window a crack to let some air in, then let the curtain fall.

"Zeke," I said, "I'm going out there and make some coffee, and I want you to take a shower." I turned around and looked at him. "Then we're going for a walk."

He groaned.

"You need fresh air. Jesus, Zeke. I've only been here ten minutes and I feel like my lungs are full of scum."

"Just a few more minutes."

I shook my head. Through the bedroom door I could see the shambles in the living room. "We're getting out of here."

He groaned again, but then he began to move. Slowly, but there was progress.

At the bedroom door, holding a dull beige towel around his hips, he looked out at the living room.

"Fuck," he said, putting his hands up and pressing down his head.

I waited until I heard the shower running before I went out to the kitchen. There, I moved a dog-eared copy of *Zen and the Art of Motorcycle Maintenance* off the stove, and opened the window over the sink to let in some more air. I couldn't find the coffee filters, so I emptied the one he'd used last time and rinsed it, then poured into it the last tablespoon or so of coffee grounds from a package on the counter. I dumped several tablespoons of instant into the glass coffee pot to make the brew strong enough. While I waited for the kettle to boil, I went outside onto the back verandah.

It was chilly there in the shade so I wandered around to the front, depressed at the sight of empty bottles, the scum of green across the water in the rain barrel, rusted tools and litter in the clearing, stumps and scrub.

We'd been walking in silence for quite a while, up the road, away from the cabin, when he finally turned to me and said, "What day is it?" and I knew he was on his way back.

"Monday," I said.

"Why aren't you at work?" His sunglasses were iridescent in the light, and I couldn't see his eyes.

He was wearing the long black coat over blue jeans and a dark blue sweater, and the clothes made him seem more substantial than he had when I'd found him in his bed. Still his face not only looked pale, but thin, and I was sure he was losing weight. In the kitchen I'd found some bread in his small refrigerator-freezer and had toasted two pieces for him, but he'd refused to eat them.

I told him about quitting the Purple Parrot, about the argument with Mark, about the protest and the article in the paper. The last was as much news to him as the first, and I thought about how much he'd isolated himself out here. Before, his insularity had been an attraction, and a protection, but today it seemed like tunnel vision, pig-headedness. I found myself growing irritated as I explained to him what was going on, and why. There was an election coming—how could anyone not care?

When I was finished talking, Zeke turned, and bent, and kissed me. There was still a faint liquor smell to his breath, and I suddenly saw him as someone else might see him—as a hung-over, seedy-looking, middle-aged burnout. I imagined Ben waking up in a room next to where his mother lay next to a tortured writer who turned the place upside down when he got drunk, and knew it was impossible. The whole thing was impossible.

A knot rose in my throat.

"You've got to get away from that shit, Maggie," he said, shaking his head. He rubbed his eyes beneath his sunglasses. "It's no good for you."

"Not yet," I said, swallowing. "Not yet."

"I want you out here with me."

"I know you do," I said.

"I need you, too. You've seen…. I need protection from myself."

We walked a little farther and then I said, "What happened, Zeke? Last week you were so happy about everything."

He let my hand go, pushed his hands into his pockets. "It got too big," he said. "They always get too big—need more time than I can give them. When I realized it was happening again, I just went off the edge." He took his hands out of his pockets and put them out, palms up, side by side, as though he were weighing something. "Time and money. It always comes down to that." He shoved his hands back out of sight.

"But you've done so much on it already," I said.

"Not enough. No where near enough."

"Is it that other character?" I asked him. "The new one you were telling me about?"

He kept walking, didn't answer.

"Why don't you just get rid of him, Zeke? Go back to what you had?"

He stopped and turned. "A book's not a tractor trailer," he said angrily. "You don't put pieces on and take them off again. I need his voice, and I hear his voice. I can't just get rid of him."

"Well, maybe…."

"Don't," he said, holding up a warning finger. "Just don't. I shouldn't have told you anything—I should never tell anyone about my work. You can't possibly understand it, Maggie. You aren't in there with me. I know it's too big. *I* know I can't do it." He jabbed a finger into his chest. "What *I* know is what is true." He spun in anger in the roadway, punching his hand up into the air. "It's brilliant and it's huge, and I have no fucking money. How can I write a sentence, knowing that? Knowing I can't afford to finish it? Jesus! It's killing me. It's killing me."

Suddenly he put his head back, and he shouted at the top of his lungs, "It's killing me! Do you hear that? You've got your wish, you bastard!" He whirled away from me into the middle of the roadway, threw his arms wide and his head back and, his coat blown open, shouted at the sky "Fuck you! Fuck you! Fuck you!"

I turned away, fearful that someone would hear him, see us, after all—perhaps fearful too, or superstitious, that he'd be stricken down where he stood. But whatever god or muse he was shouting at allowed him to keep it up until his voice was gone and, spent, he dropped his head and stood still, his breath coming hard.

He stood that way in the roadway until his breathing slowed.

"Did you call about the grant?" I asked him after a few minutes.

He glanced up at me and I thought he was going to laugh but instead, pulling the cigarette pack out of his pocket, he said, "Yeah, I did." He came and stood beside me and, cupping his lighter against the breeze, lit the cigarette. "I'll need to be here at least another six months before I'm even eligible, and it could be another six months before I find out if it's approved or not."

"That's not so long."

He shrugged. "I'm going to run out of money before that."

"How long before?"

He took a deep breath and said, "I've got less than a thousand left. That's it."

"Maybe it would be good if you had to get a job," I said.

He tensed and turned away.

"Wait a minute. Let me finish," I said. "What I mean is maybe you could find a job that just got you into the city once or twice a week. Or into Waldham or Osier, even better. I'm worried about you, Zeke, sitting out here all by yourself with no phone, no money, no contact with anyone but me, nothing to think about except the book. It's got to make everything seem worse than it is."

"When the writing's going well, Maggie, alone's the only place to be. You need to understand that."

"And when it's not, it makes you crazy."

We began to walk again. He shrugged. "That's why I want you here."

"For the bad times?" I said, angry now. "What about the good ones? What about those times when you do need to be alone? Will I just make myself scarce?"

He shrugged and put his arm around me. "We'll deal with that when we come to it." He took a deep breath. "All that matters is that I feel a whole lot better now." He put both his arms around me, pulled me closer, pulled my face into his shoulder. After a moment, I moved and he said, "No, don't." He took a deep breath and let it out. "I feel so safe right now."

I wanted to be gone.

I looked at my watch. It was nearly one o'clock and we were still a long way from the cabin.

"Drive me into Waldham," he said. "I'll get the truck, get some groceries –"

"Okay," I said. "Okay."

"Get the phone reconnected."

I looked at him. "How did you call about the grant, if the phone's not connected?"

He glanced at me, amused. "Walked down the way a bit. Farmer let me use his phone." He put his arms out wide and strode down the road ahead of me.

"I actually feel like getting back to work," he called back over his shoulder. "You're a miracle worker, Maggie."

"You'll get it done," I said.

"Sure I will," he said, turning, grinning, arms still akimbo, walking backward and still increasing the distance between us. "We'll get it done. Together."

"At least think about the part-time job," I called. "It's not such a bad idea. Until the residency thing kicks in. You're bound to get a grant after that. You're such a good writer, Zeke."

We didn't go back to the cabin, but took the car from the road where I'd left it. He remained cheerful on the way into town, thinking up ways to earn enough to stay alive and still leave time for his work. "I could sell those bookcases now they're empty," he said laughing. "Sell the books as well. Why not?"

His mood had improved so much by the time we reached Waldham that he wanted me to drive up behind the town to some secluded wooded area, but I told him I could not. I had to get back, I said, feigning disappointment, anxious to be gone.

I told him I'd see him in two weeks.

"The minute that election's over," he said.

"Well, within a day or so," I said. He'd never know when the election was over anyway.

I left him standing by the side of the road, bedraggled and pale behind his sunglasses, one hand lifted in farewell, and I wondered what in the name of God had happened that had made me lose my mind.

33

"Where were you?" Ben asked when I got into the house. He didn't appear to have moved from his position on the couch in the four-and-a-half hours I'd been gone, but he'd eaten the sandwich and the soup.

"I told you that already," I said, opening the box of Popsicles I'd bought and offering them to him. "Feeling any better?"

He was looking at me, not at the Popsicles. "Mrs. Drummond called."

I swallowed. On the way out to the cabin, I'd thought of phoning Alana to ask for her support, but it had seemed too complicated—it would have taken so long to explain, I couldn't explain it, not explaining would have been even more difficult, there was still the matter of her birthday which I'd done nothing about, I'd talked to her on the weekend, it was unlikely she would call today—and in the end I'd crossed my fingers and hoped she'd never know.

"Do you want one of these?" I asked him, holding out the box, a gnawing feeling in my stomach.

He took it and began to rifle through it. "You lied to me," he said.

"Not a lie exactly. I was just trying...."

He was looking up at me.

"Okay," I said. "You're right. I'm sorry."

He went back to looking through the box.

"I just needed some time alone. It's been a long, tough haul. Tense, you know?"

"Where'd you go?" He handed the bag back to me and leaned forward to crack his Popsicle in half on the edge of the coffee table.

"For a drive, out in the country," I said, taking the box back into the kitchen to put it in the freezer.

Like I'd ever go for a drive in the country by myself.

Thank God it was over. I hated this.

"Actually, lots of people called."

"What?" I came back to stand in the doorway. "Like who?"

He was looking at the television set, not at me: beyond him, a soap opera, mute.

He shrugged one shoulder. "Some lady from the campaign office. Then Mr. Maxwell. Said you had some stuff they needed."

The campaign materials. Still in the back seat of the car.

Oh, shit.

"Then Dad."

"What did he want?"

"To talk to you. I told him you were with Mrs. Drummond, and he got me to look up her number."

I went back into the kitchen and put the milk away. Came back to the doorway. Ben was flipping channels, but still hadn't increased the volume.

"And after that, Mrs. Drummond called."

"Right."

I felt sick, but he wasn't finished. "Then just before you came home, some man phoned and asked for you. Wouldn't leave his name. Said he'd phone back later."

He turned and looked at me over the back of the couch. Our eyes met, and it was like he knew everything, every nasty detail.

On the way to the campaign office, I stopped at a phone and called Zeke's number. It was still disconnected, which gave me a brief moment of hope that it hadn't been him who'd called. I took all the campaign stuff that had been in the car into the office, gave it to Dagmar, apologized and told her I'd be back later to help. I didn't ask where Archie was, or Victor.

I drove into Old Watchford, making a detour to avoid having to drive past the Purple Parrot, and went down the back laneway into the parking lot behind Sanderson and Lebel. It was just after four-thirty, but Alana's van was still there. I pulled into an empty stall beside it, turned the engine off, and waited.

She came out of the building about quarter to five, and I got out of the car when I saw her. She was surprised to see me, pleased, relieved.

"I've been worrying about you," she said, hurrying over to me and giving me a hug.

I began to sob and she moved her head back to look at me. "What's happened, Maggie? What the hell's going on?"

"Got a few minutes?" I said unevenly.

"Of course I do. Do you want to go for a walk?"

I shook my head. "Let's sit in my car."

I'd intended only to apologize to her for involving her in the lie, but when I started, it all came out. She'd taken my hands in hers when we got inside the car. I left them there, but I turned my head away while I told her about the Purple Parrot and the protest and everything that had happened in the past few weeks and, finally, about Zeke.

"It's over now," I said at last, turning to look at her.

I'd realized while I was talking to her that he still had my notebook. She must have noticed when that thought crossed my mind because she said, "You're sure?"

"Absolutely," I said. It was over. I was sure.

After a long time she said, "Are you going to tell Archie about this?"

I looked at her in horror. "Of course not. Why would I do that?"

She shrugged. "I guess I don't know. I just wondered."

I shook my head. "Archie and I—well, it's not like you and Vern. I've told you that before. If it was, this would never have happened in the first place." I took a deep jagged breath. "He's a good man. Archie's a good man. I'm not saying he's not that, and I don't want to hurt him. That's the last thing I want to do."

I asked her what she'd said to him.

"Only that you weren't with me. That there must be some mistake. Oh, God," she said. "Oh, Maggie." She shook her head. "I doubt it's over this easily—and it's going to be tough, no matter what."

"It'll be tough in my own head, but I got lucky in a lot of ways. It could have been much worse." I looked at her. "I feel terrible about mixing you up in it."

"If I'd known, I'd have been more help." She seemed to consider something for a moment, then she said, "I *am* pissed off that you didn't tell me earlier. I have to be honest about that. How many times have I seen you, talked to you since this started? You've been going through all this, and you haven't said a word."

"I was scared. I didn't think you'd understand."

"Why not?"

"Principles. Remember Swimmer?" I tried to smile. "You have more principles than I do."

She closed her eyes and pressed her lips together.

"Not that I don't envy you your principles. I do."

She opened her eyes again and looked at me. "You've known me a long time. Am I that one-sided? I might have understood— I do understand—at least how you feel, if not what you did. You should have given me a chance."

I closed my eyes. "I'm sorry."

"Look," she said, leaning over and putting her arms around me. "I'm here for you, and I always will be. You caught me off guard, that's all."

I nodded.

She sighed. "I have to get going. Are you going to be all right?"

I nodded again, then pulled back to look at her. "You're not going to tell Vern about this, are you?"

"No," she said, "I'm not. Now there's someone who really wouldn't understand."

I smiled.

She sighed and picked up her purse. "Anything you want me to do?"

I shook my head. "It feels better just to have said it."

It did. I felt unburdened.

She opened the car door. "Just don't use me as an excuse without warning me in future."

"I'll never use you again," I said, shaking my head. "Never use anyone again."

I was certain that was true.

34

The next ten days in my memory go past as a single, long and hectic push toward the finish line. I spent every day and evening at the campaign office, and I must have knocked on close to a thousand doors. Archie and I went out separately now for the door knocking so that we could cover more territory, and there were several other door-knocking teams as well. I was nervous at the beginning, but Bob Sanders frequently came with me and it got easier with time. When asked, I found myself delivering the Conservative campaign platform with ease and with conviction, and Bob helped me pull myself together and keep going when things got tough. I was determined to get Archie re-elected: that helped pull me through as well.

Victor was admirable, a whirlwind of energy and ideas. As promised, he managed to get Archie on almost every radio and television station in town in the first few days after the protest, and he'd schooled his candidate well in making the best use of these opportunities. Archie managed with surprising dexterity and calmness to answer questions about the demonstration and the threat to his seat, to stress the importance of the party over the candidate, and to move the interviews onto broader campaign territory.

The campaign workers who'd been spooked by the demonstration gradually returned, and our spirit of optimism seemed to come back with them. One day soon after the protest, when someone was making final arrangements for the hotel ballroom we'd booked for election night, I remember listening to his end of the conversation and noting that he wasn't referring to it as the Victory Party any more. But in the days afterward, when Archie was doing such a great job with the media and everyone was working so hard on the campaign, the term gradually came back into use.

Part of it was Victor, who referred to the Victory Party almost every time he gathered us all together for our daily—and sometimes even twice-daily—motivational talks. He'd stand on a table and punch the air and leap down onto the ground and punch it some more, and leap to a chair, to another table—If we just do this and this and this "we're going to win and win and win!"—and everyone would cheer and clap and believe him, and then we'd all get back to work. Even Bob Sanders and Archie's dad at last agreed, albeit grudgingly, that Victor was finally earning his keep. Not that they liked him any better for it, it was clear, but they seemed to be relieved.

To Victor's glee and the more private relief of other of Archie's campaign workers, five days before the election a young man stepped forward and announced himself to the media as the unsupported illegitimate son of the Liberal candidate in the riding next to ours. Victor was convinced this would cast a pall on all the Liberal candidates in the city, particularly in light of their push to make non-custodial parents more legally responsible for the well-being of their children. St. James, the Liberal in our riding, was Archie's only serious competition; Victor was taking bets that the other two candidates would collect less than a thousand votes between them.

We lived and breathed the campaign, often sending out for pizza or picking up hamburgers rather than going home for meals. Ben came and went by bicycle pretty much as he pleased— unwilling to stick around the office too much or to complain about having been abandoned because he knew he'd be put to work. I don't know how many times I promised him, home for an hour or so to run a few loads of laundry through or to toss out and replace expiring food in the refrigerator, that after the election was over, he'd have a full-time mom again. Finally, he asked me to stop saying it.

"I don't need a full-time mom," he said.

Archie was totally focused on the campaign, distracted by it even when we were alone, which wasn't often. He never once mentioned or referred to the afternoon I'd gone missing. Maybe, I thought, he'd decided Ben had been wrong or confused, that I'd meant some other female friend—but I didn't know for sure. If he ever mentioned that afternoon, I was ready to give him the same answer I'd given Ben, but I couldn't bring myself to raise the subject.

I thought about Zeke a lot, and dreamed about him several times. My queasiness about his behaviour the last time I'd been out there began to fade—he was an artist, after all, allowed to go off the rails from time to time. I missed him, and found myself aching for the mornings and afternoons of lovemaking and possibility we'd had before things went off the track. I'd felt beautiful and talented out there, and two decades younger. He'd made me feel that way.

I missed his arms around me, the long angle of his hip and leg beside mine in his bed, the look in his eyes when he was thinking about his writing, the small scar above his eye. His freedom and his vision. The memory of him standing in the roadway, his head back, his coat flared out, shouting at the sky, the gods, made me smile.

The Sunday before the election, there was an all-candidates forum at a community centre not too far from the campaign office. I hated all-candidates forums—they often got raw and nasty—and I'd managed to avoid the two previous ones, which had, but Victor insisted I be at the one that day.

Archie's parents were there as well. It had been weeks since we'd had a regular Sunday dinner together, and we decided they'd come home with us afterwards, and we'd order Chinese food. We had the sense that we could take a small breather after the forum, then give the final push on Monday. Tuesday, it would be done.

Archie was already up on the stage when I got there, seated behind a long white-clothed table along with the three other candidates and the moderator. There was a microphone at each seat, and two were placed in the aisles of the hall for questions from the audience. Archie, impeccably dressed in a grey suit, looked relaxed and handsome. He was chatting amiably with Chet Markham, the Socred candidate, who was seated to his left.

The auditorium was almost full. I put my jacket on the seat Victor had saved for me next to his, near the front, and turned to locate Edward and Millicent, who were several rows behind us. I waved at them, then I went to find a bathroom.

I could still taste the bitters I'd swallowed before I left home, and I had the bottle in my handbag in case I needed another shot later on. I was nervous, but I kept reminding myself that according to the latest polls, the Conservatives were still miles ahead everywhere in the province, and of Victor's theory that the demonstration had allowed people to get the urge to protest out of their systems, that even its reverberations were behind us now. In the bathroom, I smoothed my hair, straightened my suit, and prepared myself to go out there and look like the auditorium was the best place on earth to spend a Sunday afternoon.

On the way back to my seat I ran into Edna Lazenby. I hadn't seen her since the night of the Stovers' party, but she was wearing one of Archie's buttons, and she seemed pleased to see me.

"Isn't this exciting?" she said, looking around the auditorium. "I just love political campaigns."

"I'll be glad when it's over," I said, looking down at her red crimped hair and thinking that it looked exactly the same as it had the last time I had seen her. Not a neat crimp less or more, I was sure of it. It was as though she kept her scalp on a shelf and pulled it on each day, but I could see the scalp itself so it couldn't be a wig.

"I'm sure you will, dear," Edna said. "But it looks as though he's survived your little episode quite nicely."

"My little episode?"

"It did look as though you were working for the opposition for a while there, didn't it?"

"I was absolutely not—"

"Oh, I know you weren't, my dear. I'm just saying how it looked."

She patted my hand. "Don't worry. He'll be fine in spite of it."

The moderator called for order and I made my way to my seat. Sitting beside Victor didn't make me feel any better: his legs were crossed and his right foot was moving up and down. He was nervous, too.

The moderator explained that there were four topics that each candidate would address on a rotating basis, starting from a speaking order that had been drawn from a hat, for a maximum of three minutes each. After the introductory speeches, there would be a break, followed by questions from the audience.

The candidates were now rifling through their notes. Archie, straightening his tie at the same time, looked relaxed and self-confident. Sharon St. James, on the other hand, looked tired and her mouth betrayed her tension.

The first topic was education. Janine Lampert, the New Democrat, extolled the virtues of an educated populace, insisted that education must be universally available, and began to attack the Conservative record on education until she was finally brought to a halt by the moderator well after her allotted time. The applause was friendly, but not enthusiastic.

St. James shook the same tree, but started farther up the trunk. The tension I'd seen earlier manifested itself as anger as she denounced the short-sightedness of the Conservatives, citing cuts and legislative changes affecting schooling from kindergarten to university. She was eloquent and forceful, and she was rewarded with several bursts of spontaneous applause. I began to feel uncomfortable again, and focused my attention on maintaining my composure as she wound up by enumerating the Liberals' plans for educational reform—or "restoration," as she called it. St. James finished in exactly three minutes, and when Archie began to speak, the applause for her had not yet stopped.

Archie took an avuncular approach, suggesting more with his tone than his words that the previous two speakers had no clear grip on reality. He explained, as if he were talking to Ben, why it had been necessary to introduce a program of restructuring and reorganization in the educational system, showed that these measures had been in line with the contributions made by other sectors to the province's debt reduction program, and gave examples of how private enterprise was stepping in to pick up the slack by funding school-based programs. He quoted new statistics to show that the province's students remained competitive on a national level, and he explained that with new revenues, some areas previously curtailed could be given another look during the next four years.

The audience was attentive, quiet, polite, and I began to breathe again. But just as the moderator was lifting his hand to show that Archie's three minutes were done, a voice at the back yelled, "What about communications, Townsend? You gonna give them another look?" And another voice shouted, "Yeah! What about Bellamy and Cato?"

I closed my eyes as the moderator called for quiet. After a moment, he was granted it, and Chet Markham was allowed to speak.

On the next subject, which was health care—a red-flag topic even at the best of times—Archie was to speak second, and my heart was pounding before he started. Sure enough, the heckling started as soon as he began—"Bellamy and Cato" "Bellamy and Cato" from the back, over and over again. I turned in my seat and saw about twenty people standing along the back of the room, pumping up and down the familiar purple signs with the little white parrots on them. As I turned again toward the front I began to wonder if Mark and Fiona were back there, or Anna and Sylvie. I didn't want to know.

It took the moderator several minutes to regain control. All four of the candidates were watching the demonstrators, Archie looking angry, the other three quite cheerful.

When it was quiet enough to hear him, the moderator asked Archie if he would be good enough to address the Bellamy & Cato question, so that we could get on with the forum. That set everyone off again. The group with the signs cheered, but a lot of other people in the audience shouted their disapproval at allowing the protesters to have their way, allowing them to disrupt the meeting.

Archie straightened his tie and stood up.

Victor's foot was going up and down, up and down, and I was so nervous I had to press my hands into my lap to prevent their shaking from being visible.

By standing, Archie had removed himself from the range of his microphone, and he spoke loudly and clearly to make himself heard at the back.

"I absolutely will not speak about Bellamy and Cato. I have addressed it far too often, and the issue is irrelevant to most of the people in this audience. I have been asked to speak about health care and that's what I will do." People near me applauded and cheered, but the ones at the back started booing, and someone yelled, "Chicken!"

"Bellamy and Cato and health care are the same!" someone else back there shouted. "They're about people losing jobs!"

There was a lot of noisy support for that—some of it from the audience now as well as from the back—and other people were shouting at the moderator to get them to shut up, and the moderator started shouting into the microphone, yelling at everyone to sit down and be quiet.

A steady chant emerged from behind all the confusion, and gradually picked up steam. "Anyone but Townsend. Anyone but Townsend. Anyone but Townsend."

Horrified, I kept my eyes on Archie. He was still standing, and he was talking calmly about hospitals and home care. It was almost impossible to hear him and nobody but me and possibly Victor, his foot still moving, was likely even trying to listen to him anyway.

The moderator banged on the table and called for order, but the anyone-but-Townsend chant kept up, and other people continued to yell at one another and at Archie, and then suddenly things got really noisy at the back and the chant stopped, and Archie, looking surprised, finally stopped speaking and just watched what was going on back there. I turned around as well.

Someone had called the cops, and about four of them were trying to wrestle the protesters out of the room, and the protesters were protesting that, and cameras were flashing everywhere. Suddenly, it seemed, everyone was quiet. My heart was still pounding hard, but the police gained control quickly and the moderator said into his microphone that the forum was over, and around us people started pushing chairs back, talking quietly as they left. I saw that two uniformed policemen had appeared on the stage, one at either end of the candidates' table.

Archie still stood, his shoulders straight, looking stolidly out toward the auditorium. I saw a tiny muscle in his jaw move but that was all.

"Sit still," Victor said to me, and I did sit still, for maybe fifteen minutes more until the room was finally cleared of everyone but the candidates and their teams.

"Can we go now?" Janine Lampert asked.

"Give me a minute. I'll find out," said one of the cops, who left the stage and walked across the auditorium and went out through the doors at the back.

"Isn't politics fun?" Chet Markham said.

"I suppose your people had nothing to do with this," Victor said mildly to St. James' manager who was sitting a few seats away.

She glared at him. "We don't need to get underhanded," she said. "This will be a cake-walk anyway."

I looked around the room, toward the double doors at the back where a few people were still milling about. There was no sign of Archie's parents, and I hoped they'd already gone to our place, out of harm's way. Archie had finally sat down and was now gathering his papers together as though nothing had happened.

The cop finally came back and said that we could leave if we wanted to. "There are still people out there, out front—reporters and whatnot. But it's quiet. Nobody's very tense."

"They've done what they came to do," Victor said quietly.

We stood up, waiting for Archie to join us.

"Victor," I said quietly, turning to him, "tell me again that you've never lost one yet. I need to hear it now."

He looked across at me, pulling on his cuffs, and smiled. "I've never lost one yet," he said. "That make you feel any better?"

"No," I said. "It doesn't."

35

Millicent and Ben were playing double solitaire at the dining room table when I got home. Edward was watching television.

"It'll be all over the papers tomorrow," Edward said glumly. "It's the end of the road for him."

"Hush," Millicent said. "Don't say such things. You're alarming Ben."

"I hope he loses," Ben said flatly.

"This never would have happened if Sanders had been running the show," Edward said.

"It was a government decision," I said wearily, hanging up my jacket. "It had nothing to do with his campaign manager."

I went upstairs to change out of the suit and into jeans and a sweatshirt. When I came back down to the kitchen, thinking of ice and drinks, the phone rang.

"Some guy's been calling you all afternoon," Ben said, looking over at me. "Wouldn't leave a message."

There can only be so much adrenaline in one person's body,

and you'd think after it's pounded around a system a dozen times in one day it would lose some of its power, but it flooded me again as I reached for the extension on the counter.

It was Josh, for Ben.

I handed over the receiver, collected a tray of ice, and went into the dining room. "A drink," I said to Millicent and Edward. "I think we could use a drink."

Why would he be calling? Why now? Oh, God. Why now?

"Where's Archie?" Edward asked.

"He'll be here soon," I said, stepping down into the family room. "What would you like, Edward?"

"We didn't order dinner," Millicent said. "I didn't know what we should get."

"That's fine," I said, attempting to keep my voice even. Who cared about dinner at this point? "We'll wait till Archie gets here."

"I wonder what he'll do," Edward said. "He can hardly go back to teaching."

"He's not going to lose," Millicent said. "It's unthinkable."

The front door opened and in the diversion caused by Archie's arrival, I poured myself a sherry and drank half of it down.

Edward was pestering Archie about Victor—"You could have won this thing"—and Millicent told him to calm down and be more positive for a change.

Archie hung up his coat in the front closet, and strode past his parents and into the family room. I moved away from the liquor cabinet with my sherry, and Archie took my spot and started dropping ice cubes into glasses. We didn't look at one another.

Edward followed behind, still nattering at Archie.

"Just be quiet for a minute, Dad," Archie said. "Do you want a drink?"

"Yes I want a drink," his father said. "And don't tell me to be quiet. This is a disaster, Archie. You made a big mistake."

"The moderator should never have let it get out of hand," Archie said, pouring scotch into a glass and handing it to Edward.

"That's not what I'm talking about," Edward said.

Ben, who I'd been hoping would stay on the phone, appeared in the doorway to the kitchen. "What are you going to do for a job?" he asked his father.

"You be quiet, too," Archie said to Ben, handing a sherry to his mother.

He poured himself a soda water, no alcohol.

"Maggie," Millicent said, her cheer sounding slightly forced now. "We'll order everyone's favourite. That'll make us feel better. Let's get out a piece of paper and make a list."

"I'll get you some paper," I said. "You can make the list."

I went into the kitchen and dawdled near the phone where the paper and pencils were kept, sipping on the sherry.

"I was pretty scared," Millicent was saying. "Worried about you, Archie. Things were getting violent."

"Oh, phooey," Edward said. "These things get hot, but they don't get violent. It's the fallout that worries me. All over the papers in the morning—day before the election. That's no good at all."

"I don't want to hear another word about it," Archie said. "From anyone. It's not over until it's over. Isn't there something else we can talk about?"

There was a moment of silence, and then Millicent said, "Well, of course there is. There's dinner. What do you want, Archie? You like egg rolls, don't you?"

"I haven't eaten an egg roll in ten years," Archie said, his voice suddenly sounding tired. "They're fattening."

"Then what?" Millicent asked. "How about you, Ben?" She called, "Maggie, where's that paper? Time to make a list."

"Onion cakes," Ben said. "With hot sauce."

I came back with the pencil and paper and handed them to Millicent. "We could just order dinner for four or something," I said.

"But there are five of us."

I closed my eyes for a moment, opened them. "I'm sure they'd make enough for five if we asked them."

Millicent looked thoughtful, then shook her head. "They always put chicken balls in the standard orders. Do you know how much cholesterol there is in chicken balls?"

I suppressed a laugh that I knew could send me into hysteria. "All right," I said. "You go ahead." I was feeling dizzy, even from the one glass of sherry. "You and Ben decide."

"Of course that Purple Parrot business didn't help," Edward said to Archie, with a glance at me. "That was unfortunate." He looked at Millicent. "Make sure they don't put in any MSG."

"Are you saying this is my fault?" I asked him.

"Of course he's not," Millicent said. "Onion cakes and what else, Ben?"

"Hot sauce."

"No. What else for food."

"I'm not saying that," Edward said, "but it was unfortunate. Archie might have looked stronger otherwise."

Archie was standing near the liquor cabinet, glass in hand, lost in thought. I wondered what was going through his head. Was he thinking about his future, his alternatives? Was he feeling his life come crashing down around him, wondering what the hell he'd do?

The phone rang, and my heart stopped as I realized Archie was going to get it. He bent to pick up the receiver next to him. Whoever was at the other end of the line spoke for several moments. I couldn't take my eyes off Archie and he slowly lifted his eyes to meet mine.

"It's for you," he said.

I nodded, the rest of my body frozen for a moment. "I'll get it in the kitchen."

I walked as if through batting into the kitchen and picked up the receiver.

I could hear him breathing, or Archie breathing, or both of them. "Hello," I said.

"Mrs. Townsend," Zeke said.

"Yes," I said.

I heard Archie replace the receiver in the other room.

"Are we alone on the line?" His voice sounded sepulchral, slow.

"Yes," I said cautiously.

"Good," he said. Then paused, then said, "I need you to come out."

"I can't," I said, forcing cheer into my voice. "Not now, I'm afraid. We've got family over."

"You must. I need you to be here."

"Why?" I said more quietly, alarmed by the way his voice sounded—he was more than drunk, deeper than drunk, farther away than drunk.

There was no answer, and there was silence in the other room as well. I knew they were listening to me, curious. What had he said to Archie in those long moments?

In the quiet, I could hear my heart pounding and my skin was damp and cold. Wildly, I thought of simply hanging up.

"Please," I said quietly, swallowing. "Can't you just tell me what's happened?"

"I'm scared," he said. The eerie, measured emptiness in his voice frightened me as much as the words.

"Of what?'

He didn't answer.

"An hour," I said, taking a deep breath. "I'll be there in an hour. Just wait for me, and I'll be there."

I heard him replace the receiver.

I took another deep breath as I hung up the phone. I stood in the kitchen for several minutes, trying to think of how I could talk my way out of this one, knowing I could not.

"Beef and pea pods," Ben said quietly. It was the first sound I'd heard from the family room since my conversation with Zeke began.

"Righto," Millicent said. "Now we're getting somewhere. Grandpa likes chow mein."

She was carefully writing it down when I came into the dining room. The other three were looking at me: Edward, Ben and Archie.

"I have to go out for a little while," I said.

"Now?" Ben said, and the thinness of his voice must have reflected what he saw in the expression on my face. "Why now?"

"We haven't even eaten dinner," Millicent said, looking up from the little piece of paper. "What's happened? Tell us what has happened."

"You go ahead without me," I said. "I've got this friend.... In serious trouble. I've got to go and help."

"Mrs. Drummond," Ben said insistently, staring at me hard. I shook my head. "No. It's someone else."

"Who?"

"Archie?" I said. "Can I talk to you for a minute?"

I collected my jacket and he followed me outside.

When I turned to speak to him, he was standing between me and the light from the house and I could barely see his face. He was on the step, I was on the ground, and he seemed to tower over me, a pillar.

"I need to explain," I said, but I had no idea what I was going to say.

Archie put out his hand as though he were going to touch my shoulder, then he let it drop.

"He said he was a vacuum-cleaner salesman," he said, his voice even. "He said he'd talked to you earlier this week, that you'd asked him to call back. He said his name was Avery. I think he was drunk." Archie took a breath, raised his head. "If he's not a vacuum-cleaner salesman, I don't want to know about it until Wednesday. Do you understand that?"

I nodded.

He nodded, too. "Then go."

"What about you?" I asked, my throat tight.

"I'll eat. Then I'm going to work out at the club."

My skin felt clammy, cold in the evening air. I slipped my jacket on.

He said, "At least it all makes sense now. Finally makes sense."

"What does?" I said, buttoning. I looked up at him.

He lifted a shoulder. "Everything that's happened in the past few weeks."

"It's not that way," I said. I took a breath. "This has nothing to do with the protest, the Purple Parrot—nothing."

"I told you I didn't want to talk about it."

"Then don't say 'It makes sense'. That kind of statement invites discussion. Argument. Something."

He sighed, then shook his head. "All right. It does not make sense. All right?"

For several moments we stood like that, his eyes unreadable in the shadows, but after all these years I knew what would be in them. Nothing. No pain. No anger. Not even condemnation. He wouldn't let those feelings into his mind, at least not yet, and he wouldn't ever let himself show them on his face.

When at last I turned and began to make my way down the sidewalk to the car, I could feel those eyes still on me—making me smaller and smaller as I walked away.

36

I drove up the highway fast, aching at what I'd left behind me, afraid of what I'd find ahead. I pulled over to call him from a phone booth, first in Osier, then in Waldham, but his number just rang and rang.

After Waldham, I found that familiar landmarks had disappeared into the dark, and I slowed, sped up, slowed, sped up, looking around for buildings, signs, a fence that might jog my memory and send me forward with more confidence—fearful of the time my indecision was costing me.

Finally I found his laneway and turned in, and as I did I saw the light from a fire flickering through the trees. I inched the car along the rutted path, sure he'd set the place aflame and at the same time willing him to appear in my headlights, vision and energy restored. As the trees began to thin into the clearing I knew that the fire must be in the pit beyond the cabin, that reflections of its light were licking up the branches of the trees.

I pulled in beside the truck and leapt out of the car, ran into the dim-lit cabin, calling his name—calling as I pushed open his bedroom door and flicked the switch and saw that he was not there in the tumble of sheets and blankets and the clutter of books and towels and cans, calling as I made my way through the devastation of his living room, which was now complete—he'd pushed over his worktable, and his computer lay smashed and broken in pieces on the floor.

Light danced through the back window, and I heard the crackle of the fire.

"Zeke!" I shouted as I ran to the screen door and pushed it open. "Zeke!"

He was on the ground on the far side of the fire, leaning against a log, his hand around a bottle in his lap. His wide-brimmed hat was on, pulled low, and in the poor light cast by the small fire, it looked like he was sleeping, but when I called again he didn't move. I ran down, around the fire pit, and kneeled and shook him. No response. I knelt closer and felt his slow breath going in and out.

Enraged with him now, I pressed my hands against his shoulders, pushed and pulled him, trying to shake him awake, pushed and pulled and shook until I could move my arms no more. I sank down onto the ground beside him and wept against his slowly moving chest.

Gradually I became aware of our surroundings, saw in the dimness that the ground was littered with white papers, folded papers, some of them near the embers at the edges of the fire, some resting against the logs that formed a circle around the pit—still others scattered here and there around the clearing. Some were neat paper airplanes, others clumsy shapes, folded only once or twice.

His hand lay across a stack of papers at his side, cupped up, and on the ground beside it there was another bottle, empty. A finger of flame went up and I saw the markings of his paper aircraft, the heavy black lines across his text.

I saw that I must leave him the way he was—wrap his coat around him, build the fire up to keep him warm, and then sit with him till he woke up. I hoped it would be many hours before he came around: that sleep would start to heal him on the inside before he could see what he had done.

Shifting to get up, to look around for firewood, I reached out and touched his forehead and found it cold. I ran my hand down his cheek, along his chin. His face was cold and damp, and his breathing seemed to have grown more shallow. Alarm set in again as I looked down at the bottle in his lap, the empty one beside his hand.

"Zeke!" I shouted, grabbing the collar of his jacket on each side and pulling his face close to mine. "Zeke!" I shouted at him. "Wake up! Wake up! Wake up!"

He was so heavy that I couldn't pull him enough to get him sitting, much less standing, so I leaned him back again against the log and ran inside to find the phone. I clawed through books and papers, knocking over ashtrays, standing lamps back up, but at last I found it near the empty bookcase that had once so neatly held his boxes of paper clips and reams of paper. I lifted the receiver to my ear, and found it dead. I pulled gently on the cord and watched it come free, its ends in wire tatters. He'd pulled it from the wall.

I dropped it and ran outside again, trying once more to pull him to his feet, shouting at him to wake up wake up wake up— but I couldn't move him, couldn't get him to respond.

I had to leave him, to get help. I moved his feet as far as I could from the fire, little more than embers now. As I did so, he slid sideways down the log and came to rest on the ground at an awkward angle. Even dragging at his coat, I couldn't move him any more.

I ran inside and grabbed blankets from the bed, ran out and piled them over him, then ran toward my car, digging in my purse to find my keys. My hand made contact with the bottle of bitters, and I pulled it out and went back and left it by his head, a talisman to protect him while I was gone.

I drove fast into Waldham, not knowing exactly where to go— coming up with nothing when I poked through my memory of the town for a hospital or police station. I found a pay phone outside the Waldham Inn.

The dispatcher was skeptical about sending help when I told him Zeke was drunk, but I insisted that Zeke was barely breathing, that his skin was growing cold—and finally he responded to the hysteria in my voice and agreed to send an ambulance. I gave him the directions, then got back into my car and started back again.

I found the fire blazing high and his silhouette huge against the trees. I ran from my car around the cabin, and found him lurching around the yard, scrabbling at the ground.

"Zeke," I yelled, relieved beyond measure to find him on his feet. "Zeke!"

He turned and a low growl came from somewhere deep inside him.

"No," he said. Then louder, "No."

He fell to his knees and crawled toward the fire, and by the time I reached him he was clawing at the embers, tearing the fire apart.

I grabbed him by the shoulders to pull his hands away. "Don't," I shouted. "It's too late. You can't...."

He turned and smashed out at me behind him. "Leave me alone," he shouted. "You leave me alone with this."

He clutched his hands against himself, dropped forward until his head was against the ground, and began to keen with pain.

37

I've been in this small mountain town for nearly six weeks now, staying in the basement suite of a house that Alana's parents own. A young couple, teachers, with a baby, live in the upstairs suite. In order to avoid being home during those hours when their domestic bliss is most likely to fall apart, for their sakes as well as mine I've taken to walking out first thing each morning and late every afternoon. As I've watched summer settle into this part of the province, I've thought about time passing, and the way it inevitably numbs and heals whether we're ready for that or not.

I came up here to try to put the pieces of Gran's story together, to try to weave those tatters and scraps of paper memories into some sort of cohesive whole. Back at the Purple Parrot, I used to feel that my jottings about Gran connected me to her directly, if imperfectly—that I was edging closer to her truth. But by the time I got up here, I'd moved so far away from the person who'd once written in that notebook that I'd lost my sense of Gran completely. That sense hadn't been there when I needed it the night of the fire, and I couldn't seem to get it back.

By the time I realized that I wasn't going to be able to do what I'd come up here to do, a week of rain had started and the town was grey and dirty, dismal, the mountains hidden day after day by a shifting gauze of cloud. Upstairs the baby was feverish, crying, the parents short-tempered, not only shouting at one another, but dropping so many hard objects on their floor that I began to suspect that the quiet below them was driving them mad with envy, and they were determined to drive me out.

It might have been quiet down here, but the floor was littered with my frustration, torn and balled and scattered—and the discarded pieces of paper drove me mad with memories of Zeke. I was crawling with irritation at the sound of the baby's crying, at those inexplicable thumps, even at the more predictable sound of the furnace grumbling to life again, again, in the room that was next to mine.

I began to see what he'd been through. I couldn't work, but I couldn't not work, either. I couldn't bear to just sit and think, and I didn't want to leave. I was still fraying at all the edges. I wasn't ready to go back.

One afternoon I returned from a long, cold walk, a bottle of wine in my bag the only way I could imagine getting through the night. But before I opened it, I put down on paper a few words I'd been thinking about while I was walking.

"I first saw Zeke Avery again the night of Archie's nomination," I wrote, and immediately I stopped hearing the baby, the thumps, the furnace. For a month, I had to remind myself to eat, to sleep. Writing and walking was all I wanted to do, and I looked up to find that I was on the mend. Remembering was healing, after all, but I'd had to deal with the recent past before I got back to Gran. I'm almost ready for her now.

My first instinct after the ambulance left that night was to clean the cabin up, make it look like nothing bad had happened. I had some idea at that point that I might be able to restore things back at home as well. I would pay whatever penalty was exacted, and learn to live with whatever I had left.

I methodically went around the yard, picking up pieces of manuscript that were still whole or partly whole, holding them to my chest and carrying them inside. I folded the blankets I'd taken out to cover him, and brought them in and put them on his bed. I gathered the bottles from around the fire pit, emptying them as I went, and stashed them on the verandah with the others. I found a plastic pail and drew water from the rain barrel to put the fire out, soaking my skirt in the process—it was the skirt I'd selected that morning for the forum, but it seemed that I'd been wearing it for weeks.

I started on the living room, picking up books and shoving them back into the bookshelves, emptying ashtrays into cans, straightening lamps and tables. I was getting so tired I could barely move, so the more I saw there was to do, the faster I tried to do it. I went from living room to kitchen, kitchen to bedroom, bedroom to kitchen to bathroom, straightening, smoothing, sorting. Then, my arms full of paperbacks and mugs, I sank down onto the couch and wept.

I wept for Zeke, and for his book. For Archie, and his campaign. For my job at the Purple Parrot, and all the people there I'd never see again. I wept for my son, who would never understand, and for his grandparents. And for myself. Mostly, I wept for me. I wept a kind of clarity into myself, and saw that there was no way to undo the damage that had been done. Here or anywhere else.

Beginning to shake from the wet and cold, I went to find one of the blankets I'd put away, flicking the light switch in Zeke's bedroom. There, slid half-way under the bed, was my notebook.

I sat down onto the bed and lifted it, and held it to me as though it were a flotation device and I were sinking—my fingers running over and over the elastic bands that held it closed. I willed her to rise up from those pages, to stand between me and the destruction I had made. That he had made. That we had made together. I willed her to hold out her courage like a shield while I slipped past behind it, past the rubble of the past few days and weeks and the havoc yet to come, to somewhere quiet and protected. I willed her to hide me until it was safe for me to come out again.

I rocked, arms across my belly, clutching the notebook to me, head down, eyes closed. Crying "Gran," "Gran," "Gran," until I fell asleep.

I awakened hours later, the blanket wrapped around me, to the sound of a robin calling. I looked toward the window, but it seemed completely dark. I felt a deep, sick, empty feeling, as though death had found me and were waiting at the door. It was a feeling I knew well. I had held it at bay for all these years, but it had always been there, as familiar to me as my reflection in a glass. It was fear and loneliness together, and it had been resting beside my heart ever since Gran had started to get sick. And now I had no defenses left, no way to fend it off.

At last I stood. I locked the doors, the back one from the inside, then the front, locking myself out. I walked around the cabin as the sky began to pale. I found the bottle of bitters by the log at the fire pit, and slid it in my bag beside the notebook.

In Osier, I rented a motel room, and I stayed there pacing, thinking, weeping, getting nowhere with any of it, past or future—and only occasionally, for brief moments, sleeping. Later in the day, I went over to the hospital and asked to see Zeke Avery, but he'd been transferred to the city. The next morning, feeling deathly ill, I showered and drove back home.

There was no one there when I got in. I took another shower, made up my face, and went out to vote for Archie.

As the only member of the Conservative Party in the city who lost his seat in the last election, Archie was courted by a dozen private businesses—a process he seemed to enjoy. He accepted a position in the oil industry, and entered the world of free enterprise—the virtues of which he'd been so fond of extolling while he was in the Legislature.

His hours at work were as long as they'd been as an elected official, but even when he came home early, he'd usually find me buried deep in bed. I was unable to stir myself before ten a.m., too depressed to get dressed before noon.

I'd assured him that the thing with the vacuum-cleaner sales-man was over (For once remembering a name, he'd said, "No. It was Avery. From the nomination meeting"), and that was the end of it as far as he was concerned. Counselling was for wimps and football players. He was busy. He didn't want to think about it. We'd talk about it later. There was a dinner on Friday night he would need me to attend.

I finally called Alana, and she walked out of Sanderson and Lebel in the middle of the day and drove over to my house. She found me hair uncombed, shivering despite the heat outside. She put her arms around me, and let me sob it out onto the shoulder of her silky, turquoise jacket. At last, she said, "It sounds to me like you're not finished with this little dream of yours. Face it or forget it, Maggie. In this condition, you're useless." She pulled fresh tissues from the box, pressed them in my hands. "Now get up and make some coffee."

That was the call that started to get me here.

By some amazing coincidence, Dagmar has gone to work for the same company as Archie, and when I called home on Friday night, Ben told me his father was working late. That's okay with me—a relief, if anything—but she'd better not get maternal with my son.

"When are you going to be finished with your breakdown?" Ben asked me a week or so ago.

"What makes you call it a breakdown?"

"That's what Dad calls it," he said. I'd heard him hesitate before he spoke—already trying to figure out how to protect his parents from each other.

"It's not a breakdown," I said. "Maybe it was, but it's not now. It's like I flew apart before I came out here, and now I'm putting myself back together again."

"So you're going to be okay."

"I am," I said. "But it won't be easy, Ben. The pieces aren't going back together the way they were before."

There was silence at the other end of the line.

I sighed. "I'd rather talk to you about this face to face. I will. As soon as I get back. But you have to know that I love you. I love you and your father loves you. That hasn't changed, and it never, ever will."

The silence grew, and then he said, "If you loved me...."

I hesitated, trying to think of some way to make it right, to make him understand. But finally I just said, "I know."

I've been using the bottle of bitters as a paperweight, and a reminder. Now that I've stopped writing about Gran, her lesson has started to sink in. She found her peace in the people she was with, in the objects that surrounded her, in the way she held her knitting, in the music on the radio. Her ability to accept herself, and the immediate situation she was in, was what made her strong and still.

That's all it was.

It may take me a while to learn how to put that into practice for myself, but it's what I have to do.

Tomorrow Zeke will leave the house in town where he's been staying. I will meet him at the cabin. He needs someone to help him manage out there—his hands are still hard for him to use, and he's just beginning to get the hang of living without alcohol—and I need a place to stay until I find something in the city.

We've come to an agreement that may last a day, a month, or years. It doesn't matter. He's no longer twenty-two, full of dreams and the potential to fulfil them. Nor am I. This time we'll each be building, bit by bit, on what we have right now, instead of trying to drag a future from the past. I'm eager to see him. Ready to begin.